Please turn to the back of the book for an interview with Philip Luber

More praise for the work of Philip Luber

"His engaging characters are intricately connected, yet they stand distinct and clear like columns throughout the story. A classy writer."

—JANE LANGTON
Author of *The Shortest Day*

"[Luber's] books are top-choice reading material with tight plotting, well-drawn characters, and thoughtful writing. . . . Luber is one of those rare storytellers who can tell a riveting tale and imbue it with just the right mix of wisdom and warmth, emotion and knowledge. . . . Whether he is telling us about religious struggles, clinical psychology, family dynamics, or New England architecture, he does it with a subtle but talented hand."

—*Maine Sunday Telegram*

"He has an assured hand when it comes to creating characters who exhibit depth."

—*Publishers Weekly*

"HAVE MERCY ON US, Philip Luber's fourth Harry Kline novel, has a puzzler of a plot, cunningly constructed and laced throughout with surprisingly tender developments in his protagonist's love life. Luber writes with his usual quiet assurance, drawing on his dual professional skills as both forensic psychologist and author."

—DIANNE DAY
Author of the Fremont Jones series

By Philip Luber:

DEADLY CONNECTIONS
FORGIVE US OUR SINS*
DELIVER US FROM EVIL*
PRAY FOR US SINNERS*
HAVE MERCY ON US*

*Published by Fawcett Books

HAVE MERCY ON US

Philip Luber

FAWCETT GOLD MEDAL • NEW YORK

A Fawcett Gold Medal Book
Published by The Ballantine Publishing Group
Copyright © 1999 by Philip Luber

www.randomhouse.com/BB/

Library of Congress Catalog Card Number: 98-96892

ISBN 0-449-18330-0

Manufactured in the United States of America

First Ballantine Books Edition: April 1999

10 9 8 7 6 5 4 3 2 1

ACKNOWLEDGMENTS

I thank my wife, Cindy Mate, and my daughter, Holly Elizabeth Mate-Luber, for the many ways they helped me while I wrote this book

Robin McGrath, Paul O'Brien, and Paula Surrey read the manuscript in progress and offered many helpful comments.

I thank Len Whetherbee, Concord's real-life police chief, for his consultation.

Tara Venukrishnan provided information about the effects of physical trauma.

Robert Kinscherff allowed me to use one of his witticisms.

The friendship of Greg Adams, Lenny Gibson, and Jerry Kogan lurked in the background as I wrote this book, as did the memory of my mother, Ruth Luber, and the love of my father, Bernard Luber.

Best wishes go to Alan and Eleanor Luber, Estelle and Julius Mate, Elaine and Bill More, Donna and Joe Stachowicz, and Patrice Weiman and Jim Mate.

As always, I thank my editor, Susan Randol. I am grateful for the artwork of Carlos Beltran and the copyediting assistance of Peter Weissman. Thanks go also to Joe Blades, Mark Rifkin, and Laura Paczosa at Ballantine Books.

A hunter told me that he once saw a fox pursued by hounds burst out on to Walden when the ice was covered with shallow puddles, run part way across, and then return to the same shore. Ere long the hounds arrived, but here they lost the scent.

—from *Walden*,
   by Henry David Thoreau

1

All things being equal, I preferred to remain alive.

That was a stupid expression, I thought. *All things being equal.* What things were people talking about when they said that? Other than the left and right sides of a mathematical equation, are two things ever truly equal?

I once heard another father tell his children, "I love all of you equally." But that was surely a crock. I don't know much about love—who the hell does?—but of one thing I'm certain: We love different people differently, not equally.

Thomas Jefferson wrote that all men are created equal. But he wasn't counting slaves and freemen equally. And women were obviously not in his equation at all. Of course, historians tell us that neither of those facts prevented Jefferson from enjoying carnal bliss with one of his slaves.

Even identical twins have different fingerprints.

Of course, I supposed the Red Sox and the Celtics had equally poor chances of winning their respective championships that year.

I was obsessing again. Anxiety always did that to me.

I checked my watch. I checked my odometer. Traffic was light, and with luck I would make it from Concord to Cambridge before the morning rush hour kicked in.

I was on my way to meet with Jamie Ray: a woman who might soon—literally and figuratively—hold my life in her hands.

All things being equal, I preferred to remain alive.

2

"If a skull cracks in the forest," said the police chief, "does it make a sound?"

The medical examiner paused in his examination of the unidentified corpse. "This one definitely made a sound, judging from the configuration of the fracture. But I wouldn't call this a forest. Maybe in Thoreau's time it was, but not now." He glanced around at the pines and hemlocks, and the path that led thirty yards down a gentle slope to Walden Pond. "Anyway, why do you ask such a strange question, Chief?"

Concord police chief Alfred Korvich leaned against a tree, shading his eyes from the early morning sun. "I was referring to the old riddle. You know—'If a tree falls in the forest, does it make a sound?' Just a little humor, Doc. To take the edge off of . . . this." He gestured at the slender, bloodied female form lying faceup in front of the medical examiner. "Just a little humor."

Detective Kay Wheaton said, "Very little humor, if you ask me. Besides, you left out the most important part. 'If a tree falls in the forest, *and no one is there to hear it,* does it make a sound?' *That's* the riddle."

The medical examiner made certain his latex gloves were snug, then began to examine the pulpy head wound in earnest. "Actually, Chief, it's simple physics. An event gives rise to vibrations, and vibrations give rise to sound waves. The waves travel through a medium, like air . . ."

2

Kay Wheaton watched and listened as the medical examiner explored the dead body and lectured Chief Korvich about sound and the human ear. She thought some of the anatomical terms had an oddly erotic flavor: *Cochlear fluid. Tectorial membrane. The organ of Corti.* But she knew that the chief, whose eyes had quickly glazed over as soon as the medical examiner began his discourse, likely didn't appreciate those nuances.

Kay did another quick visual survey of the scene. They were standing where Henry David Thoreau's cabin once stood, near the far northwest corner of Walden Pond, about fifty yards from the train track that extended from Boston to Fitchburg. Four Concord police officers had sealed off the scene, setting a wide perimeter. A half-dozen onlookers had gathered, and the officers were keeping them at bay.

The corpse lay between two of the short granite posts that marked what was once the boundary of the one-room cabin. It was eight o'clock on a late August morning, and the sun had been up for two hours. Shortly after sunrise a jogger had called the police station to report his gruesome find.

"Only in Concord," the detective said, more to herself than to the others.

"What do you mean?" asked Chief Korvich.

"Only in Concord would a jogger come equipped with a cellular phone."

The medical examiner stood and stretched. "So you see, Chief, the answer depends on how you define sound. On one hand, you could say yes, sound exists whenever vibrations cause sound waves, whether or not someone is there to hear it. But if you define sound as a sensation that's detected by a receiver, like the ear, then the answer is no. Either answer can be considered correct."

Next to the body lay a blood-splattered, palm-sized edition of *Walden*.

The victim wore a thin necklace that looked like it was made from gold. A simple cross dangled from it. Other than her clothing, it was the only personal item apparent: There was no wallet or anything else to help them identify the victim.

Detective Kay Wheaton put on gloves, then leaned over and inspected the cross. "It looks very old," she said. "There appear to be two letters here, initials, perhaps. The first one is definitely a C. It's hard to make out the second one. It may be another C, but it could also be G. It's hard to tell because of this scratch on the second letter. Take a look."

Korvich examined the letters on the cross. "You're right. It's either C.C. or C.G. At least that tells us something."

"Something," Kay Wheaton agreed. "But not much."

The medical examiner said, "I'm ready to turn her over now. Will you give me a hand?"

Korvich stepped forward and put on a pair of gloves. Kay watched the two men slowly roll the corpse onto its front. She noticed the rigidity in the dead body, and she knew the killing had occurred at least several hours earlier.

"Holy shit," Korvich said when the corpse's posterior side came into view.

"Ditto," the medical examiner said.

The three of them stared at the massive wound on the back of the victim's head. You probably couldn't even call it a head anymore, Kay thought, so obliterated it was. The medium-length blond hair was completely matted with dried blood.

The medical examiner kneeled next to the body and peered at the mangled mess for several seconds. "There were at least two blows to the back of the head. One in the parietal region, and another down here in the occipital region." He stood. "I can't give an accurate count on the number of times she was hit in her face, either."

"Overkill," Korvich said.

Kay winced and said, "That's putting it mildly. Any other injuries?"

"Nothing obvious," the medical examiner replied.

"Any defensive wounds?"

"None."

"Which blow killed her?"

"Take your choice."

"How long ago?"

The medical examiner shrugged. "Judging from the advanced rigor and low body temperature, anywhere from nine to twelve hours ago."

Korvich said, "Sunset was seven-thirty, give or take. Maybe she and whoever killed her came through yesterday evening at around that time, after everyone else was gone."

Kay Wheaton noted the dirt and organic debris that clung to the back of the dead woman's clothing. None had been stuck to her front before they rolled her over. A couple of feet away from the corpse, near one of the granite posts, there was a small pool of coagulated blood.

She closed her eyes for a moment and tried to visualize the scene that unfolded the previous evening. Then she said, "The woman is standing right over there when the attack begins. She's struck from the rear. She falls forward, but she doesn't hit the ground, which is why her front was still clean before you turned her over a few minutes ago. She falls instead onto this stone pillar, and blood drips from her head onto the ground, right over here."

A commuter train rumbled past the nearby western edge of the pond, right to left, heading toward the town of Lincoln and ultimately into Boston.

Detective Kay Wheaton continued her imagined description of the murder. "She's perched on the pillar, and her assailant strikes her again on the back of her head. Now she falls off the pillar and lands on her back, the position she was still in when the jogger found her."

Korvich said, "Which means the injuries to her face came after she was already lying on the ground."

"One strike after another." She nodded toward the medical examiner. "Too many for the doctor to give an accurate count. Her head was caught between the ground and the killer's blows."

The sound of the train disappeared in the distance. Some sort of bird chirped—Kay never could tell one from another—and a few more walkers joined the crowd of the curious outside the sealed area.

Alfred Korvich scratched his cheek. "Are we looking at a rape here, Doc?"

"I don't know. They'll do an internal exam during the autopsy in Boston."

Kay said, "I doubt that he raped her. There's no ripping or displacement of her clothing. If he was going to rape her and kill her, he wouldn't have her get fully redressed between the one and the other. What sort of weapon are we looking for, Doctor?"

"Maybe one of those rocks over there." He pointed at the pyramid-shaped stack next to the cabin. The mound was several feet high, and several of the stones were at least the size of a baseball.

"What *is* that rock pile?" Kay asked. "How did it get there?"

Korvich said, "You mean, you've never been here before?"

She shook her head. "Nature's not my thing."

The police chief grinned. "It's an old custom. Visitors leave stones to mark the fact that they were here. They say it's been going on for a hundred years."

Kay Wheaton went to inspect the pile. No bloodied rock was immediately apparent. "I'll have the uniforms do a systematic scan of the area after you authorize the removal of the body. Maybe they can find the weapon."

The medical examiner reached into his pocket and produced a small ruler. "I just want to make a few more rough measurements of the wounds, in case moving the body jostles things around."

Kay silently read the words on the carved-wood placard near the rock pile. She presumed they came from *Walden*.

I went to the woods because I wished to live deliberately, to front only the essential facts of life. And see if I could not learn what it had to teach, and not, when I came to die, discover that I had not lived.

She thought: *Okay, Henry. So now we know why you came here. But why did she come here? And who the hell is she?*

The detective turned her back to the murder scene and walked the short distance to the edge of the water. Off to the left, a half mile away, a small beach lined the pond's short eastern edge. Beyond it and up a small incline was Route 126, and across the road were the parking lot and gift shop.

Murders weren't supposed to happen in this wealthy and privileged town, Kay Wheaton knew. Yet this was the second homicide in Concord since she began working there two years earlier. That figure didn't include the three people who died on Route 2 the previous winter when a drunk driver plowed into their car.

"Hell of a way to start the day," Chief Korvich said, suddenly appearing at her side.

"I know. I left the Cambridge Police Department to get away from scenes like this."

Korvich gestured toward the onlookers. "Well, too many witnesses now. Otherwise we could drag the body to the other side of the pond, make the Lincoln police deal with it. Maybe next time."

"There's not supposed to be a next time," Kay said. "In Boston and Cambridge, sure. But not in Concord."

The police chief sighed. He picked up a small flat stone and tossed it sidearm, low to the water. The stone skimmed the pond's surface, bounced once, then sank. Two sets of small concentric circles spread out, melted into one another, and then faded away.

Korvich looked directly across the pond to the Lincoln side. He said, "The prettiest ones are the first to die."

"How can you tell she was pretty? Her face is so caved in, I don't think I'd recognize her if she was my own sister."

"Huh? No, not the dead woman. That maple tree over there, across the water. We're still a week away from September, and it's already turning bright red."

"What about it?" Kay asked.

"It's the weaker trees that have the hardest time adjusting to the temperature changes in the late summer. That's what makes the leaves turn color. So the prettiest ones are actually the weakest ones, the ones that are gonna die before the others."

"Interesting," she said, sounding anything but interested. To her, a tree was just a tree, and no particular tree was significantly different from its neighbors.

"I'm surprised you've never been to Walden before."

"Like I said, nature isn't my thing."

"To do good police work in Concord, you have to understand the town's history. This pond is a big part of that history. Study the town and you'll learn some interesting things."

"For example?"

Korvich smiled. "Have you seen the Minuteman statue up at the North Bridge?"

"Yes."

"A long time ago the town made a cast of the Minuteman just in case they ever needed to repair it. Then about ten years ago, the National Guard asked to use the cast to make a copy of the statue for their headquarters. The town put it to a vote, and they turned the Guard down."

"Why?"

"Some crap about protecting the town's heritage by keeping its uniqueness. A bunch of bullshit about how special Concord is, and how it would lose some of its specialness if it started to lend pieces of itself to other places. But the way I see it, Concord is exactly like every other town. Because in every town, even Concord, you can find nice guys and assholes on every corner. The only thing different about Concord is how different they think they are."

Korvich skimmed another stone off the water surface. Once again it bounced one time and sank on the second contact. "I never could do that very well," he said.

Kay bent down and found a circle-shaped flat stone. She flung it over the pond, where it bounced up four times before piercing the surface on the fifth hit.

"Impressive," said Korvich.

"Simple physics, just like the doctor said. It's all in the angle and the velocity."

"Have you been to a tour at the Old Manse?"

"I've passed by," she replied, "but I've never been inside."

"When you go there, ask one of the guides to tell you about the French wallpaper in the dining room."

"What about it?"

He smiled. "Ask them. Takes the fun out of it if I tell you."

He gestured toward the murder scene. "So—how do you want to proceed?"

"The usual stuff. Bag her hands, tag any forensic evidence we can find on or near her. Get credit card receipts of the purchases at the gift shop yesterday evening, then try to track those people down and find out if they saw anything. And in the meantime, try to identify the victim. We'll see if her fingerprints tell us anything, see if one of the cars in the lot belonged to her. Check any missing person reports that come in to the state police, especially for someone with initials C.C. or C.G. Maybe Forensics can tell us whether the second letter on the cross is a C or a G. When we figure out who she was, we'll be a step closer to finding the murderer. Because she probably knew the person who killed her."

"What makes you think that?"

"She was struck from behind while she was standing still. If a woman goes into the woods by herself, and if a stranger approaches from the rear, she'll turn to face him. But she didn't turn around, because she didn't come here alone. She came here with someone she knew, and he killed her."

Alfred Korvich considered what she said for a moment, then said, "You should talk to Davey Waterstone."

"Who's he?"

"A rich guy in town, sort of a loner. Lives off his inheritance and spends a lot of time in these woods. Someone gave him the nickname the Lord of Walden. I guess he considers himself a keeper of the flame. Maybe he knows something that can help you. Maybe he'll hear something he can pass on to you. Maybe this woman has been here before, and he knows who she is."

"Is there anyone else you think I should speak with?"

The police chief turned away from Walden Pond and faced the crime scene. Kay thought she saw him smile slightly. He said, "Talk to Harry Kline."

"The psychiatrist? Why should I speak with him about this?"

"Because it seems like every time someone gets murdered in Concord, Harry Kline winds up at the center of it."

3

I unbuckled my belt and unzipped my pants. "In the past twenty-plus years," I said, "only three other women have seen my penis."

She didn't reply. She continued doing what she was doing.

"Sorry," I said. "That was a stupid thing to say. I guess I'm a little nervous."

"That's all right, Harry. I understand."

And with that comment Dr. Jamie Ray, my new urologist, donned a latex glove, dipped a finger in lubricating jelly, and positioned herself behind me. She proceeded with insertion.

"Ouch!"

"Sorry."

"That definitely is *not* one of my erogenous zones."

"Thank you for sharing that with me, Harry. And now, please hold still."

After ten or fifteen seconds of digital penetration and palpation, she withdrew, discarded the glove, and began to wash her hands. "What are you waiting for?" she asked.

"Huh?"

"As you were, soldier."

I stood there, distracted, with my pants still around my ankles.

She said, "You can put your penis away now, Harry."

"Oh. Right. Sorry." I pulled my pants up and sat in the chair across the desk from her. "So—what do you think?"

"There does appear to be some enlargement. Not necessarily something to be concerned about if that were the only thing out of the ordinary. But as you know, it *isn't* the only thing out of the ordinary."

"You're referring to the PSA result."

"Yes," she replied. "It's a concern."

Prostate Specific Antigen: A few days earlier the results from a routine physical contained a troublesome reading on that screening test for cancer. My internist suggested that I see a urologist. Bobby Beck directed me to Jamie Ray. Bobby was my best friend, and Jamie was his younger cousin. She was in her mid-thirties, about ten years younger than Bobby and me. She came from the Midwest and had recently opened a practice in Cambridge.

I said, "What do you suggest?"

"I'd like to do a biopsy, to take some prostate tissue."

I had forgotten most of the limited urology training I received in medical school. Like proctology, dermatology, and many of the other -ologies, that training had little long-term relevance to a psychiatrist. But I had a notion that snipping away at my prostate gland would be a complicated matter. I said, "How do you get the tissue?"

She gave me a you-must-be-kidding look. "Think of your prostate as being like Provincetown, or Hilton Head, or the Florida Keys."

"Because it would make a lovely vacation spot?"

"No. Because there's only one main road that will get you there."

"And that no doubt is the road you just traveled a couple of minutes ago."

"Yes. But today I was traveling light. I'll require some baggage for the biopsy."

I cringed. "Small enough to carry on, or will you have to check it at the gate?"

She stared blankly for a moment, then began to laugh. "Bobby was right," she said. " 'Harry Kline is a funny guy.' "

I exhaled, long and slow. "May I ask you a question?"

"Yes."

"Does being a urologist make it difficult for a woman to develop romantic relationships? Do men keep wondering how they measure up? Do they shy away from you because your expertise makes them nervous?"

She laughed and said, "You really *are* incorrigible, aren't you?"

When she stopped laughing, I said, "May I ask you another question?"

"I can hardly wait."

I was surprised at the quiver and crack in my voice as I asked, "Do you think I have cancer?"

There was a subtle shift in her demeanor: a softening around the eyes, a warming in her voice. She leaned closer to me. "Oh, Harry—I think you may."

I wanted a more specific assessment. "From zero to a hundred, what do you think the chances are that I have it?"

She paused, either to figure out an answer, or to figure out whether or how to tell me what that answer was. "At least fifty percent."

"In other words, greater than fifty percent. More likely yes than no."

"Yes. More likely."

"Greater than seventy-five percent?"

Dr. Jamie Ray sighed. "I don't know, Harry. It's all fruitless conjecture, and that doesn't help anything. It's early. Let's go one step at a time. I'd like to do the biopsy as soon as possible, then wait for the results before making any other plans. I know it's hard not to begin to spin out scenarios. But the less of that you do, the better off you'll be for now."

We talked for a few minutes about the prebiopsy routine, which included a megadose of antibiotics the night before, and certain bodily function stuff that is best left undescribed.

"And afterward," she said, "you'll need to refrain from ejaculation for two days so the system can heal."

"I think I'll survive."

"I'm glad to hear it. Call my nurse this afternoon to schedule the procedure. And I recommend that you ask someone to drive you home afterward, because you may feel a little weak and there may be some discomfort." She smiled and said, "Now—may *I* ask *you* a question?"

"Sure."

"Who was the third woman?"

"You've lost me."

"You said only three other women had inspected your plumbing in the past twenty years. I assume your wife was one, and the woman you're with now—what did you say her name is?"

"Veronica."

"Veronica would be another. So who am I missing?"

I shook my head. "A temporary thing. It's not something I'm particularly proud of."

"Why? Did it occur during your marriage?"

"No, of course not. It happened after my wife died."

She smiled. "Well, that means you were always faithful to your wife. Strength of character. Very important for someone dealing with the possibility of cancer."

I stood to leave. "Well, on that happy note . . ."

She stood and shook my hand. "Call me if there's anything I can do, Harry. My cousin says you're the best friend he's ever had. I want to take good care of his friend."

"You're not coming on to me, are you?"

She laughed. "No, I wouldn't do that to you. Besides, isn't Veronica a cop?"

"FBI."

"Well, I never try to steal a man from a woman who knows how to use a gun."

When I reached the door I turned and asked, "How long will it take for the results to come back?"

"It usually takes about two weeks."

"And if the results are positive?"

"That's when we begin to talk about your options."

"For example."

"Radiation. Various types of surgery. We'll have plenty of time to discuss it if the results come back the wrong way. There's one option you would have if you were an old man, but that you won't have."

"What's that?"

"The option of doing nothing. You're forty-four years old. Too young to outlive the effects of even the slowest form of prostate cancer. If you do have the disease, and if you do nothing about it, then eventually it will kill you."

4

It was a little after nine o'clock when I left Jamie Ray's office. I had no patients scheduled, and I was content to drive around for a while, so I avoided the highway and drove up Trapelo Road, through parts of Watertown, Belmont, and Waltham.

Veronica was busy with paperwork at home that morning. I was in no particular hurry to get home because I was in no particular hurry to face her with my news. I hadn't told her about the abnormal PSA results from my physical, or making an appointment with a urologist. I guess I had been hoping that my internist's concern was unfounded: that Jamie Ray—reputed to be a magician with a penis or a prostate—would give me a pill or prescribe a special diet and send me on my merry way. I knew all along that it was a ridiculous fantasy. But sometimes a little denial can go a long way.

I thought about my late wife as I drove home. Janet was only thirty-two when she died. Once her illness was diagnosed, there was little hope for her. The pancreatic cancer was vicious in its effects. But it was merciful in its brevity, and it took her quickly. She'd been gone now for eight years.

One day as Janet lay dying, I wondered how I would react if I were in her place. Back then I supposed that I would tell everyone about my plight if I were dying: The more sympathy I got, the better I would feel. And maybe that's how I would react in a little while: after my biopsy was performed, or when the results were known. But I didn't want to talk about it with anyone at that moment: not my parents, not Bobby Beck, not even Veronica.

I certainly didn't want to talk about it with my daughter. Telling her would be the hardest part. There was no point in alarming her now, before I knew anything for certain; I would wait until there was a reality that couldn't be avoided. She was only four years old when Janet died. The thought of her grieving for a parent all over again was too much for me to handle just now.

I switched on the car radio and turned to a mid-morning sports call-in show on the AM dial. A caller with a thick Boston accent was trashing the Red Sox in general, and Roger Clemens in particular. "Three years ago he signs his twenty-million-dollar contract, and each year his butt is two inches wider. Just one year left after this one, and then good riddance to the lard-ass. Hey—can I say lard-ass on the radio?"

You can say anything you want, I thought. *We're all going to die, so what the hell does it matter?* Well, I was getting ahead of myself there. I knew I'd have to guard against inflicting my anxiety on those around me.

The clutter of Waltham was replaced by the woods and fields of Lincoln. Tract houses gave way to luxury homes and estates, and Trapelo Road metamorphosed into Sandy Pond Road.

I drove past the DeCordova Museum and the Gropius House. I crossed an open expanse of Lincoln conservation land, and I turned onto Route 126 just a quarter mile below the Concord town line.

Something was going on at Walden. A Channel 7 news van from Boston was parked by the main path to the pond. There were two Concord police cruisers and one from Lincoln. The gate to the parking lot was closed.

Leaning against the parking lot gate was a hand-lettered poster that said, "The End of the Innocence." I knew it was the title of a song by Don Henley, the rock musician. He founded a conservation group to help ward off real estate development in the area, and now and then he flew in from California to help publicize the effort. I assumed Henley was somewhere beyond my line of vision, over the ridge and down the incline, standing alongside the famous pond.

I was tense and restless. I thought exercising might reduce my stress. So I headed toward the southwest part of town, and shortly after ten o'clock I arrived at the Thoreau Club.

Years earlier the property owners cleared away acres and acres of trees; installed a lodge, a gym, three pools, and eight tennis courts; and named the place after the godfather of the environmentalist movement. It was high irony, and something the cantankerous Thoreau likely would have appreciated.

I did a light workout on the weight resistance machines, swam a few laps, then relaxed in the Jacuzzi. All the while I tried to push away every thought. But as I sat in the hot bubbling water, I remembered someone once telling me that using a Jacuzzi could cause your sperm count to shrink. I thought, *Too bad it doesn't shrink tumors.*

I changed into my clothes and got ready to leave the club. As I walked through the lodge, I glanced through a window toward one of the tennis courts. I saw a silver-haired man with broad shoulders engaging in an agitated conversation with his doubles partner. I couldn't hear what they were saying, but the silver-haired man had a flushed face and was gesturing intensely with his racket. I didn't know his name, but I had seen him around the club a few times. No matter what the season, he always appeared tan and fit. And he always played tennis as if he were waging trench warfare on the Western Front.

He seemed especially riled up today. *Relax, buddy,* I thought. *Life is too short.*

Life is too short. I wondered: Would impending death make a man more impatient? Or would it instead lead him to greater tolerance for the imperfections of his friends, lovers, and tennis partners?

I didn't want to have to find out.

On my way home I tried to decide how to break my news to Veronica. *There's no time like the present,* I thought, trying to steel myself for the task—and then, more simply: *There's no time.*

I walked into the house a minute or two past noon. Veronica was in the den watching the Channel 7 midday news. I said hello and asked her how her morning had been, but she held a hand up to quiet me and kept her eyes focused on the television. A reporter was standing, microphone in hand, next to the pathway that leads down the incline to Walden. The word "live" was superimposed onto the bottom right corner of the screen.

I sat next to her on the couch. Still facing the television, Veronica said, "They don't know who she is."

"They don't know who *who* is?"

"The victim," she replied. "They haven't identified her yet."

"Victim?"

She looked at me and said, "A woman was beaten to death at Walden Pond."

She returned her gaze to the news report a moment too late to read the words on the hand-lettered poster that had flashed onto the screen for a few seconds. She said, "What did that sign say? Do you know?"

"Yes." It was the placard I had seen when I drove past the pond. I placed my palm over the back of Veronica's hand. "It said that this is the end of the innocence."

5

Melissa ran into the house as Veronica and I were finishing lunch. "I'm going next door to Emily's house." She opened the refrigerator and grabbed a can of Diet Coke. "See ya," she said, and headed toward the door.

"Hey, hold on," I said. "I want to talk with you about something."

My daughter froze in her tracks and turned around with a sigh of exasperation. "What?"

"Well, for starters, I'd like to say hello. You were still asleep when I left this morning. This is the first time I've seen you today."

"Where did you go?"

"I had a meeting in Cambridge. How was your tennis lesson?"

"Good." Melissa tapped one foot against the ground over and over again: a sign of her restlessness. "Is that all? Emily is waiting for me. Her sister's gonna take us for a walk in the woods."

We lived near the North Bridge, site of the Battle of Concord and the shot heard 'round the world. Our home had once been a farmhouse, and the property abutted a wooded conservation area.

I said, "No, that's not all. Sit down, sweetheart. Veronica and I want to discuss something important with you."

"Okay, okay. I'm sitting." She plopped herself on the high

stool near the cupboard. "What is it?" She glanced at the clock, impatient.

I said, "A woman was murdered at Walden Pond. They found her body there this morning."

Melissa pondered that for a moment. "Was she raped?"

"I don't know." I didn't recall hearing my almost-thirteen-year-old child use that word before.

"Who was it?"

"She hasn't been identified yet. And they don't know who did it, or why."

"How was she killed? Did someone shoot her?"

"The news reports say she was beaten to death."

"Oh." She gazed at the floor for a moment. "Oh!" She looked at Veronica. "Beaten to death?"

"Yes, honey," Veronica replied.

"Are *you* okay?"

"I'm fine, honey. Really."

I stood and carried our lunch dishes to the sink. Melissa stepped down from the stool at the same moment. We were standing inches away from one another, and I realized once again how tall she had grown in the past year. She noticed me looking at her, and she averted her eyes and turned away.

I said, "I don't want you walking in the woods today."

"Why not?"

"Weren't you listening? Someone was killed in the woods, and the person who did it hasn't been caught."

"But that was different woods," she said, whining. "It's practically on the other side of town."

"It's a three mile walk from here. Someone could cover that distance in less than an hour."

"Oh, sure, and he's coming right over here to rape twelve-year-olds."

There was that word again. "Jesus Christ—I can't believe you're arguing with me about this."

"Don't say 'Jesus Christ.'"

"Listen to me," I said, my voice getting louder.

"Don't say 'Jesus Christ'! You know I hate it when you say that!"

"Please," Veronica said. "Let's everyone calm down."

I took a deep breath. "You're right, Melissa. I shouldn't say that."

"Can I go now?"

"You can go to Emily's house. But I want you to stay away from the woods. Any woods. That includes Estabrook Woods, and the woods between our field and the wildlife refuge."

She pouted. "I wanted to go swimming at Walden tomorrow."

"*That* is completely out of the question."

She looked at Veronica: the beseeching expression she had when she wanted Veronica to side with her against me.

"Your father is right, honey."

"Fine!" my daughter replied, but her tone of voice said it was anything but fine with her. She stomped out of the kitchen and out of the house.

I said, "When did I begin to lose control of this situation?"

"About thirteen years ago, minus two weeks."

"That was a rhetorical question."

Veronica placed her hand over mine and patted it. "Well, that was a rhetorical answer."

"There's no such thing as a rhetorical answer."

"Sure there is. Look it up." She touched my cheek, then went to the sink and began to load the dishes into the dishwasher.

I looked out the window and watched Melissa pass through the grove of trees that separated our property from Emily's place. "I was more comfortable talking with her about murder than about rape."

"I know. I could tell."

"Did you notice the way she looked at you as soon as I told her the murder victim was beaten to death?"

"Yes," Veronica replied. "She was trying to protect me. She takes after her father. I don't need you to do that, either one of you. But I do like it when you try."

She was wrong, of course. She needed protection sometimes. Everyone needs protection sometimes.

Veronica's mother was beaten to death, killed by an intruder when Veronica was only nine years old. Veronica witnessed the murder. It affected her in every way I could imagine, and no doubt in ways I would never be able to understand. It even affected her career choice. She once told me why she became a prosecutor, and then an FBI agent: "I wanted to hurt people who hurt other people."

Melissa knew about Veronica's mother. That was why she reacted with concern for Veronica when I told her about the woman who was beaten and killed at Walden Pond.

Protection: I told myself I was protecting Veronica by not mentioning my prostate screening results, and then by keeping secret my appointment with the urologist. But maybe I was simply protecting myself: avoiding mention of something I wanted to pretend wasn't happening. What was that old expression? *Denial is a river in Egypt.*

Tired from the mental strain of denying my mental strain, I got into bed earlier than usual that night. I was reading a book when Veronica came into the bedroom a short while later. She said, "You're still planning to paint the barn doors this weekend, aren't you?"

"Yes."

She unfastened the sash on her robe and walked toward the bed. "I'd like to take Melissa to my aunt Marilyn's beach house. Stay over tomorrow night, come home Sunday night. Just to get away from Concord, and not think about the murder."

"Sounds like a good plan."

"I guess I still feel like I have to ask your permission."

"What do you mean?"

"She's not my daughter. My rights are limited."

"Well, I guess that's a complicated subject."

"I know. But it's just that sometimes . . ." Her voice trailed off.

"Come here."

She let her robe slip off her shoulders and fall to the floor. She crawled into bed and pressed herself against me.

I lay on my back. I held her close. I said, "This has been a rough day."

She sighed and placed her arm across my chest. "Yes."

The longer a secret festers, the harder it is later to make things right. I didn't want to keep my worries hidden from her any longer. "I want to talk with you about something."

"What is it, darling?"

"I'm glad you and Melissa are close to one another, because if anything ever happens to me—"

She placed a finger against my lips: a gesture to be quiet. "This isn't the time to talk about those sorts of hypotheticals."

"But there's something I want you to—"

"Shush." She placed her lips on mine, running her fingers across my chest as she kissed me. Then she trailed her tongue along the width and length of my chest, breathing on me as she licked, sending chills through me as her breath hit the wetness.

She draped a leg over me and kissed me again: tongues probing. We lay entwined like that for several minutes, touching and tasting. I felt myself harden against her.

Veronica rolled onto me, covering my body with hers. She pulled into an upright position, straddling me. And then she lifted herself up and brought her body down onto me.

I pressed down on her hips as I thrust slowly upward. She froze for a moment, then accelerated slowly into a steady pace. We made unhurried love to one another: rich and passionate, without frenzy.

At the end she shuddered and spasmed, her body jerking wildly above me. Then her muscles tightened around me, and I spilled into her.

She collapsed on me, licking and kissing my chest feverishly, then more slowly, more slowly, until she came to rest in my arms.

We lay there silently, our racing hearts and rapid breathing gradually slowing down.

After several minutes I said, "Jesus Christ. That was incredible."

"Don't say 'Jesus Christ,'" she replied, and we both broke into hysterical laughter.

Veronica rolled onto her side, facing me. She propped herself up on her elbow. She ran her free hand through my hair, a gentle and loving touch.

She said, "Melissa really hates it when you say that."

"I know. Blasphemy from the godless Jew."

"Well, she's Jewish, too."

"The jury is still out on that," I said. "She doesn't know what she is."

"And neither do you."

"No, I don't know what she is, either."

She said, "I meant, you don't know what *you* are."

"I know what I am. I just don't want to do anything about it."

"How long has it been since you were in a synagogue?"

"Not since Janet died."

"She was thirty-two, wasn't she?"

"Yes."

"And her birthday was earlier this month."

"That's right."

"So if she died in February, that means . . ." Veronica performed the calculations in her head. "I'm a month older now than she was when she died. And that means I'm the oldest woman you've ever made love to."

"You do pretty well for an old woman."

She leaned toward me and placed her head on my shoulder. I said, "You used to hate talking about Janet."

"That was when I didn't know for sure if you loved me."

"I do love you."

"I know, Harry. I know." She lightly stroked my chest. "Did you have a nickname for her? You know—a term of endearment that you used only for her?"

I hesitated, uncertain what to make of her uncharacteristic foray into the privacy of that relationship. "I used to call her 'angel.' Pretty ironic, isn't it?"

She said, "We're all wingless angels."

"I don't understand."

She said, "It's from something I read in high school. 'The earth is a depot, where wingless angels pass the time waiting for the long ride home.' It always made me think of my mother."

"I like it."

"I do, too." She pulled closer to me and kissed my cheek. "You know what I wish?"

"What's that, darling?"

"I wish that I die before you do."

"But you're twelve years younger than me."

She laughed softly. "Don't get me wrong. I want to live a very long life. But I want to die before you do, because I couldn't bear living without you. I never want to lose you."

She pressed her entire body to mine and held me tight. She said, "What is it you wanted to talk with me about?"

"Some other time," I replied. "Not right now."

Some other time. She slipped into a quiet sleep while I watched the time pass by on the nightstand clock.

6

"Alfred Korvich is an idiot," Bobby Beck said.

I held my phone in one hand and scrambled an egg with the other. "Why do you say that?"

"Didn't you read the *Boston Globe*? This is what our articulate police chief had to say about the murder yesterday. 'This matter is under investigation, and our investigators will be out there investigating until everything is completely investigated.' I mean, could you possibly think of a more stupid thing to say?"

"He may not be the most polished guy in the world, but Korvich is far from stupid."

"Oh, that's right—I forgot. You actually *like* the dumb son of a bitch."

"Let's just say we've come to an understanding. He sort of grows on you."

"Pal of mine," Bobby said, "so do venereal warts."

"And you would be an expert on that matter, I suppose."

"Hey—we were discussing your *schmeckel*, not mine. What time do you want me to pick you up on Monday morning?"

"A little after eight. The biopsy is scheduled for nine. Your cousin said the procedure would take about a half hour."

"How are you doing with all of this?"

"I'm trying not to think about it too much."

"How is Veronica handling it?"

"She doesn't know yet. That's why I asked you to drive me."

"Oh." He paused. "You should tell her."

"I know."

I walked a mile down Monument Street into the center of town: past the path to the North Bridge, past the house that bore a hole from a Redcoat musketball that was fired almost two and a quarter centuries earlier, past the colonial homes that comprised so much of the heritage of the town.

I bought paintbrushes at Vanderhoof's Hardware. As the clerk rang up the sale she said, "Quite a thing, what happened at Walden yesterday, don't you think?"

"Yes," I said. "Quite a thing."

"It's like, everyone who comes in wants to talk about it, and at the same time they don't want to talk about it. You see what I'm saying?"

"I see what you're saying," I said, pondering that nonsensical construction for a moment.

"I just hope the poor woman didn't come from around here."

She came from somewhere, I thought. *If not here, then someplace else.* But there was no point in getting into that.

"Well, you have a nice day now, sir."

She handed the receipt to me. As I stepped toward the door I saw an acquaintance and his young daughter. Phil and I nodded at one another. When he and Holly approached the cashier, she said, "Quite a thing, what happened at Walden yesterday, don't you think?"

A murder, savage and unsolved, so close to home: I wanted to talk about it and yet I didn't want to talk about it, so I guess the clerk was right in her assessment of things. Between the Walden homicide and the renegade cancer cells that might be setting up camp around the almond-shaped gland behind my rectal wall, I guess I had plenty to talk about and not talk about.

A familiar figure was seated on a bench across the street from the town square. Davey Waterstone was only a few years older than me, but his hair had gone entirely gray. He wore it pulled back into a ponytail, and this morning there was a day's growth of stubble on his face in matching color. He sat perfectly still with his eyes focused on the ground. People walked past him in either direction, but he didn't change his pose or posture.

"Town's pretty empty today," I said as I sat next to him.

He remained quiet for several seconds. Then he said, "The last Saturday in August. All the rich folk have flown the coop. You're looking for someone in particular, you can probably find him in Nantucket or on the Vineyard."

"*You're* rich, but *you're* still in town."

"*You're* still in town, too, and from what I hear, you're doing pretty well yourself."

"I'm comfortable," I said. "You're rich. An important distinction, especially in this town."

"Why—do you need some money?"

"I think I'm all set for right now," I said. "What would you do if I said yes?"

"I'd ask you how much you need."

"What if I said twenty thousand?"

He shrugged. "I suppose I could do that."

"But why?"

"Why not? I can afford it. A dollar to a homeless person in the subway, twenty thousand to an acquaintance in need. Not all that much difference between the two if you have enough. Hell, maybe I'd be better off if I started giving money away. I don't spend it. It just grows and grows. Like crabgrass."

"An interesting analogy," I said.

"You think I'm joking, don't you?"

"Actually, you sound quite serious."

A couple with two small children and three cameras walked by.

"Tourists," he said. "Wonder what they make of our quiet little town on this particular day. I'm sure they didn't count on murder when they put Concord on their vacation itinerary. Not exactly something the chamber of commerce would put in a tourism brochure."

Davey Waterstone watched the tourist family as they walked down Main Street. He said, "They talked with me about it already."

"Who? The chamber of commerce?"

"No. The police. Some detective came, said she heard that some people call me the Lord of Walden."

"Was it Kay Wheaton?"

"That was her name. You know her?"

I said, "She arrested Alex Mason's kid for that incident at my house last year."

"Oh, that's right. One of your patients was killed."

"Yes."

"So this makes three straight years with a homicide in Concord. I never thought I'd see the day."

"Why did Kay Wheaton want to talk with you?"

"Showed me pictures of the victim, asked me if I had ever seen her at Walden. Not that anybody would have an easy time recognizing someone with half a face."

"Sounds gruesome."

"I've seen worse, unfortunately."

"In Vietnam," I said.

"Yes, in Vietnam."

"Did you recognize her?"

Davey Waterstone shook his head. "Never saw her before, as far as I know. But like I said, there wasn't much there to recognize, so who knows? I told the detective that the woman probably didn't come from around here. Other than that, I don't know anything."

"Why do you think she wasn't local?"

"She said the only thing they found on the woman was a pocket-sized version of *Walden* that they sell at the gift shop. Very condensed, just has the most familiar passages. Sort of a *Reader's Digest* version. The mark of a dilettante. Someone from this area would most likely want the real version, and probably would own it already."

I checked my watch. "I've got to get going. I had new barn doors installed last week, and I need to paint them."

"Well, take care of yourself, Harry. You never know."

"You never know what?"

"You never know anything. The older I get, the more convinced I am of that."

"You're not that old."

"I'll hit the big five-oh next month. What's the line from that Beatles song? Something about memories that stretch out longer than the road ahead of us."

"Something like that," I replied. "You sound a little depressed."

"Is that a professional opinion?"

"It's a friend's opinion."

"What makes you think I'm depressed?"

"For one thing, the way you talk about giving away money."

"I thought that was something manic-depressive people do when they're high."

I said, "Manic people spend money wildly for things they don't have any use for. Depressed people don't care what happens to the things they already have."

He thought about that for a moment. "I have more money than most people. My *money* has more money than most people. The entire Waterstone fortune, nurtured by generations of tight-assed, penny-pinching WASPs. I have everything I need, I have no one to share it with, and I have no one to save it for. Twenty thousand dollars is chicken feed, and fifty fucking years is fifty fucking years." He paused. "Sorry for getting carried away there. How old are you?"

"Forty-four."

He grunted. "That's how old Thoreau was when he died."

"Well, on that comforting thought, I'd best get moving." I stood. "What did he die from?"

"Tuberculosis, supposedly. Who the hell knows? In 1862 they probably didn't know what people died from most of the time unless you fell into a thresher."

I wondered if prostate cancer was a known entity back then. There would have been no screening tests, and the only way of detecting it would have been on an autopsy.

"Was Thoreau autopsied?"

"His writings have been dissected up the yin yang. But I don't think he ever had that particular pleasure himself. Why?"

"Just curious," I replied.

"People tell me I'm a curious person all the time." He smiled for the first time since I joined him. Then the smile faded into a yawn, and Davey Waterstone said, "Maybe I *am* depressed. Or maybe I'm just tired. But most of all, I'm angry as hell that somebody would spill blood at Walden. I hate what people are doing to those woods. Every day they leave their crap there—candy wrappers and condoms and disposable diapers—and real crap, too, for that matter. Then there's all that talk about development in the area. And now someone commits murder right where Thoreau built his home. It's enough to make me sick."

7

After lunch I laid down the primer on the new barn doors. Working at a leisurely pace, I finished late in the afternoon. I washed up, then had an early pizza dinner at Papa Gino's.

When I arrived home at five-thirty, a metallic-blue Toyota with no one in it was parked in my driveway. I didn't recognize the vehicle. A minute or two later Detective Kay Wheaton turned the corner of the house, coming from the direction of the entrance to my office.

"Reminiscing?" I asked.

"Something like that." She gestured toward my office entrance. "It took me less than a day to close the last homicide case in town, so I'm already behind that pace this time around."

A year and a half earlier one of my patients was killed shortly after he left my office. Kay Wheaton handled the investigation, and the day after the slaying, two students from Concord-Carlisle High School were charged.

I said, "I heard that the matter is under investigation, and that your investigators will be out there investigating until everything is completely investigated."

She smiled. "The chief doesn't like talking to the press."

"With good reason."

"What is it between the two of you, anyway?"

"It's a complicated relationship. I used to sleep with his sister."

"He has a sister?"

"That was a joke. I have no idea if he has a sister. It's hard imagining him having any family at all. Easier to think of him being hatched fully grown in a genetic experiment at some underground bioengineering lab."

"He thinks highly of you, too. Yesterday morning at the murder scene, one of the first things he said was that I should talk with you."

"Did he say why?"

"He said that whenever someone is murdered in Concord, Harry Kline seems to be mixed up in it."

"Then I suppose you'll want to know if I have an alibi. What time were the two of you at Walden?"

"Eight o'clock."

"I believe I have that one covered. I was at my doctor's office in Cambridge at that time." *With my best friend's cousin's finger wedged up my ass,* I thought.

"The medical examiner puts the time of death at around sunset Thursday."

"Hmm. I was home alone. No one to corroborate my story. Are you going to read me my rights?"

"Damn it. Why are you giving me such a hard time, Harry? And why are you being so cavalier about such a horrible thing?"

Chastened, I said, "I'm sorry, Kay. I guess it's just gallows humor. Do you have kids?"

"No. I'm not married. Why do you ask?"

"My daughter and her friends go to Walden two or three times a week during the summer. She was there Thursday afternoon, apparently just a few hours before that woman was killed. The thought makes me uneasy, especially when the police haven't made an arrest yet."

"Is that supposed to be a shot?"

"No, of course not."

"All right, then," she said. "Christ, talking to you always gives me a headache."

"You shouldn't say 'Christ.' "

"Sorry. I didn't realize that was an issue for you."

"I'm trying to turn over a new leaf."

"I never know when to take you seriously."

"There's a lot of that going around."

"I thought you were Jewish."

"I am," I said. "How close are you?"

"Not close at all," she replied. "I'm Methodist."

"I mean, how close are you to making an arrest?"

"Oh. Well, let me see. We don't know who the killer is. We don't know who the *victim* was. We don't have any witnesses. We don't have a murder weapon. Except for some dark hairs on her clothing that obviously didn't come from her, we don't have any forensic evidence."

"And so the investigator continues her investigation until all the investigating is complete."

"This isn't funny, Harry."

"I know. It's just my way of dealing with things. Walk with me behind the house. I have something I need to take care of."

Outside the barn, I removed the paintbrushes from the thinner in which they were soaking. Kay glanced up at the second-story apartment that had been carved out of the original barn structure. "Was that there when you bought the house?"

"No. My late wife and I had it put in shortly after we moved here."

"How long ago was that?"

"About fourteen years ago."

"You must know the town fairly well by now."

"Everything is relative. Walk around town, you'll find elderly people living in homes their grandparents were born in."

"The chief says I should make more of an effort to learn about the town. Do you know anything about the Old Manse? That place just down the road from here, next to the North Bridge."

"Descendants of Ezra Ripley still lived there until fifty or sixty years ago. The Trustees of the Reservations own it now."

"Who was Ezra Ripley?"

"The parish minister during the Revolution. Ralph Waldo Emerson's step-grandfather. Why are you curious about the Old Manse?"

"The chief said I should inquire about the French wallpaper in the dining room. Do you have any idea why?"

"Maybe he's thinking of redecorating his home."

We walked around the house and back to her car. I said, "Davey Waterstone told me the crime scene pictures you showed him were pretty brutal."

"Is he a friend of yours?"

"More an acquaintance than a friend."

"Actually, I wondered if he might be one of your patients."

"Why do you say that?"

"He seems odd. They say he practically lives as a hermit. He has a huge estate next to Estabrook Woods, and they say he avoids the mansion and stays in an old trailer on the property."

"There's no law against that, is there?"

"I think it's unusual, that's all. That, and all the time they say he spends in the woods at Walden."

"He's a war hero, Kay. He earned the right to be as odd as he wants to be, and he has enough money to do it any way he wants to."

"What sort of war hero?"

"Vietnam. Some sort of counterinsurgency project."

"Behind enemy lines, stuff like that?"

"I don't know. He doesn't like to talk about it. Lots of Vietnam vets don't like to talk about it. It's important to respect that."

"No need to get upset, Harry. He can live in an outhouse if he wants to, war hero or no war hero. I didn't come here to argue with you."

"Why *did* you come here, Kay? You haven't said."

"I'm not sure. I came out Monument Street because I wanted to check out the Old Manse, but it was closed for the day when I got there. I stopped here on the spur of the moment. I'm not making any headway on the Walden murder. I guess I hoped I might get a little inspiration if I revisited the scene of the last killing. Everything fell into place quickly with that one."

On a cold night, the winter before last, Richie Conover exited my office and stumbled upon two vandals who were spray-painting my house. He shouted at them, then ran after them when they took off down the driveway.

I heard his shouts. I ran outside. I saw two figures struggling in the wooded area next to the driveway.

I ran toward them. Just before I reached them, one of the figures fell to the ground. And then the one that remained standing, reeking of beer, dropped me with a punch to the head.

The vandals fled. There was a sudden brief rustling on the ground just a few yards away. Then I heard a strange and sickening sound: like someone choking and wheezing at the same time. And then all was still.

I reached into my pants pocket and pulled out my key chain. I aimed the weak beam of the small flashlight in the direction of the noises I had just heard.

Richie Conover lay motionless on his back. His eyes stared upward, unblinking.

I crawled toward him on all fours, cutting my hand on the same jagged-edged broken beer bottle that he had been struck with.

Blood poured from a wide gash in the jugular area of Richie Conover's neck. I ripped my shirt off and pressed it against the hideous wound. Holding the shirt in place, I was able to feel a weak but steady pulse. Seconds later the weak pulse became irregular. And after a half minute his pulse was no more.

And thus, on a cloud-darkened frigid winter night, with his blood and my blood dripping on the hard ground, Richie Conover died in my arms.

Kay Wheaton said, "You were brave that night, Harry."

"You're not going to go all mushy on me, are you?"

"Don't hold your breath. Besides, you're attached, if I remember correctly."

"You remember correctly. Anyway, I don't know if I was brave. Mostly, I was just stupid."

"One can be both at the same time." She stepped into her car. "Do you want to go to the Old Manse with me tomorrow afternoon? You can bring your daughter and your womanfriend."

"They're away for the weekend. I don't know. You can give me a call if you want to."

"I could use the company," she said. "Murder always makes me feel lonely."

8

I got an early start on the barn doors on Sunday, and by mid-morning I was finished. The telephone answering machine was flashing when I returned to the house. The counter indicated two calls.

The first message came from Veronica. She said she and Melissa would be home before dark.

I didn't recognize the male voice that left the second message. "Hello, Vee? Veronica? Vee, it's Steven . . . Long time, no see. Geez, what a cliché. Anyway, I heard you're living in Concord. I'm going to be there tonight. I'll be staying somewhere called the Colony Inn. To tell you the truth, I'd really like to see you. You know, catch up on things . . . Well, is this the stupidest message you've ever gotten, or what? Talk to you soon, Vee."

His halting words notwithstanding, the stranger was confident that Veronica would know him from just his first name. Yet it was a name I had never heard her mention.

When Janet and I were together, we knew almost everything about one another. We shared in each other's separate memories of things that had happened long before we met: grade school teachers, first loves, childhood hopes and teenage fears. It was as if our love had taken us back in time, connecting us to one another from the earliest parts of our lives.

Things were different with Veronica. Often she guarded herself from me. And I guess I guarded myself, too: I probably would have told Janet about my prostate screening results as soon as I learned about them, and would have taken her with me to the appointment with the urologist.

Well, enough of that for now. Enough ruminating about my health. Enough longing for a particular intimacy that might never be repeated. And enough wondering about the guy without a last name who knew Veronica well enough to call her Vee, but who didn't know the correct name of the inn he would stay at that night.

I drove past the *Colonial* Inn—not the *Colony* Inn—in the center of town a short while later. I was on my way to the Thoreau Club. I didn't know if I would feel like exercising later in the week, postbiopsy; so I wanted to hit the machines and swim some laps while I was still able to do so. I drove west on Main Street, past Concord Academy and the public library, underneath the railroad tracks and across Route 2.

It was a warm summer morning, the last Sunday in August, and my prostate was enlarged and a killer was on the loose, and I didn't want to think about any of that.

The silver-haired man with broad shoulders, who had been so angry with his doubles partner on Friday morning, was on one of the courts again when I arrived at the club. He was playing with customary ferocity, but this time he was playing alone.

He had reserved some practice time for himself, and this was a new one on me: Not only had he booked the court, but he was using *both* of the club's ball machines. He stood at the net while the machines fired alternating volleys at him from the left and right sides of the baseline. With each return he beamed, triumphant—as if he had vanquished a flesh and bone opponent, and not some metallic foe running on electricity and compressed air.

The machines ran empty. Then he turned and saw me watching. "Hey, you," he shouted. "What are *you* looking at?"

I shrugged and turned to leave.

"Yo," he called. "Get your racket."

"Excuse me?"

"I've seen you play before. You can give me a game. Go get your racket."

"Just like that?"

"Just like that," he said.

"I don't think so."

"Why not?"

"Why not?" I repeated.

"I asked you first."

I didn't know what to say.

"What are you—chicken?"

"Sure," I replied. "Cluck. Cluck."

I turned away again and walked toward the lodge. I heard the thwack of taut nylon strings against the nap of a tennis ball, and a second later the ball whizzed past my right cheek.

I wheeled around and moved toward him. "Hey, you little—"

He laughed out loud. "Come on, come on. It's just a little tennis ball. Listen—name your favorite charity."

"Name my—what?"

"A charity," he said. "Get your racket. Whoever wins two games out of three. Beat me and I write a two-hundred-dollar check to your favorite charity."

"Just like that."

"I told you already," he said. "Just like that."

"And if you beat me?"

"You can buy me a burger at the snack bar." He paused. "Come on, Kline. You've got at least ten years on me. What do you say?"

"You know my name?"

"I've seen you around. We've got something in common."

"What's that?"

"Alex Mason hates both of our guts."

"Who are you?"

"Max Rothman."

I thought I might have heard the name before, but I couldn't place it.

Before I could ask him why Mason hated him, he spoke again, softer this time. "Come on, Kline. Please. I'm running out of people who are willing to play tennis with me."

I think it was that plaintive admission, more than the prospect of winning two hundred dollars for a good cause, that persuaded me to play. I went downstairs to my locker and got my racket, then joined him at mid-court.

He won the spin of the racket. "My serve," Rothman said, grinning. "Just remember, I like my burgers well done."

He aced me with his first serve: a speeding, spinning missile that hit near the baseline and continued on its journey, untouched by my racket. I managed a feeble return from the left side when he served for the second point; it dangled lifelessly above the net, and Rothman angled a chip shot well outside of my reach. I did only marginally better on his third and fourth serves, and just a few minutes after we began I was down, one game to none.

Max Rothman had more power than I did, but the extra years had cut into his mobility and range. I was able to use that to my advantage when I took over the serve in the second game. I kept him on the baseline, and I ran him back and forth along the width of the court. He began to wear down. I took him to deuce, then snuck a passing shot down the left sideline for a point advantage.

It was game point, advantage to me, so I crushed the serve as hard as I could, hoping to surprise him with an extra burst of power. The serve caught the net and dropped on my side. It was the first time either one of us had failed to get the first serve in. I let up on the second serve, not wanting to double fault. Like a pitcher's change-up, the slow-moving serve confused Rothman's timing, and his return sailed over my head and beyond the baseline. We were tied at one game apiece.

We switched sides for the third and final game. As we passed each other on the sideline I noticed his reddened face and quick, shallow breathing. "Let's take a break," I suggested. "I'll get us some water and then we can finish."

"No! No breaks allowed. It's my serve now and I don't want to break the rhythm."

"All right, if you say so. I was just trying to let you catch your breath."

"I say so!" he bellowed. "Worry about yourself."

Max Rothman double-faulted for the first point, and he double-faulted for the second point, and with each bad serve he smacked the rim of his racket against the ground.

He won the next point with another service ace. But when he rushed the net after his next serve, I caught him with a lob to the back right corner, and now we stood at double match point, in my favor.

Rothman struck his third service ace of the match, but I still had him at match point.

I caught his next serve solidly, my best return yet. But Rothman rushed the net again, and he guided a drop shot perfectly into the right forecourt. I ran in, lunged at the ball, and hit a lucky soft line drive over his head and toward his backcourt. I lost my footing and fell on all fours, in no position to make another play if he returned my shot.

Rothman spun completely around and took off after the ball, like an outfielder trying to chase down a fly to deepest center field. And then I realized three things: He would never reach it. It had only a fifty-fifty chance of landing in bounds. And because Rothman was between me and the ball, only he would be able to see where it landed.

The ball hit somewhere in the vicinity of the baseline. Rothman stopped in his tracks and stared at the spot where it landed. I stood and headed toward my baseline, uncertain where my shot had landed, but knowing Rothman would call it out of bounds regardless, and realizing I would have no grounds for argument. We would be at deuce, and I would need to endure his serve once again.

But Max Rothman didn't turn to face me. He stayed locked in position, staring at the baseline on his side of the court. Then he flung his racket to the ground and kicked it toward the sideline. "Shit!" he shouted. "Shit, shit, motherfucking shit!"

He walked to the sideline without making eye contact. He picked up his racket, grabbed his equipment bag, and headed toward the locker room. "I'll mail you a check, asshole," he muttered, and then he was gone.

9

I asked Kay Wheaton why she decided to become a cop.

"My father was on the job," she replied. "I was the only girl in the family, and he never paid attention to me. I thought I could force him to notice me if I followed in his footsteps."

"Most fathers dote on their only daughters."

"Well, my baptism pictures and high school graduation pictures were on the same roll of film, if that gives you any idea."

We were standing on the North Bridge, the wooden footbridge that spans the narrow river in the shadow of the Old Manse, a short walk from my house.

She said, "This is a very pretty place."

"Most battlefields are. People were killed here. It's easy to lose sight of that, precisely because it *is* such a pretty place."

Children were playing and feeding ducks on the east bank of the peaceful stream. Maybe it was my imagination, but parents seemed to hover especially close on this Sunday afternoon, two days after the discovery of the Walden Pond murder victim.

On the other side of the river, visitors strolled to the crest of the low hill: toward the stately building, once a private residence, that was converted years ago into a visitors' center for Minuteman National Park.

Kay said, "What in the world were British soldiers doing all the way out here, anyway?"

"They were looking for gunpowder they heard the rebels

had hidden in Concord. They lined the east side of the river, where those kids are playing. The Minutemen gathered across the river. When the Redcoats fired, the Minutemen fired back. That was the first time Americans returned British fire. It hadn't happened at the Boston Massacre or in Lexington. That's why they called it the shot heard 'round the world. You could say the Revolutionary War started right here."

"And *you* could probably get a job as a park tour guide," Kay said. "Go on. I'm listening."

"Ralph Waldo Emerson's father was six years old in 1775. He watched the battle from the second floor of the Old Manse."

"Isn't six years old a little young to be a father? And why do they call it the Old Manse?"

" 'Manse' is a Scottish word for a clergyman's residence. Emerson's grandfather was a minister."

We continued across the footbridge and came to the statue: a life-size figure of a Minuteman grasping the handle of a plow in one hand and a musket in the other. Kay read aloud the Emerson verse that was chiseled into the statue's base. " 'By the rude bridge that arched the flood, their flag to April's breeze unfurled. Here once the embattled farmer stood, and fired the shot heard 'round the world.' "

We stepped aside so an elderly woman could take a picture of her grandchildren standing next to the statue.

Kay said, "The chief told me your town wouldn't let the National Guard copy the statue for its headquarters."

"I'm afraid he's right," I said. "A lot of pious talk about preserving the town's unique heritage, and I'm sure some people sincerely felt that way. But for a lot of people, that was just a smokescreen for their own elitism. By the way, that's what started the bad blood between Alex Mason and me. Alex opposed the Guard's request. He and I argued about it at town meeting. Voices rose. Intelligence was questioned. Motives were impugned. He said so many stupid things that even his friends laughed at him. He thinks I goaded him into making a fool of himself, and he's never forgiven me for that."

"Does that bother you?"

"A little. It's a small town. Alex is rich. Alex is influential.

And on those few occasions when he musters enough energy to pluck his head out of his ass, he's pretty smart. And he's so full of himself that *he* probably blames *me* for what happened to his son."

Tommy Mason was only seventeen when he got drunk and vandalized my house. He probably thought he was doing a favor for his father. But now he was doing a prison sentence for manslaughter.

Kay said, "By the way, he's back in town."

"Who?"

"Tommy Mason. A few weeks ago he was transferred to NECC."

It was a state prison farm, fenceless, near the Route 2 rotary. I said, "I'm surprised they put him in a minimum security prison so quickly, and so close to his home."

"Well, like you said—Alex Mason is rich, and Alex Mason is influential."

We crossed back over the bridge to the Redcoats' side. We passed the grave of five British soldiers who died at the battle on that April day in 1775.

Kay said, "I'm sure that killing someone was the last thing on Tommy Mason's mind when he and his buddy came to your house that night. I can't say the same for whoever killed my unidentified corpse Thursday evening."

"What do you mean?"

"Whether you do it coldly or in the heat of passion, you don't bludgeon someone to death from behind by accident."

"No, I suppose not."

"And in this case, I think the victim knew the assailant."

She told me her theory: that no woman alone in the woods at dusk would keep her back toward a stranger.

"All right, then," I said. "The killer knew his victim, and maybe by the time they got to Thoreau's cabin he was intending to kill her. Do you have any idea who they are? Or were, in her case." When Kay didn't reply, I said, "Are you allowed to talk about things like that while you're still investigating?"

"I'm not sure there *are* any rules in this situation, Harry. I don't have to worry about telling you what I know, because basically I don't know a damn thing. She didn't leave a car in the lot, or if she did, the killer drove it away. We got the credit card slips from the gift shop and tracked down everyone who charged a purchase that day. They're all accounted for, and no one saw anything suspicious. She wore an old gold cross with faded initials on the back. We're pretty certain the initials are C.G. No one with those initials has been reported missing in the past week."

I pointed at a break in the stone wall that lined the path, and we passed through it and headed toward the Old Manse. "When I told my daughter about the murder, the first words out of her mouth were, 'Was she raped?' "

"She thinks like a woman. How old is she?"

"She'll be thirteen a week from Saturday."

"Well, the victim wasn't raped. You can tell your daughter that if you think it will make her feel safer. And if I'm right about the victim knowing her killer, that should make your daughter feel safer, too."

"Why?"

Kay said, "If he knew his victim and killed her intentionally, it's less likely we have someone out there who will kill again at random."

"A few years ago a mentally ill man I knew killed a series of people. I helped the FBI track him down. That's how I met Veronica. She and I had to inform a couple in San Antonio that their daughter had been murdered. It was the most difficult thing I've ever done."

"I know what you mean," she said. "I've had to do that, too. And sooner or later, it will have to be done with the family of this latest murder victim. I wonder if anyone misses her yet. Is there someone, somewhere, waiting for news, worrying what they'll hear when that news comes?"

I said, "What if you never identify her? Wouldn't that be even worse for her family—never to know what happened?"

She shrugged. "You heard what your friend Davey Waterstone said about the condition of the corpse. If that happened to someone you loved, would you want to know?"

I didn't have an answer for that question.

We entered the Old Manse through the gift shop. Kay identified herself to the young woman behind the counter and said she needed to ask some questions about the French wallpaper in the dining room.

"I just work here on weekends, detective, and I don't know much about the house. There's a tour finishing in a few minutes. I'm sure Margaret the guide will be happy to answer your questions before she starts the next tour."

She said it quickly, as if it were one long hyphenated word: Margaret-the-Guide.

As if on cue, the door between the gift shop and the old kitchen swung open, and a well-coiffed woman in her sixties led a small group of people into the room.

Kay took a step toward the woman, but I grabbed her lightly by the arm. "Wait," I said. "Let's go on the tour."

"Not today, Harry. I really don't—"

"You said you wanted to learn more about Concord. And I haven't been inside the house since my first year in town. Come on—you might enjoy it. My treat."

She smiled, and we fell in line with a couple from Ohio and three elderly women from Hartford. Margaret-the-Guide said, "The old parsonage, as Nathaniel Hawthorne once called it, was built around 1770 for the Reverend William Emerson and his family." And for the next half hour we learned about the succession of fabled residents and the important events they witnessed.

In a first-floor room that looked out on the North Bridge, our guide told us that Nathaniel and Sophia Hawthorne lived in the Old Manse for the first three years of their marriage. "In March of 1844, Sophia gave birth in this house to their daughter, Una. If you will, take a close look at this windowpane, right over here."

One of the Hartford women said, "There's something scratched into the glass, but I can't make it out."

Margaret-the-Guide smiled. "One winter day there was a fierce ice storm. Sophia etched these words into the windowpane. 'Una Hawthorne stood on this windowsill, January twenty-second, 1845, while the trees were all glass chandeliers. A goodly show which she liked much, though only ten months old.' "

I was drawn to the old glass and the faint markings. I stood there even as the others began to file out of the room. Though the Hawthorne girl lived and died long before me, I could picture her so clearly: standing at this very window and watching with wonderment. And I could picture another little girl as well, gazing through another window on another Concord winter day . . .

"What is it, Harry? Is something wrong?"

"No . . . not really. I was just remembering something."

"They're heading into the dining room now. Let's go, okay?"

A huge stuffed owl was perched in a glass case in the dining room. Our guide told us that one of the residents in the late 1800s always had to throw a sheet over it when she walked into the room, so eerily did the owl's eyes seem to follow her wherever she stood. I looked at the owl; he seemed to look directly back at me. I moved a few feet to the left, then several feet to my right. No matter where in the room I stood, the owl's eyes did, indeed, appear to track me.

The wallpaper—a design of pale green vines on a black background—looked new. Kay said, "That isn't the original wallpaper, is it?"

"No," replied Margaret-the-Guide, "but it is an exact copy. The original wallpaper was hung in 1780 when Reverend Ezra Ripley lived here."

"I've been told there's an interesting story about the wallpaper."

"Yes, there is." Margaret-the-Guide hesitated for a moment, as if uncertain whether to tell what she knew. "Ezra Ripley always said it was a French imitation of an English product. But when the trustees restored this room in the 1970s, they pulled down what was left of that 1780 wallpaper and found the stamp of England's King George on the back. Well, I thank you for your attention, ladies and gentlemen, and I invite you to pass some time in our gift shop on your way out of this wonderful old house."

Kay and I stepped outside. "I don't get it," she said. "French, English—what difference does it make?"

"In 1780 the colonies were still at war with England. They were boycotting British goods. This wallpaper was contraband, and it was passed off as a French product."

"In other words . . ."

"In other words," I said, "Reverend Ezra Ripley, town minister and staunch patriot, was a smuggler and a hypocrite. He probably put it up by the light of the midnight oil so the Sons of Liberty wouldn't find out what he was doing."

"What do you suppose they would have done to him if they found out?"

"As my father sometimes says, he would have gotten a slow death, by hanging."

"But hanging is a quick death."

"Only when they hang you by the *neck*."

Kay considered the story of Ezra Ripley's wallpaper as we walked along the path toward Monument Street, then back toward my house. Then she smiled and said, "You Concord folks are really something else, aren't you?"

10

Early that evening, still alone in the house, I stepped into my daughter's bedroom. I couldn't recall the last time I had gone in there without Melissa being present. Hell, I hardly ever went into her room these days even when she was there. She was growing, and she was changing, and as she entered her adolescence there came a distance between us that was unfamiliar and disconcerting.

She used to throw herself into my arms when she said goodnight. We seldom embraced now; touching was limited to pecks on the cheek or light, brief pats on the shoulder. Veronica saw this, and her explanation was no doubt informed by her recollection of her own experience as a girl. She said, "Your daughter's breasts have come between the two of you."

That distance seemed especially pronounced whenever we talked in her room. Even now, standing there alone in her private space, I felt like an intruder: alien, adult, male.

I walked to her window seat and gazed outside.

Uma Hawthorne stood on this windowsill, January 22, 1845, while the trees were all glass chandeliers.

I recalled a winter morning, more than eight years earlier, when Melissa stood in that same spot and looked at the snow-covered field.

I remembered: Janet's parents had stayed with Melissa at our house overnight, while I remained in Janet's hospital room for the end we all knew was near. And in the early hours of that February morning, my wife died as I held her in my arms.

I returned home and walked upstairs to Melissa's room, and I waited quietly for her to stir. When she finally opened her eyes, I tried to say the lines I'd rehearsed—about God loving Janet too much to see her suffer any longer, and Janet going to heaven where she would watch over us forever. But I couldn't get the words out.

Without expression my four-year-old child said, "Mommy's dead, isn't she?"

"Yes, sweetheart. Mommy's dead."

She walked slowly to her window seat and gazed out at the field beside our house. For several minutes she sat there, motionless: no tears, no wailing, no reaching out to me in anger or pain. I tried to hug her, but she pulled away. I tried to get her to talk, but she kept her thoughts buried inside. She turned a blank stare to the snow outside.

The moment Margaret-the-Guide told us about Uma Hawthorne watching the winter trees, I thought about that morning when Melissa looked out her window.

If Kay were still there, I would have told her I was wrong earlier: Informing that San Antonio couple that their child was dead was the *second* hardest thing I had ever done. The hardest thing was telling Melissa that her mother was gone.

Perhaps one day, sooner than I had heretofore imagined, Bobby or Veronica would be bringing more sad news to my daughter. . . .

Take one thing at a time, I thought. *Tonight Veronica and Melissa will be home. After my daughter is asleep, I'll talk with Veronica, really talk this time.* She had a right to know.

Melissa said, "I've really gotta go," and she ran into the house and headed for the bathroom.

"I'm glad you're here," Veronica said. "I'm too tired to carry these suitcases. We were up late. You know how my aunt gets when she's in one of her energetic moods." She opened the trunk. "We listened to the news on our way home. I didn't hear any mention of the Walden murder."

I pulled the suitcases from the car and carried them toward the house. "According to Kay Wheaton, there's nothing to report."

"Who's she?"

"The detective on the case. You remember her. She handled Richie Conover's murder last year."

"Oh, right. I forgot. I only met her once." We entered the kitchen. Veronica sat and leaned back in one of the chairs, exhausted.

"I saw her this weekend and she told me a little bit about the case. We went over to the Old—"

Melissa came into the kitchen and headed for the refrigerator. "Dad, I learned the most amazing things about eastern religions from Aunt Marilyn. Did you know she used to live in India?"

"Yes, she told me about that once." I noted without comment that Melissa had just referred to Marilyn as her own aunt.

Veronica's aunt Marilyn was a manic-depressive woman in her fifties. Years earlier, in between two successful careers and a few psychiatric hospitalizations, she went to India and joined an ashram, in search of whatever it is ashram-joiners search for.

Just then the front doorbell chimed. I left the kitchen and went to see who was visiting, unexpected, on a Sunday evening.

The man was taller than me, and younger, with dark hair, a rich tan, and a look of confusion on his face. "I hope I have the right house," he said. "I'm looking for Veronica Pace. My name is—"

"Steven!" yelled Veronica, who had followed me to the door without me knowing it. She rushed past me and fell into the man's embrace. "I can't believe it's you."

They kissed each other on the lips. "Did you get my message, Vee?"

"Message? No, I just got in. I haven't checked my messages yet. How *are* you? What are you doing here? My God, you look terrific."

She hugged him, lingering a little too long to suit me. Then she saw me out of the corner of her eye and broke the embrace. "Oh—Harry Kline, this is Steven Farr. Steven, this is Harry."

He extended his hand. "Harry, nice to meet you. Geez, Vee. What's it been? Ten years?"

"More like twelve years plus. The end of my junior year, remember?"

"Oh, yeah. That's right." He looked a little uneasy, as if he had been reminded of something he would rather not think about.

I stood there quietly, the odd man out in this conversation, hoping for an explanation that would tell me who this person was and how he fit into Veronica's life.

With a slight hesitation, Veronica said, "Steven was my . . . boyfriend in college."

"Well, love, you had lots of boyfriends," he said, as if to diminish the importance she had just placed on their relationship. I wondered if he did that for my benefit or his, or if I was just reading too damn much into every nuance.

He turned to me and said, "To tell you the truth, your ladyfriend here was one hot shit back then."

Who the hell was this man whose arm was still curled around my girlfriend's waist?

11

Bobby pulled out of my driveway and headed down Monument Street toward the center of town.

He said, "I still think you're too old to be referring to Veronica as your girlfriend."

"Then what am I supposed to call her?"

"How about 'my womanfriend'?"

I shook my head. "Sounds like someone you play bridge with, or go with on a senior citizen's group tour to the Catskills."

" 'Companion'?"

"Nope. That's a home health aide."

" 'Partner' is a good term for someone you're screwing. My law partners screw me all the time."

"Cute."

"How about 'lover'?"

"Sounds gay."

"How enlightened of you. What do you mean, 'sounds gay'?"

"Every gay or lesbian person I've ever known referred to their significant others as their lovers."

"There you go," Bobby said. "Call Veronica your 'significant other.'"

"That sounds like a term in a statistics book. Also, it raises the question, what is an *in*-significant other?"

"Well, I guess that leaves us with 'cohabitant,' 'concubine,' or 'love-bunny.'"

"Perfect."

He said, "My parents went through this years ago when my brother started living with someone. They had no idea what to call her. 'Slut' just didn't have the right ring to it."

In the center of town we drove by the Colonial Inn, where Steven was staying. Then we passed the rectory for St. Bernard's Catholic Church.

Bobby said, "There's your priest friend."

Father John Fitzpatrick, the pastor at St. Bernard's, was a good friend to me and to my daughter. He stepped into the street without looking, prompting rigorous horn-blasting on Bobby's part.

I said, "I wonder—if you accidentally run over a priest, is that a mortal sin or a venial sin?"

"Probably neither. It's probably a good deed—a *mitzvah*—because the priest goes to heaven on the express train instead of having to wait for the local."

"You're a very wise man."

"Thank you," Bobby replied. "Look on the backseat. I have something for you."

I turned around and saw it: a doughnut-shaped pillow.

He said, "I thought you might need that on the ride home."

"A very wise man," I said. "And thoughtful, too."

We took Lexington Road out of the center of town, then turned onto Cambridge Turnpike in front of Ralph Waldo Emerson's house.

"You're sure Veronica never mentioned this guy to you before?"

"She's not big on talking about the past. I guess over the years she had to spend too much energy trying to keep the past from dragging her down."

"You mean the business with her mother's murder."

"Right."

"Makes sense. So—is this guy good looking?"

"I guess so, if you like the tall, well-built, chiseled-features movie star sort of look."

"What's he doing in Concord?"

"He said something about a rendezvous with a friend. I

didn't get to hear much about him. He and Veronica went to the inn for drinks and some catch-up conversation, and I was asleep by the time she came home. I was planning to tell her about my prostate situation last night, but she was with Steven, instead."

"You still haven't told her anything?"

"No, I haven't."

"If you don't tell her today, you may need to come up with something creative to explain why you can't sit down."

"Any suggestions?"

"She's Protestant, right?"

"Episcopalian."

"Just make up some Jewish holiday and say you're observing it by remaining standing all day."

The road we were on merged with Route 2, and we headed east into Cambridge.

I said, "Steven said Veronica used to be a real hot shit."

"I didn't realize people still use that expression."

"Neither did I. I wonder—how does it come to pass that comparing someone to warm excrement can be considered a compliment?"

Bobby and Jamie greeted each other warmly. She waited until Bobby was out of earshot to ask if I had followed my pre-procedure ingestion and extrusion instructions. Then she led me into an examination room.

The air was cold.

I changed into a johnny and laid facedown. The examination table was cold.

Jamie said, "The probe may cause some discomfort, or it may not. Different people experience it differently."

The lubricating jelly was cold.

"I'll be using ultrasound to guide the placement of the probe. It has a punching device in the tip, and I'll take about a half-dozen tissue samples through the rectal wall. You'll probably experience discomfort, but it will be over quickly. Well, Hilton Head, here we come."

The probe was cold, ice cold.

"Yow!! What the hell are you doing?"

"Try to lie still, Harry. When you move or tense your muscles, the natural movement of the sphincter tends to push the probe out, which makes the procedure take longer."

"Thanks for sharing that with— God*damn*, that hurts."

Jamie Ray's hand on my back was soft. Her perfume was sweet. The pain she inflicted was indescribable.

"Holy fucking shit! Goddamn it!"

"All right, Harry. I'm going to take the first sample now."

Searing pain: red-hot, jagged, slicing, piercing.

"Jesus H. *Christ*!"

Bobby pressed the elevator button in the hallway outside Jamie Ray's office. "What does the H in Jesus H. Christ stand for, anyway?"

"You heard me say that?"

"Pal of mine, people in Chelsea and Dorchester heard you say that."

We entered the elevator and began our descent. I said, "I think it stands for 'haploid.' "

"Haploid?"

"It's a term from genetics. It means, having only half the standard number of chromosomes. Which is what you would expect from a virgin birth."

"Oh." He thought about that for a moment. "You're jerking me around, aren't you?"

"That's what the word means. But yes, I'm jerking you around."

"Just checking."

I waited while Bobby brought his car to the front of the building. I was weak and fatigued, but by the time he came for me, most of the pain had subsided.

"Want the pillow?"

"No, I'm all right. I feel pretty drained, but otherwise I'm okay. The good thing is, if I had any lingering unconscious doubts about my sexual orientation, they're gone forever. That probe was without a doubt the most intense physical pain I've ever experienced."

"I infer from the colorful progress reports you shouted out every few seconds that you wouldn't recommend this procedure."

"I'll die before I do that again."

"Let's hope it doesn't come to that."

We headed west on Mount Auburn Street until we came to its junction with Fresh Pond Parkway, which we followed toward Route 2.

Bobby said, "I cleared my schedule until late this afternoon because I wasn't certain how long you would need me. I guess you don't feel like coming back to my house for some tennis, do you?"

"No, thanks."

I told him about my match the day before with Max Rothman. I said, "I had seen him around the club, but yesterday was the first time I met him. Surprised the hell out of me when he called my final shot inbounds."

"He's a surprising guy. Hard to predict."

"You know him?"

"We've met. You know who he is, don't you?"

"No." .

"He's the developer who bought the old Logan tract, near Walden Woods."

I thought for a moment, trying to jog my memory. I wasn't very interested in the issue, so what I heard sometimes didn't stick with me. "It has something to do with affordable housing, am I right?"

Bobby nodded. "He's trying to make an arrangement with the state to put in two dozen units for low income families. Nice tax incentives for him if he can pull it off."

"You're opposed to that, aren't you?"

"Thoreau did some of his best seed observations on that land. And it's just too damn close to the pond not to have a runoff effect. I spoke against the proposal at the Planning Board hearing where his permit was considered. They haven't put it to a final vote yet. And several of us are working at the statehouse level, talking to people on Beacon Hill. Trying to persuade them to order more environmental studies. Trying to get the tract designated as a landmark. Trying a variety of things to stop Max Rothman from developing the land."

"I wonder what Rothman thinks about the murder."

"I doubt he thinks much about it at all. It doesn't help him, and it doesn't hurt him. He's a pretty driven guy, and he's only going to focus on things that directly affect his plans."

"He impresses me as someone who can be very unpleasant when he doesn't get what he wants. Hey—as long as we have the time, turn right onto Huron Avenue. A little detour for old time's sake."

"You want to go to Hutchinson Street?"

"Yes," I replied. "Take me to Hutchinson Street. Please."

"You're sure?"

"I'm sure."

He sighed, then put his right turning signal on. At the light, he turned. "When will Jamie have the results of your biopsy?"

"They should be back at the end of next week or early the following week. Either right before or right after Melissa's birthday."

"How is Melissa doing, now that the summer is almost over?"

"Your goddaughter is pissed that I don't want her walking in the woods until they catch whoever killed that woman at Walden. Also, she's wearing bras."

"Most girls are by that age, I suppose."

"About fifty percent," I said.

"The figure is probably lower if you live in Cambridge or Berkeley. And much higher in Dallas or Revere."

"You and Cheryl are coming to her birthday party a week from Saturday, right?"

"Yes." He paused. "I still say I should be going to her bat mitzvah."

"Ah, shit. Let's not get into that today. Okay?"

"Okay."

It was a sore point between us: my allowing Melissa to grow up without a formal religious education. We had argued about it several times. Once, when the discussion got heated, he tried to bring the specter of my late wife into play. "This is *not* what

Janet would have wanted," he had said, and he probably was right. But today he had the decency not to push the issue.

I said, "Melissa is interested in religion. She's interested in all religions. She thinks about it and reads about it more than I ever did. For example, have you ever heard of Kurban Bayram?"

Bobby pondered that for a moment. "Skinny kid, very friendly? I think he was a year behind us at Tufts. Wasn't he in Theta Chi?"

"No, you idiot. Kurban Bayram means 'Sacrifice Holiday.' Muslims celebrate Abraham's faithfulness to God by sacrificing rams, like he did. Boy, I hate that story."

"You hate Kurban Bayram?"

"No. The story about Abraham in the land of Moriah, where God told him to kill his son as a sacrifice."

"I thought that happened on Highway 61."

"You're thinking of the Dylan song, you moron. I mean, what kind of God would do that?"

"But God didn't go through with it," Bobby said. "It was just a test. After Abraham passed the test, God told him to sacrifice a ram instead. Thus clearing the way for the glorious celebration of Kuban . . . whatever."

"I'm serious. I hate the Old Testament God. All of those plagues, all of that pestilence. And the smiting. Who the hell wants a God who does all that smiting? A God that vengeful?"

"Vengeful, perhaps," Bobby said, "but at least he's intelligent. The New Testament God is kindly but stupid."

"Why do you say that?"

"Look at what He let the Romans do to *His* son. I know that the whole crucifixion-resurrection thing was supposed to show that Christ really was the Messiah. But this is God we're talking about. He's supposed to be smart. Couldn't He come up with a better plan?"

I meant what I said to Bobby about the Old Testament deity. But we both knew what really lay behind my personal rift with God, if truly there were a God: the loss of my wife, and the despair it took me so long to overcome.

Bobby parked at the curb in front of the three-story apartment house on Hutchinson Street. We stepped out of the car and looked up at the third-story apartment Janet and I shared early in our marriage, when I was in my residency training at McLean Hospital.

I said, "There were some good times here. A part of me has always stayed here, if that makes any sense."

"I think what you mean is, a part of this place has always stayed with you." He put his hand on my shoulder.

"I wonder what she would have thought about what I'm going through. I wonder what she thinks about it now, if there is such a thing as 'now' for her. I told you what Janet's father said about *her* cancer, didn't I?"

Nathan Jacobs was a difficult man: overbearing and controlling. Several months after Janet died, her parents visited Concord for a few days. One evening the two of them were sitting in the den, unaware that I was just about to walk into the room. I overheard Nathan say to his wife, "None of this would have happened if we'd kept Janet with us in Connecticut. There were plenty of boys there she could have been very happy with."

I appeared in the doorway just as he finished his words. Our eyes met for a moment.

Rita Jacobs, whose back was toward me, didn't see me. She said, "Janet was very happy with Harry, dear."

I waited for him to say something appropriate to her: to acknowledge that it was his grief talking, that it was foolish to think of me as the carcinogenic agent responsible for Janet's death.

But his only words were, "I've said all I'm going to say on the matter."

I turned to Bobby and said, "So Nathan blames me, and I blame God, and the only thing that really matters is that she's gone."

We turned and walked back to his car.

I said, "I love Veronica. I want to stay with her forever. But every now and then I think about Janet, and I wonder. You know?"

"I know, pal of mine. I know."

12

Veronica was at her office in Boston, and Melissa was at Crane Beach with the family of one of her friends. I rested for a while after Bobby dropped me off at my house. Then I drove to the pizza shop on Thoreau Street for lunch, across the street from the commuter train depot.

Davey Waterstone was seated alone at one of the few tables in the room, the only sit-down customer in this predominantly take-out shop. He invited me to join him, and we waited for the clerk at the counter to tell us our orders were ready.

"You look like shit," he said.

"That's a relief."

"Why is that a relief?"

"Because that's how I feel. I'd hate to feel like shit and not get credit for it."

"Rough morning in the office? All your patients running out of Prozac at the same time?"

I shook my head. "I'm closed for business until a week from tomorrow, the day after Labor Day."

"A lot of you shrinks take this time of the year off. Is that a derogatory term to use, 'shrinks'?"

"During my residency at McLean Hospital, we used to call ourselves shrinks-in-training. 'Shits,' for short."

"A healthy percentage of Waterstone forefathers passed through McLean. Foremothers, too. Maybe I should say, an unhealthy percentage. Back then, it was the place to be if you were rich and nuts. I come from a long line of rich nuts."

The clerk called out Davey's number. He called mine a minute or two later. Davey returned to the table with a vegetarian sub and a bottle of sparkling water. I had a small pepperoni pizza with extra cheese, and a twenty-ounce bottle of Pepsi to wash it down.

He said, "Afraid your cholesterol level is running too low?"

"I want to be unhealthy when I die."

"Keep that up and you will be."

That's what I'm afraid of, I thought. "That reminds me," I said. "Did you hear what happened at the O.J. trial this morning?"

He checked his watch. "Nothing, yet. It's not quite nine o'clock, L.A. time. Today's session hasn't started." He paused. "Oh. I see. This is a joke you want to tell me."

I said, "The final blood tests are in. His lawyer tells O.J. that there's bad news and there's good news. The bad news is, the DNA results leave no doubt about his guilt. O.J.'s blood is at the murder scene, Nicole's blood is in the Bronco, Ron Goldman's blood is in O.J.'s house."

"And?"

"The good news is, O.J.'s cholesterol is down to 140."

Davey Waterstone took a swig from his bottle of water. "Using a knife like that, real up close and personal. Much harder on the person than using a gun."

"Why would it be harder on someone to be knifed than to be shot?"

"I'm talking about the killer," he replied. "Harder to get over a knifing than a shooting."

I suspected he had experience with both of those things, either firsthand or vicarious, in Vietnam.

"Up close and personal," Davey repeated. "Like the woman at Walden. Whoever killed her probably has that video running through his mind, continuous loop. Unless he's kept himself drunk."

"Or unless he killed himself afterward."

He pondered that for a few moments. "I hadn't thought about that as a possibility."

"Me, neither, until right now."

He picked up his knife. "They cut these subs in half, but I like them in quarters."

With two quick and deft movements of the knife, he turned two sections into four. Then he held the knife up and studied it for several seconds.

"Something wrong?" I asked.

"I'm just thinking. They say whoever sliced up Nicole Simpson knew her, because you don't brutalize someone like that unless you want them dead very badly. And you don't want someone dead that badly unless you have a relationship with them. If that's true, then the same thing would hold for the Walden woman."

"Kay Wheaton thinks the victim knew her killer."

"She talked to you, too?"

I nodded.

He said, "Did she show you the pictures?"

"No. And I didn't ask to see them."

"Smart move. They're not easy to forget. They say the crime scene pictures in the O.J. case are the same way."

"Do you think O.J. did it?"

"Let me tell you, Harry. It doesn't take any special genius to kill someone. And O.J. is no genius. It doesn't take much. Something happens, and you don't expect it. And then you don't expect to do what it is you wind up doing, but you do it anyway. Funny thing is, it almost always feels like self-defense to you when you do it, even if you're not really in physical danger. If you have time to think, you tell yourself there's no other way, that it's justified. Or you tell that to yourself later, when there's no point in letting yourself feel any other way about what it is you did." He paused. "Am I making any sense?"

"I think I understand what you're trying to say."

He laughed. "That sounds like something you read in a how-to-be-a-psychiatrist handbook. All-purpose shrink response, number two hundred fourteen."

He stared at the knife again, and then he set it down. Then he looked directly at me, all mirth gone. "You know what surprises me most about murder, Harry?"

"What's that?"

"That more of us don't do it, and that it doesn't happen more often. That woman at the pond. Why her? I don't know that. But it only takes a minute to become a killer. I *do* know that. *That* I know."

He turned his attention to his sub and attacked it with gusto, no more disconcerted by our conversation than he would have been had we been discussing our socks. But I was imagining the pepperoni on my pizza as scabbed-over wounds, and the extra-thick cheese layer was like gelatinous scar tissue.

The door swung open and a tall man with a youthful but harsh countenance strode past us and up to the counter. I didn't recognize him. Davey saw him and muttered something under his breath.

The tall man must have telephoned ahead, because his order was waiting for him. He paid for it—some sort of sub, wrapped in foil to keep the heat in—then walked briskly toward the door.

He passed directly in front of us. He stopped in his tracks, glared at Davey, and said, "Why don't you do something useful for a change—like, get a job?" Then he continued toward the door.

I said, "Who in the world—"

The tall man changed his mind about leaving. He stopped, whirled around, then strode back toward Davey. "What will it take to make you realize that people are more important than your fucking trees?"

"No matter how hard you and Max Rothman try, Robert, those trees will be here long after you're gone. Why don't you go back to Cambridge, or Brookline, or wherever you keep that rock you crawled out from."

"I've got as much business being in Concord as you do. My grandmother—"

"Yeah, yeah, I know—your grandmother was a whore."

"That's right. Don't forget it."

"You know, I really like saying that. 'Your grandmother was a whore.' "

"Go fuck yourself, Waterstone."

The tall man stomped out of the pizza shop.

I felt like I had tumbled into a meeting of some secret society, where the players communicated with gestures and meaning-frought phrases that were incomprehensible to the uninitiated.

"Davey, who the hell was he?"

He snickered. "That was Robert Butler." He wiped his face with a napkin, smiled broadly, and stood up. "That was Robert Butler," he repeated as he walked away, "and his grandmother was a whore."

He laughed, and then he was gone.

13

Bobby said, "Robert Butler?"

"Butler," I repeated into the phone. "As in, 'The butler did it.' "

"I heard you the first time. I'm just surprised you don't know who he is."

"I'm drawing a blank. From what Davey Waterstone said, I gather the guy moved to town recently."

"He has family roots here," Bobby said, "but he doesn't live here. He's from Cambridge. He's an outside agitator. Robert Kennedy Butler."

"Outside agitator? The way you say that, you sound like one of those sheriffs from Alabama or Mississippi during the civil rights— Hey! Robert *Kennedy* Butler!"

"Now you know?"

"Now I know. And he's about as humorless in person as he is in his letters to the *Journal*."

Butler directed a community-action organization that lobbied for the creation of affordable housing for low income families. In letters to the *Concord Journal* he contended that racism and elitism—the desire to keep certain types of people out of Concord—lay behind the efforts to torpedo the development of the old Logan tract into low-cost residential units.

Bobby said, "He's tied in with your tennis buddy, Max Rothman. Maybe we can all do doubles sometime."

"Is his name really Robert *Kennedy* Butler?"

"That's his real name. His father shamed the Concord Butlers by marrying a Jew from Brookline, turning Democrat, and giving substantial sums of money to the NAACP. I think he worked for Bobby Kennedy at some point, or raised money for him. Thus Robert Kennedy Butler."

"Well, it was a hell of a weird scene. Davey Waterstone called Butler's grandmother a prostitute, and Butler agreed with him. In fact, he seemed damn proud of it."

"A prostitute? That doesn't make sense."

Bobby put me on hold for a few seconds. When he came back on the line he said, "I'm going to have to take another call. Are you feeling okay?"

"Good enough."

"You need anything, you let me know. Right?"

"Right."

"And tonight, tell Veronica what's going on. Right?"

"Right."

"Take care, pal of mine."

After we ended our conversation I went into the den to lie down for a while. As I walked into the room there was a sudden, sharp throb somewhere deep inside my lower body: not too intense, not too prolonged, just a reminder of my morning ordeal in Jamie Ray's examination room.

Veronica called to tell me she planned to take the early commuter train out of North Station. "I invited Steven to come over. I'm going to pick him up at the inn on my way home. I thought we might grill those swordfish steaks for dinner."

When she said "we," she was referring to me. Veronica had never met a piece of meat or fish she couldn't char beyond recognition, especially when using the gas grill in the backyard.

I said, "Is he still in Concord?"

"Yes. That's what I just said."

I knew I was being foolish, but that thought didn't please me. "We only have three swordfish steaks. I guess Melissa will be just as happy with a burger."

"Don't be silly. I'll pick up two more steaks at Stop & Shop when I get off the train."

"Two more?"

"One for Steven, and one for his fiancée."

"Fiancée?"

"Didn't I tell you? Steven is getting married soon. He expects her in this afternoon. Tomorrow they're driving up to the White Mountains to go camping."

So he had a fiancée, whom he presumably thought was a hot shit; and tomorrow they would be in New Hampshire. I was feeling better already.

Steven Farr was surprised that Veronica had settled down with a psychiatrist. "She was the least introspective girlfriend I ever had, Harry. Isn't that right, Vee?"

"I never thought about it," she said.

"That's my point, exactly. To tell you the truth, if I had to choose between the two of us, I would've said that I was the one who would be more likely to hook up with a psychiatrist. Have you ever heard of CEMA, Harry?".

"I have an Aunt Seema."

"Not 'Seema,' the person. CEMA. C-E-M-A."

Cancer eats me away, I thought. "It doesn't ring a bell," I said.

He poured his third glass of Chablis. "Chronic existential male *angst*," he said. "A condition diagnosed with alarming frequency amongst liberal arts majors who never decided what they wanted to be when they grow up. And I'm their poster boy." He flashed a broad smile, apparently impressed by his own cleverness.

There were two empty chairs at the picnic table that I had hurriedly set up after Veronica's phone call. Melissa had already wolfed down her dinner and was next door at Emily's house. And the poster boy's fiancée was a no-show.

Veronica said, "I'm so disappointed that Sandi isn't here."

"Yes," I said. "So disappointed. Really, I am."

Steven set his glass on the table a little too hard. Wine splashed onto his hand. "She planned to be in Concord last night. But to tell you the truth, she's a little unpredictable sometimes. I'm not surprised she didn't make it, but I'm a little concerned that she hasn't called. I left your phone number at the hotel, in case she gets in while I'm here."

Veronica said, "Where is she coming from?"

"Well, I'm not really sure."

"I don't understand."

He leaned back in his chair, almost losing his balance and tipping over backward. "She left Brooklyn for Concord very early on Thursday morning. I was stuck at home, working on deadline. Sandi had some business to take care of here that afternoon. She stayed at the Colony Inn—"

I corrected him. "Colonial Inn."

"Sorry. Colonial Inn. She called me when she got to Concord, said she had just checked in. The plan was for me to fly up yesterday, which I did, meet her at the inn, then drive together to New Hampshire today. We have reservations at a campground in the White Mountains."

Veronica said, "And she wasn't at the inn when you got there?"

He shook his head. "They told me she checked out Friday morning."

"And she didn't call you to tell you that?"

"She told me before she left that if she finished her business on Thursday, she might visit a friend in Amherst for a day or two, then come back to Concord on Sunday to meet me."

"And she didn't call you again after Thursday?"

"No. She knew I was busy, so I assumed she didn't want to distract me."

I said, "What sort of deadline were you working on?"

"I'm a recording engineer. An independent record producer, sometimes. I own a small studio in Brooklyn. Sandi and I live in the apartment above it. I was mixing an album all weekend. To tell you the truth, I was glad she had business out of town, because I was pressed for time and needed to concentrate. As it was, I barely had time to sleep while she was gone, and I just did finish the master tape early yesterday morning."

Veronica said, "Have you tried calling her friend's place?"

"I tried Sandi's cell phone a few times, but she was either out of range or just not using the phone."

"And you didn't call her friend's place?"

"She never told me the name of the friend. Or maybe she did, but I was just too busy to listen. She travels a lot. Sometimes we lose touch for a day or so. It's no big deal."

"Am I talking to the Steven Farr who used to give me the third degree if I answered my phone on the fifth ring instead of the second?"

He smiled. "I've changed, Vee. I'm not the same control freak I was back then. You would probably like me a lot better now."

My girlfriend and her ex-boyfriend exchanged a smile. He reached for her hand and held it for a few seconds until she pulled it away. It seemed like a good time for me to change the direction of the conversation. I said to Veronica, "I'll start to clear the table if you'll get dessert."

Veronica went inside. Steven drained the rest of his wineglass while I cleaned up.

"Damn," he said. "I wonder where the hell she is. I *hate* it when she pulls this shit."

"What sort of business brought Sandi to Concord?"

"Walden Woods. Do you know who Don Henley is?"

"Sure," I answered. " 'The End of the Innocence.' "

"Then you probably know about the project Henley created to buy and conserve private property near Walden Pond. I mixed a couple of album tracks for him three or four years ago. That's how Sandi and I met him. He got her a job with his manager. Then last year she helped coordinate the reunion tour he did with the Eagles. She did a great job, and Henley hired her to help with his Walden project."

I said, "Why did she come here last week?"

He shrugged. "To tell you the truth, I don't know many of the details. Something about meeting with a developer, trying to work on a deal to buy him out."

"Max Rothman?"

"I don't know. I don't recall that she ever told me the man's name. She was going to try to get him to visit the pond with her, talk with him there, soften him up. She wasn't very optimistic about the trip, but she said she was going to give it her best shot, no matter what happened."

No matter what happened, I thought. With that remark, my vague uneasiness crystallized into a specific concern.

Veronica returned with coffee and cake. She said, "I was going to call the inn to see if Sandi arrived, but I don't know her last name."

"O'Neill, love. Sandra O'Neill."

I said, "I need to step inside for a minute. I'll make the call."

And make the call I did, only to learn what I expected to learn: No one named Sandra O'Neill had come to the Colonial Inn that evening.

And then I called Kay Wheaton to tell her I thought I knew the identity of the Walden Pond murder victim.

14

"It doesn't match up with the little bit we already know, Harry," said Kay Wheaton. "How could she check out Friday morning if she was killed Thursday night?"

"I don't know. Maybe Steven misunderstood what the inn told him. Or maybe the killer checked her out."

"And the initials on the cross are C.G., or possibly C.C., but definitely not S.O."

"Maybe she found it. Maybe she stole it. Maybe she bought it secondhand. Maybe it was a gift and those are the initials of the person who gave it to her. Maybe the letters have some religious significance. Maybe *she* killed someone and lifted it off the dead body. How the hell do *I* know? Where are you?"

"Whoa, boy. Calm down. I'm home. The switchboard patched you through to me here."

"I know that. Where do you live? How long will it take you to get to my house?"

"Well, my plan was some aspirin for my headache. A warm bath. The Red Sox, if they're on, or maybe a *Murphy Brown* rerun. Not a wild goose chase. I mean, really, Harry—what do you have?"

I took a deep breath. "Like I said—a woman who may have enemies in Concord, who may have taken one of those enemies to Walden on Thursday, and who hasn't been seen or heard from since. I mean, really, Kay—what else do *you* have?"

She paused. "Nothing."

"Exactly."

There was silence for several seconds. She said, "You're serious about this."

"I have a bad feeling about it. Something just doesn't seem right."

She sighed. "Okay, okay. I live in Bedford. It's a little after seven now. I can be there in fifteen or twenty minutes. Did you tell this fellow you think his womanfriend may be a murder victim?"

"No. I wanted to talk with you first."

"All right. Keep it that way until I get there."

A few seconds after I hung up the phone, Steven stepped into the kitchen. He asked where the bathroom was. I pointed him in the right direction, then went outside to talk with Veronica.

I said, "We may have a problem here."

"With Steven? Don't be silly. He's harmless. It's been years since we were together."

"No, not that. I'm talking about Sandi."

"What about Sandi?"

I told her about the conversation Steven and I had, and about my phone call to Kay Wheaton.

She frowned. "You should leave the cops-and-criminals game to the professionals."

"I know. That's why I called Kay."

"*I'm* a professional. You could have told me first. This whole thing sounds ridiculous to me."

"Let's hope you're right, for your friend's sake."

Steven rejoined us, and then we all went inside. We sat in the den and made small talk. When Kay Wheaton arrived, I introduced her to Steven by name, but I didn't say what her job was or why she had come to my house.

Kay said to Steven, "I understand you haven't had word of your womanfriend for four days, since last Thursday."

He glanced at me, perplexed.

Kay continued. "Harry called me a little while ago. I'm a police detective, and four days makes your friend a missing person."

"It's like I told Harry—she pulls something like this every once in a while."

"Has she ever been missing for four days?"

"Look—just because I don't know where she is doesn't make her a missing person. She went to see a friend. She said she'd be here on Sunday. She's one day late. Why is everyone so concerned? What's going on here, Harry? Vee?"

Veronica moved next to him on the couch. She looked at Kay and said, "I think you should tell Steven why you came here."

Kay cleared her throat. "An unidentified woman was murdered at Walden Pond last Thursday evening. We need to check out all possible instances of missing persons."

He said, "So . . . this would be considered . . . routine?" He looked to Veronica for reassurance.

Kay said, "At this point, yes. This would be considered routine. Tell me—do you have a photograph of Sandi?"

"Not with me."

"At your hotel?"

"No. Back home."

"Will you tell me what she looks like?"

Except for the correspondence in approximate age between Sandi and the corpse, I didn't know enough about the murder victim to know if Steven's description ruled Sandi in or out as a possible match. The same was true for his description of the clothing she was wearing when he last saw her on the morning of the day on which the murder took place.

Kay said, "Does she wear jewelry?"

"Earrings, sometimes. No rings."

"Pierced ears?"

"No. She wears clip-ons. I don't remember if she wore any on Thursday."

"Anything else?"

He hesitated, perhaps not wanting to give voice to something that might so definitively force the issue. "She wears a crucifix. A small gold cross—at least, I think it's gold—on a plain gold chain."

"As a necklace?"

"Yes."

"Did you give it to her?"

"No. She's had it for as long as I've known her. I think she said it was handed down to her by her mother, or maybe her grandmother."

"Can you tell me her mother's name?"

"Claire, I think. She died before Sandi and I met."

"Do you know her maiden name?"

"No." His foot began to tap nervously. "I don't understand why you want to know about Sandi's mother. I don't understand why you're asking me all these questions. Vee, what does this all mean?"

Detective Kay Wheaton reached into the pocket of her jeans and pulled out a small envelope. She removed something from the envelope and laid it gently on the coffee table in front of Steven.

The sheen was dull on the old, small cross. I wondered: How many times over the years had its wearers taken communion, made the sign of the cross, kneeled in prayer, confessed their sins, sought God's forgiveness?

Steven Farr took the crucifix and studied it. "I don't know, but . . . I think . . ." He held it to his cheek. He closed his eyes. His hand and arm began to shake.

Veronica tried to steady him: She wrapped one arm around his back, then touched his quaking arm with her other hand as she leaned in against him.

His tears began to flow and his body heaved, but neither words nor any other sound could break through his shocked silence. After several seconds he emitted a low moan. All the air and energy seemed to leave him, and he collapsed against the back of the couch.

"Dear God," he whispered. "Oh, my God."

Veronica lay against his chest and stroked his face. "It's okay, baby. It's okay."

Steven looked intently at Kay Wheaton. "Take me to her. Please. I have to see her."

* * *

The remains were at the morgue in Boston. Kay called ahead to tell them we were coming. I sat with her in the front of her sedan; Veronica and Steven sat in back.

It was a quiet ride down Route 2 and along the Fresh Pond Parkway. Every once in a while Steven stirred and began to breathe heavily. Each time, Veronica patted his arm or shoulder and made a shushing sound.

We picked up Storrow Drive and headed east: on our left the Charles River and Cambridge; Allston and then Boston on our right. We passed Harvard Stadium and the business school, then Boston University and the Kenmore Square area.

"God, Vee—I don't want it to be her."

"I know, baby. I know."

"Please, don't let it be Sandi."

No doubt he sat there proposing silent bargains to God: Save her and I will be honest. Save her and I will be true. But please let it be some other man's lover lying splayed and eviscerated on the cold metal table.

It was after eight o'clock. The sky ahead of us was nighttime dark, and office lights formed a speckled pattern on the high-rise Prudential and Hancock buildings. We passed Copley Square and the Back Bay, and we crossed through the Esplanade area. Then we picked up the Central Artery and took the Albany Street exit.

The nondescript Suffolk County medical examiner's building was situated near a public care hospital and the city's two largest shelters. I wondered: chance or choice? We parked beside the building and gained access through the service entrance.

The long, cold hallway was marked by the mixed odor of antisepsis and decay. Incomprehensibly, the words of a childhood gross-out song passed through my mind: *Great big globs of greasy, grimy gopher guts. Mutilated monkey meat . . .*

A technician led us to a wide swinging door with translucent windows. Kay turned to Steven and said, "Identification is going to be difficult because of the injuries she suffered. I've arranged for her face to be covered. Is there anything else you can look for to identify her when I take you in there?"

"I want to see her face."

Veronica interrupted. "No, you don't."

"But . . ."

"You don't want memories like mine."

I thought about Veronica at age nine, witnessing the brutal murder of her mother.

Steven thought for a minute. "She has an open blister on her ankle. Her left one, I think."

"Anything else?" Kay asked.

"A small scar from an operation on her right knee. I would recognize that."

Kay pushed open the door and led Steven inside. The door swung shut behind them.

Veronica and I waited in the hallway. We were silent for a short while, and then I said, "I'm sorry for your friend."

"I know you are, Harry. Thanks."

"I didn't want to be right about this."

"I know."

I held out my hand to her. She reached toward me and—

Wham! The door swung wildly open toward us. Steven ran through it and down the hall toward the service entrance. Veronica took off after him. I ran after her. Behind me I heard the door swing open again, then Kay's footsteps keeping pace. We ran single file through the building and out the exit, flailing wildly like demented Keystone Kops.

Steven darted blindly into the street, narrowly avoiding a car. Brakes squealed. He crossed over to a building on the other side and began pounding on it with his fists.

Veronica caught up to him. She grabbed his shoulder and spun him around to face her. Then she wrapped her arms around him and pushed forward, pinning him between herself and the building.

Kay stood next to me. "Fuck," she muttered. "I really, really hate this." She walked to her car and stood in the street: leaning against her door, watching the scene across from her.

I could hear Steven crying. He and Veronica slid slowly down the wall and to the sidewalk. She cradled him in her arms and together they rocked slowly.

Kay was there on business. Steven was there because he had

to be there. Veronica was there for Steven. I was superfluous, the scene was painful to see, and I was ashamed to admit that I wished I hadn't come with them.

I glanced up and down the block. There were others sitting and lying on the ground: the ragged homeless who hadn't made it to the shelters on that warm summer evening.

The suffering of the few, the suffering of the many: Why would a just God allow it to exist? And what right would an unjust God have to be worshiped as a God?

I walked aimlessly a few yards down the sidewalk, embarrassed to be watching the gut-wrenching intimacy between Veronica and her former lover.

I came upon a lone figure, a bedraggled woman sitting and swaying in the shelter of a refuse-littered doorway. I thought about my daughter sitting and swaying on her window seat the morning Janet died. Was there a connection? What was that connection? I wondered if this woman's salvation and my own were linked in some way I couldn't possibly hope to understand.

I reached into my pocket and pulled out a dollar. "Excuse me," I said. "May I give this to you?"

She stopped rocking and looked up at me, eyes and skin as black as coal, an impassive, impenetrable expression on her face. She took the dollar.

I headed back to the car. I thought I heard the woman mumble something as I left. I turned to face her again, twenty or thirty feet away. I called out, "Excuse me—did you say something?"

"Yes . . . I would like to say something." Then she sat quietly, as if waiting for me to come closer.

I walked back to her.

"I would like to say something," she repeated.

I leaned down. Our eyes met. I looked for a sign of life or hope or faith in her eyes and found none. I said, "What do you want to say?"

She whispered, "I wish I had a home."

"I know. I wish you did, too."

"This is America, ain't it?"

"Yes."

"I mean, this is America, ain't it?"

"Yes, it is."

I turned and walked away. I thought: *Sweet land of liberty.*

My friend Father John Fitzpatrick once told me that a man can find a hundred reasons to believe in God merely by slowly turning and looking at the world around him.

But on this night, in this place, I couldn't find even one.

15

"This is my fault," Steven said.

I poured decaf for the three of them and water for myself, then rejoined them at the kitchen table.

Kay said, "Why do you think it's your fault?"

"Because I should have been with her. She wanted me to come. But, no, I was too busy doing *important* things. Too busy to be there when she needed me the most. So now instead of marrying her, I have to bury her."

Veronica groaned. "Damn it, Steven. You think everything that happens is happening to *you*. You've always been that way."

"Sorry."

All was quiet for a moment, and then Veronica said, "No, I'm sorry. I shouldn't jump on you like that."

"What she means," said Kay, "is that we all feel bad about your friend. But we need to put our own feelings on hold right now. Focus our energy on the person who *is* to blame for this."

"I understand," Steven said.

"Why did you stay in Brooklyn?"

He told her about working around the clock, shut in his studio, to finish a recording project.

"What kind of car did Sandi drive?"

"A Honda Accord. White, four doors." Steven told her the license plate number.

Kay said, "We'll start looking for it immediately. There

might be important forensic evidence inside it. Did she carry a cell phone?"

"Yes."

"That's good. What's the number?"

He told her the number. "Why is that good?"

"If the killer stole it and tries to use it, we may be able to locate where the signal is coming from."

I remembered that the L.A. police used cell phone signals to locate O.J. Simpson in the Bronco. I decided no one would want to hear anything about O.J. at that particular moment.

"While you and Veronica were standing across the street from the morgue, I called my chief and briefed him on what had happened. Sandi's name will probably be on the news stations tonight. And it will certainly be in the Boston papers in the morning."

"Oh, great," he said, with obvious sarcasm. "No privacy in death."

"No," said Kay. "No privacy. I want to get the word out."

"Why?"

"Two reasons. First, there's a possibility the killer wanted to hide her identity. She didn't have any identification on her, and her car is missing. And if the killer did try to keep her identity hidden, then releasing her name works against his interest, even if we don't know exactly why that's so."

"True," Veronica said. I was glad at least one of us had followed Kay's reasoning.

I said, "What else? You said there were two reasons to make her name public."

"The second reason is much more straightforward. The more people who know about it, the more memories get jogged. Maybe Sandi said something to someone she talked to up here, something that can help us figure out who was with her in the woods."

Steven said, "I already have a pretty good idea who was with her." He told Kay what he had told me earlier: Sandi had hoped to take a developer out to Walden to try to make him more amenable to being bought out.

"Max Rothman?"

"That's what Harry asked me. I don't know the man's name."

As she had done with everything else Steven told her, Kay wrote Rothman's name in her notebook. "After we finish talking, I want you to make a list of her closest friends and associates. I need to talk with them as soon as possible."

"Do you really have to get them involved with this?"

"Four full days have passed since she was killed. Almost all homicides that are solved get solved in less than that time. So we're running behind, and with each day we'll get further behind. I need to talk with them. I need to learn as much as I can about Sandi, as fast as I can. And I need your house keys."

"My . . . why?"

"I'll fly to New York tomorrow, hook up with a detective there, go to your place to look for any information about Sandi's activities that might implicate anyone."

"I'll come with you."

"I'd rather you stay here."

"I really don't like the idea of you and another stranger being in my—"

"Listen, Steven. No one wants to jam you up. I don't care if you have dope or kiddie porn or overdue library books. It's Sandi's things I'm interested in, not yours. If you would prefer that I get a warrant, which will slow things up even more—"

"You won't find anything illegal. I would rather be there, that's all. Otherwise it just seems too cold, strangers sifting through her stuff."

Veronica leaned closer to him and spoke softly. "Kay is right, Steven. You would just be in her way. Besides, don't you want to take care of funeral preparations?"

He winced when she asked that question. "I can't begin to tell you how much this all really sucks." He sighed, reached into his pocket, and grabbed his keys. He slid them across the table to Kay.

"Thank you. Now, before long someone in the press will figure out that the Steven Farr who's staying at the Colonial Inn is the Steven Farr who was planning to marry the Walden Pond murder victim. When they ask you to talk with them—please don't."

Veronica said, "I want you to stay here with us, Steven. We have an apartment above the garage. I don't think you should stay by yourself at the inn, now that all of this has happened."

Kay said, "I like that idea myself."

Veronica turned to me, awaiting my comment.

"Sure," I said. "Not a problem." I figured I could be magnanimous, under the circumstances.

Veronica said, "If Kay is finished asking you questions, I'll take you over to the inn now so you can get your things."

"I'm finished," Kay said.

Steven said, "If it's okay with you, Vee, I'd sort of like to go there alone. Just to have a few minutes to think."

Veronica passed her car keys to Steven, and he stood to leave.

Kay said, "I'm sorry for all of this, Steven. I promise you I'll do my best to find Sandi's killer. Now, please write the list of people for me to interview. Also, the names of people who saw you in Brooklyn last Thursday."

"Saw . . . me?" He stared at her with a blank expression for a few seconds. Then, as his awareness of the implication of her question set in, his face reddened. "Are you telling me I need an alibi for—"

"It's okay," Veronica said. "Standard operating procedure, Steven."

"Okay, okay," he muttered. He scribbled some names and numbers onto a piece of paper. "These are her best friends."

"And who saw you on Thursday?"

"The only person I can think of is my assistant. And I gave him this week off. I don't know where he is."

"Well, let me have his home phone number, and I'll see if I can track him down."

Steven hesitated for just an instant. He wrote the man's name and number on the paper. Then he left to get his belongings at the Colonial Inn.

After Steven left, I said, "I saw Max Rothman at the

Thoreau Club on Friday morning, after Sandi's body was discovered. He seemed upset. Then again, the few times I've seen him, he's always looked upset."

"Upset," Kay repeated. "Upset as in sad, or upset as in pissed off?"

"The latter. Maybe 'irritable' would be a better word to use."

"Did you talk to him?"

"No."

"If you didn't talk to him, and if it was merely at the irritable level, then you probably wouldn't have noticed."

I thought for a moment. "Perhaps 'agitated' is a better word. But, hell—he always looks agitated."

"Did he appear more agitated on Friday than usual?"

"Hard to say for sure."

"Guess."

I shrugged. "I suppose so. I'll give you a definite maybe on that."

"Uh-huh." She thought for a moment, then turned to Veronica. "Is your friend Steven the violent sort?"

"Hotheaded, yes. I wouldn't use the word 'violent.' "

"Did he ever hit you?"

Veronica didn't answer for several seconds. "Not exactly. He grabbed my arm very hard once—hard enough to leave a bruise that took a few days to heal."

"Just once?"

"Just once." She paused. "I persuaded him not to do it again."

"How did you persuade him?"

"I loosened two of his teeth. I told him that if it happened again, he would lose an eye."

Kay pondered that for a few moments. "I think I'll head over to the Colonial Inn, too. Maybe I can figure out how a dead woman managed to check herself out on Friday morning."

It was almost midnight. Veronica walked over to the barn to ready it for Steven. I went upstairs. I considered waking my daughter to tell her what had transpired but decided it was better to do that with a clear head in the morning.

I lay down to rest on top of the bedspread, still in my

clothing. Veronica was still in the barn when, a few minutes later, I fell into a restless sleep.

In my dream I was standing near Walden Pond. The homeless woman I had spoken with was there. One moment she was sitting and rocking. In the next she lay on the ground, her face battered beyond recognition, a small gold crucifix around her neck.

16

Alfred Korvich called early on Tuesday morning and asked me to meet him in his office.

"What do you want to talk about?" I asked.

"If I wanted to talk about it on the phone, I wouldn't be extending you this gracious invitation to the police station, would I? Oh—and one more thing."

"What's that?"

"I would appreciate it if you don't tell your ladyfriend or your house guest where you're going."

"They're not here," I said.

Veronica was on her way to work. Steven Farr was meeting with Father John Fitzpatrick to talk about a memorial Mass for Sandra O'Neill. Sandi had expressed a wish for cremation; Steven figured on having that done in Concord and spreading the ashes at Walden.

And so shortly after nine o'clock I joined our illustrious police chief in his Naugahyde palace on the second floor of the combined police-fire station on Walden Street.

He was reading the *Boston Globe* when I stepped into his office. A few days earlier, the discovery of the corpse at Walden had been a front-page story. Today the identification of the corpse was featured on the first page of Section B, the Metro/Region section. "No major mistakes," Korvich said. "They got the story right."

"I thought the statement Don Henley issued was very thoughtful."

"Yeah, I guess so. I met him, you know, on one of his trips here. Nice guy. Doesn't flaunt his money and power at you. A good model for some of you Concord folk." He tossed the newspaper onto his desk. "Sit down, Harry. Take a load off. Been a while since we had one of our chats."

"So *that's* it. I knew there was something missing from my life."

"Funny man."

"I do my best. Why did you ask me to come here?"

"Well, I see you've managed once again to make yourself a central figure in a murder investigation."

"I'm peripheral, at best."

"*Au contraire, mon frère.* You're a very important man. And I'm going to give you the opportunity to serve your police chief in a very significant way."

"In other words, you want me to do a favor for you."

"That would be a more shortsighted, self-centered way to look at it. I prefer to think of it as an opportunity for volunteer service in the interest of the community." He drummed his fingers on his desk for a few seconds. "Tell me, Harry—what do you think of your houseguest, Steven Farr?"

"I haven't thought much about him, one way or the other."

"Come *on*, man. He used to play hide-the-salami with your ladyfriend. Doesn't that influence you a little bit in the negative direction?"

"If you work at it, you might be able to come up with an even more unpleasant way of putting that."

He smiled. "I'll make a note about that. Seriously, though—what do you think about him? Do you like him?"

"Not particularly. I feel bad for him, but I don't have any particular liking for him."

"Why not?"

"Just a gut reaction."

"Uh-huh." He leaned back in his chair. "Kay likes him."

"Is that so?"

"I thought that would get your attention. When I say she likes him, I mean she likes him as a murder suspect."

"Why is that?"

He inhaled deeply, then let it out slowly, watching me carefully all the while. He said, "I've trusted you before to keep certain things confidential in a murder investigation."

"When it suited your interest to do so."

"Of *course* when it suited my interest. We wouldn't be having this goddamn conversation if it didn't suit my interest." He adopted a more pleasant tone. "I figure I can trust you not to tell this to Farr. I would prefer that you also don't tell your ladyfriend what I'm about to say."

"I can't make that promise until I know what I'm promising to keep secret."

More finger drumming, more careful watching, and then: "Sandra O'Neill didn't check herself out of the Colonial Inn the morning after she was murdered."

"Obviously."

"Which means someone else did."

I pondered that for a moment. "Not necessarily. She probably used a credit card to check in. So when she didn't check out in person the next day, they just checked her out on their own and ran the total on her card."

"Nice deduction, Harry. Nice, but wrong. First of all, she had a reservation for four nights. Which means the front desk would have no reason to check her out automatically after the first night. Second, she left a note for the maid—or someone else did—that said she had to leave in a hurry, and would the maid please notify the front desk that she had to leave. And there was no luggage left behind."

"That does sound a little unusual, but it could happen."

"It sounds *damn* unusual, and I don't think that's what happened."

"Well, what *do* you think happened?"

He walked over to the coffee machine on top of his file cabinet. "Want some?"

"No, thanks."

"Oh—I forgot. You don't drink coffee." He sat again behind his desk. "This is what I think. The killer knows her, just like Kay said. He goes with her to Walden. Kills her. Drives to the Colonial Inn, where he knows she's staying. Uses her room key. He gathers her luggage and writes the note to the maid. Then he takes her car keys and drives her car somewhere."

"And why would he be doing all of this?"

"To get a head start. He figures no one will be able to identify the body for a while. He wants a couple of days to go by so he can get back home before the body is identified and the police start looking for him to notify him. So he doesn't want anyone at the Colonial Inn wondering why the lady in room 107 hasn't unpacked her bags and hasn't slept in her bed for one, two, or three nights. Therefore he goes back to the inn after he kills her to get rid of her stuff and her car."

"Assuming you're right, why would he come back Sunday night?"

"The camping reservation. They did indeed have a reservation in the White Mountains. And it was made in his name. So he came up on Sunday, just like nothing had happened. And he found someone both clever enough and gullible enough to drop some hints to. Enough hints that it would lead to the identification of the body."

"And I suppose that clever but gullible person would be me."

"If the shoe fits."

"I don't know. His story sounds plausible to me."

"Come on, Harry. What about all that crap about not knowing where she was, and not being concerned about not knowing where she was, from Friday until Monday? Engaged people don't act that way."

"So you think he came up here with her, and then went back to New York after he killed her?"

"It's a hypothesis."

"How many people checked into that room last Thursday?"

"She made the reservation for one person, a few weeks earlier. But maybe he came along at the last minute."

I shrugged. "I don't want to tell you how to do your job, but what you're saying sounds pretty speculative."

"Well, it's just a theory. There is one other thing. Farr told Kay that his ladyfriend called him in Brooklyn after she checked in. The phone records at the inn show she made two long distance calls shortly after arriving. One was to Don

Henley's manager in California. The other was to the camp-ground in New Hampshire. Nothing to Brooklyn."

I thought about the evidence, if that's what it was, and the theory he was offering. I had no particular investment in Steven Farr's innocence, but I still thought Korvich's specula-tions were built on slim proof.

I said, "He seems genuinely shocked by what happened. Genuine grief."

"You can kill someone and still grieve the loss."

I shifted in my chair. "What does this have to do with me? What's this great public service you want me to perform?"

"Nothing too difficult. Just keep your eye on him. He's staying in your house—"

"My barn apartment."

"Whatever. He's staying at your place. Keep your eye on him and let me know if you see anything significant."

"Like what?"

"Anything that seems unusual for a grieving fiancé to do."

"Like walking around, singing, 'Ding, Dong, the Witch Is Dead.' "

"That would be a dead giveaway, so to speak," Korvich said.

"Or if he tries to play hide-the-salami with Veronica."

"That, too, would seem worthy of note. You'll know it if you see it. After all, you're a clever fellow, Harry."

"Don't forget gullible."

"You're a clever fellow. A pain in the ass, but clever."

Pain in the ass. That expression had taken on new connotative meaning for me since the previous morning in Jamie Ray's office.

Alfred Korvich said, "Now that I've planted the seed of sus-picion in your mind, let's see how it grows."

As I walked toward the door he called after me. "Harry, all kidding aside, do you have someplace you can send your daughter for a few days?"

I turned back. "I suppose so, if I needed to. Why?"

"You want to think about the implications of what I'm saying. I'll admit we really don't have much to go on yet. But if by some chance Steven Farr really is a killer, perhaps you would prefer removing your daughter from the house while he's there."

17

Kay Wheaton was traveling light: carry-on luggage only. Tired from a late and eventful night, she fell soundly asleep on the early morning shuttle and had to be awakened by a flight attendant when they landed at La Guardia.

New York City police detective Joseph Ramirez was waiting for her at the gate. "Hey, now. I see they grow their police folk a lot prettier up in your neck of the woods."

Kay ignored his comment. He led her through the terminal and out to his car, which was conveniently parked in an emergency zone.

She briefed him about the murder of Sandi O'Neill as he drove recklessly down the ramp and onto Grand Central Parkway. Ramirez said, "So—do you suspect the boyfriend?"

"You always suspect the boyfriend, until things are proven otherwise."

"You got that right, doll."

She ignored that, too.

Ramirez said, "We did record checks, just like you asked. No criminal record on the murder victim. Steven Farr had a drunk driving charge a few years ago. Continued without a finding while he did a drunk drivers' program, then the case was filed. Nothing else on the criminal side for him."

"Anything on the civil side?"

"You mean restraining orders filed by old girlfriends, or by the murder victim? Stuff like that?"

"Yes."

"Nope. Zip. Zilch. Bupkis. Nada."

At exactly nine-thirty they arrived at their destination: a building in a section of Brooklyn that was zoned for mixed purposes. There were stores and some brownstone apartments, but nothing of an industrial nature. "Light business only," said Ramirez. "You can sell it here, but you can't manufacture it."

Ramirez was familiar with the two-story building. He said it was once an auto parts store, and that subsequently it sat abandoned for about three years. Then it was purchased and renovated. Now the ground floor was windowless, completely encased in brick. Hanging plants were visible through the windows of the upstairs apartment.

There were two doorbells. A small metal tag with the words "Farr Away Productions" hung by one doorbell. The tag next to the other bell said merely "2nd floor." As a precautionary measure, Kay rang both bells before entering.

There were three dead-bolt locks on the outer door, each with its own key. She relocked the door behind them. Once inside, there were two additional locked doors: one for the recording studio and the other for the apartment. Kay said, "We'll start upstairs," and she unlocked and opened the door that led to the staircase.

The apartment ran the entire length and width of the building, with windows on all four sides. The layout conformed to the description Steven Farr had given to Kay: a full-size kitchen at the top of the stairs, with a small dining room to its side. There was a doorway at the other end of the kitchen. It led into a hallway, which in turn led to a living room, a small office, and a guest room; and then to a spacious master bedroom.

Ramirez whistled softly. "Fancy living for this part of the city. The building was a pit before it was converted, so they probably got a good price."

Kay said, "This was Sandi O'Neill's office. Steven Farr's office is downstairs in the recording studio. I'll start in here, and you can start in the bedroom."

"What are we looking for?"

"A note or a diary entry that says something like, 'Thursday evening, meeting at Walden Pond with so-and-so, who has threatened me with bodily harm in the past.' "

"Uh, that's a joke, right?"

"Yes, detective, that's a joke, although that would certainly make things a lot easier."

"But you *are* looking for anything related to her trip to Massachusetts, right?"

She nodded. "Especially anything that relates specifically to her plans for Thursday afternoon or evening."

Situated in one of the second-story corners, Sandi's office was large, with two windows. One window looked out on the street, the other on the small lot between this building and the next. There was a desk, a computer station, three file cabinets, and an extra chair. Orderliness prevailed: cabinet drawers neatly labeled, trash can emptied, shades on both windows drawn to the exact same height, dead leaves picked off of the geranium plant on the windowsill.

Kay switched on the computer, only to find that a password was required to get beyond the opening screen. She wouldn't be able to peruse the machine's hard disk without help from a specialist.

There was a telephone and an answering machine combined into one unit. It was Sandi's business phone, with its own number. There were no messages on the answering machine.

There were three photos on the desk. The same young woman appeared in two of them, and Kay assumed her to be Sandi; the hair color and general size and shape matched that of the Walden victim, but this was the first clear look Kay had at her face.

In the first of those photos, Sandi was standing between two men who looked familiar to Kay. There was an inscription:

> To Sandi—
>   Hell has frozen over.
>   Love, Glen

Kay copied the inscription in her notepad.

The second photo showed Steven and Sandi with arms

around one another's waist, standing on a balcony overlooking what looked like the Riverwalk in San Antonio.

The final photo was larger than the others, set in an ornate antique frame. The picture had a brown hue, like an old daguerreotype. A woman in a modest dress stood in front of a curtain as if posed in a photographer's studio. She wore a small crucifix around her neck. Kay assumed that it was the cross Sandi was wearing when she died, and that the woman in the picture was Sandi's mother or—more likely, judging from the period outfit she wore—Sandi's grandmother.

Sandi's desktop was bare, except for a small empty basket that was labeled: *Replies needed.* Apparently Sandi had taken care of outstanding business before leaving for Massachusetts.

The general appearance of the office conveyed an impression of Sandi different from the one Steven had given. This was a woman who wanted her world to be neat and predictable. Surely she wouldn't go off for a few days without letting her fiancé know how to contact her.

Kay began to search through the desk drawers. In there as well, everything appeared carefully ordered: notepads, paper clips, envelopes—

A loud, shrill whistle echoed from the other side of the apartment. Ramirez was summoning her, like a man would call his dog. What was with him, anyway?

Kay left the office and walked down the long hallway to the master bedroom. When she entered the room she saw Ramirez standing by a night table. He was holding a small appointment book. He said, "Do the initials M.R. mean anything to you?"

"Let me see."

He tossed the appointment book onto the king-size bed. "Check it out," he said. "I'll be visiting the porcelain throne." He went into the master bathroom and shut the door behind him.

Kay sat on the edge of the bed. The appointment book was small enough to fit in a woman's purse, and it bore Sandi O'Neill's name on the first page. She turned to the page for the week just passed and found an entry for four o'clock on the afternoon of Thursday, August 24. It contained the initials

M.R., followed by a Cambridge phone number—no doubt a business number—that ended in two zeros. She reached for the phone, dialed the number, punched in her credit card number, and waited on the line until an automated messaging system announced that she had reached Max Rothman Enterprises.

She replaced the phone in its cradle. Suddenly she heard footsteps and an unfamiliar voice that shouted, "Hold everything right *there*!"

She turned quickly. The man was very large and very black, but she didn't get a good look at him right away because her eyes were focused on something else: the cold steel barrel of a small-caliber handgun, pointing directly at her from only eight feet away.

The first order of business in that situation was to identify herself as a police officer. But fear got the best of her, and instead she blurted out, "Who are *you*?"

"Who am *I*?" His fingers trembled on the trigger. "Lady, who the fuck are *you*?"

Kay Wheaton heard the bathroom door swing open behind her. The man glanced in the direction of that noise and reflexively moved his gun slightly in that direction.

A single shot from Ramirez's pistol ripped into him.

Kay shrieked, jumped up, and was cut down by Ramirez's second bullet.

18

On my way home from the police station, I stopped at Sally Ann's for a cherry Danish. I walked outside the shop and stood on Main Street.

The library was off to my left. I considered walking over and looking for information about prostate cancer. Then I reconsidered. Then I ate the cherry Danish.

From a viewpoint of pure self-interest, imagining Steven Farr as the prime suspect didn't bother me at all. Maybe it was jealousy: that he was once Veronica's lover, that he was intimate with her before I was. Maybe it was that he had once assaulted her. Whatever the reason, I hadn't warmed up to him, and I didn't like the fact that Veronica found it so easy to shower him with sympathy and compassion.

But the theory Korvich outlined seemed farfetched to me. I figured the most likely scenario was a stranger-upon-stranger murder: an isolated setting, with Sandi O'Neill as the convenient target of a robber or would-be rapist who went too far.

Besides: Veronica cared for Steven. For her sake, I hoped he had nothing to do with the murder.

A tall man with a brisk no-nonsense stride was walking along the sidewalk from the direction of the library. It was Robert Kennedy Butler, he of the low-income housing sympathies and prostitutional ancestry.

He glanced at me as he approached, then turned his gaze to the sidewalk in front of him, and then looked at me again with purpose. He had an expression on his face that seemed to say: I know I know you, but I don't know how I know you.

He stopped, and after a few seconds he said, "You were with Waterstone the other day."

"Guilty as charged."

"You're one of them, aren't you?"

"One of who?"

"One of the people fighting the Logan tract development. A tree lover." He paused. "Or maybe a nigger-hater."

"I'm not interested in the project, one way or another. And I suppose trees are all right in their place, but I wouldn't say I've ever been in love with one. As far as the last thing goes, it's not a sentiment I embrace, and it's not a choice of words that I condone."

"They used to call my father a nigger-*lover*. He wore it like a badge of honor. He was a Freedom Rider in Alabama."

"That took real courage."

He smiled for the briefest of instants, then washed his face clean of any such indication. He probably couldn't tell whether I was complimenting his father or merely putting him down by comparison. I couldn't tell, either.

He said, "I just wanted you to know."

"Know what?"

"Know the family stock I come from. I'm in this fight to stay, no matter what, no matter how long. Tell your friend Waterstone. You people disgust me."

He turned around and continued his purposeful walk through the town.

19

"Son of a fucking *bitch*! I can't believe you fucking *shot* me, man. I can't believe you shot me and her *both*."

"All right, already," Ramirez said. "It's a goddamn flesh wound. Consider yourself lucky, seeing as how you pulled a gun on me. You all right, Kay?"

Kay Wheaton was tying a cold compress to the man's arm with a torn pillowcase. She had already done so with her left thigh. As best as she could tell, neither wound was serious. If Ramirez had been aiming, he obviously needed more time on the practice range.

"I'm all right," she said. "Just a little woozy."

"Yeah, well, the ambulance will be here soon."

"Fuck that shit," said the man. "I been hurt worse than this. It's the principle of the fucking thing. *I'm* the one belongs here, and *I'm* the one gets shot. Lady, why didn't you *say* you were police?"

Ramirez said, "Why didn't you identify *your*self?"

"You didn't give me time, man. Shoot first, think later, that's you."

"Because you were pointing a gun at two police officers, you stupid bastard. And we didn't know who you were."

"Ah, shit, man. Ouch! Hey—ease up, lady."

"I'm sorry, Mr. Stamis. Truly, I am."

"Shut up," Ramirez said to her. "You never say that in a situation like this."

"Fuck you, man. Lady's just trying to make things right."

Kay finished tying the compress. "All right, all right—both of you. Shut . . . the . . . fuck . . . *up!*"

His name was Roy Stamis, and he was Steven Farr's assistant. Unbeknownst to them, he was in the studio when they arrived. Alerted to the presence of strangers by Ramirez's shrill whistle, he had surprised them and been shot for his trouble.

Kay said, "Why didn't you respond to the downstairs bell when we rang it?"

"I didn't see it."

Ramirez said, "What the hell does that mean, you didn't *see* it?"

"No bells or buzzers in a recording studio, man. You press the button outside, a light goes on in the control room. But I was in the john. What're you doing, busting in here like that. You got a warrant?"

"Nope," said Ramirez. "Don't need one."

"Need one 'less you got probable cause there's a crime going on. You got that?"

"You want me to think of one?"

Kay said, "There's no crime being committed, Mr. Stamis. Steven Farr gave me permission to search the apartment. These are his keys."

"Bullshit. Steven ain't even in New York. He's up in New England somewhere."

"I'm from Massachusetts. I'm a police detective there." She showed the man her badge.

"You flash that when I get here, you save me a bullet from Wyatt Earp over there. Save yourself a bullet, too. Why're you here? Is Steven in trouble up there? He okay?"

"He's all right. He's not in any trouble."

"Then what?"

She said, "Do you know Sandra O'Neill?"

" 'Course I know Sandi. She lives here. She's up there with Steven. Why?"

Neither Kay nor Ramirez said anything, and in that awkward silence, the injured man must have sensed something of the dread that brought Kay there. His eyes opened wide and his voice cracked. "What? Is something wrong? What's wrong?"

Kay tried to speak calmly, but the alarm of the previous few minutes and the tension of the previous few days made that impossible. She said, a little more loudly than she intended, "Ms. O'Neill was attacked by someone in Massachusetts. We don't know who, and we don't know why. And I'm sorry to tell you that she died from her injuries."

She thought that sounded gentler than "She was murdered," or "Somebody killed her." But if the words she used were less distressing than those other choices, she couldn't tell from the injured man's reaction.

He stood, wincing from the pain in his arm as he did so. "Oh, God!" He repeated that over and over again, feverishly rubbing his face.

Sirens sounded from a block or two away, heading toward them.

"Steven . . . was he hurt? Was he there, too?"

Kay said, "Did he go up with her?"

"No. Sandi went on Wednesday or Thursday. He and me were mixing an album. We finished real late Saturday—actually, real early on Sunday. So Steven left on Sunday. I'm off for the week, but I came by to pick up some stuff. But I still don't understand why you're here."

"I'm looking for anything that might help me understand who would want to murder Sandra O'Neill. Did she have problems with anyone that you can think of?"

"Uh-uh. Not Sandi."

Kay realized there were three sirens. One no doubt was an ambulance, and the others were probably patrol cars responding to Ramirez's call about an officer-involved shooting. The sirens came to a stop within seconds of one another, directly outside the building.

Ramirez went downstairs to open the door.

Kay was puzzled by one part of the man's story. "My information says Sandra arrived in Massachusetts on Thursday. But you said she left on either Wednesday *or* Thursday. Why is that?"

"Because I don't know. I wasn't here."

"I thought you were mixing an album with Steven."

"I was. But I started losing it. Working so hard, just couldn't stay awake. Usually I sleep on the cot in the studio when we're going at it like that. But he said I should take a couple of days off, especially since we planned to work the whole weekend."

"When did you leave?"

"Wednesday, late morning."

"And when did you return?"

"Friday morning, like Steven told me."

"Did you talk to him at all on Thursday?"

"Uh-uh. Didn't want to bother him. Ouch!" He winced again and pressed his arm against his body. "Fuck. New thirty-dollar shirt."

The medics helped Roy Stamis down the stairs. The uniformed cops asked a few basic questions, then filed out of the apartment.

Kay said, "We're going to be tied up all day filling out reports and answering questions about this shooting."

Ramirez yawned. "Hey. Shit happens."

"I hate that expression."

"You want to make sure you and me, we have our stories straight?"

"I have *my* story straight."

He glared at her for a moment. Then he shrugged and headed for the stairway.

"Hey—Ramirez."

"Yo."

"Do you carry an appointment book?"

"Me?" He snickered. "Doll, I spend half my time trying to forget the crap I have to deal with. Why would I want to remind myself?"

"If you *did* carry one, wouldn't you take it out of town if you were going on a trip?"

"Hell if I know. I don't have one, and I never go anywhere."

Kay picked up Sandi O'Neill's appointment book and tucked it in her oversized handbag.

20

Federal Express delivered the envelope shortly after I arrived home. Inside was a note that read:

Call for a rematch.
    M.R.

Attached to the note was a check for two hundred dollars, drawn on the personal account of Max and Evelyn Rothman. It bore Max Rothman's signature. It wasn't made out to me or anyone else. When we played tennis I didn't specify the charity I wanted my winnings to go to, so now he was leaving it to me to fill in the name of the payee on the check.

That could have been a matter of simple courtesy, to save me the trouble of depositing his check and writing one of my own. Or it could have been his way of keeping me honest, by ensuring that he would see the name of the final recipient when the canceled check returned to him in his bank statement. Or maybe he was simply ensuring that he, not I, would get the tax deduction.

Steven had driven Veronica to the train station and then taken her car. I assumed she had given him the spare key to the barn apartment. I hoped she'd removed the spare house key from that key ring.

He hadn't returned yet from his meeting with Father John Fitzpatrick.

I wondered how long it would take to arrange the memorial Mass and the cremation. I wondered how long it would take to get Steven Farr out of my life and back to New York. I wondered how long it would take for my biopsy results. I wondered how long it would take for me to feel like life was back to normal.

And I wondered how long it would take to solve the murder of Sandi O'Neill.

"I want it to go to someone in town who really needs it. Someone that two hundred dollars would make an important difference for. I don't want to know who you give it to. I don't want anyone feeling obligated to me, or ashamed to look me in the eye. So if I put the name of St. Bernard's Church on the check and send it to you, will you pass it on for me?"

"Ah-ha," Father John Fitzpatrick said over the phone. "Money laundering. What sport." He laughed. "Certainly, my boy. But why mail it? Why not come over for lunch today at the rectory and simply bring the check with you?"

I met John Fitzpatrick two and a half years earlier, shortly after he became pastor at the larger of Concord's two Catholic churches. We fell into an easy friendship, and he had also been kind to Melissa as she went about her task of trying to figure out what, if anything, to believe in.

He never chided me for not providing or arranging religious guidance for my daughter: for allowing her to reach the age of almost-thirteen without feeling grounded in an identifiable faith. And it was probably easier for me to have him as a friend than it would have been if I were Catholic; had I been of his faith, I would likely carry too much psychological baggage into a relationship with a priest.

Bobby didn't like me having John Fitzpatrick as a friend. He didn't like anything that might take Melissa—or me—even further away from our Jewishness than we already were.

Veronica, an Episcopalian by upbringing, was wary in the beginning, too. When I returned home after my first social visit to the rectory, Veronica wore one of her more skeptical expressions as she said, "Well, what did the two of you do, anyway?"

"We walked over to the inn for a drink, then we went back to his place. Talked, played some music. John has a terrific album collection."

"You call him by his first name?"

"Sure." I was perplexed. "Is that sacrilegious?"

"I don't know." She furrowed her brow and then, intending no humor, said one of the funniest things she ever said to me. "Well, what the hell. I guess there are *worse* people you could be hanging around with."

I pocketed Max Rothman's check and walked into the center of town. The rectory was on the town square, across from Town Hall, diagonal to the Colonial Inn.

"Harry, my boy. Come in, come in. I've already set the water up to boil, so the pasta will be ready in no time. Ah-ha. The famous check for two hundred dollars, won not through honest labor but through an unholy wager." He snatched the check out of my hand. "I'll relieve you of this, and you'll feel better in no time."

We walked into the kitchen. On the long counter by the window was something I hadn't seen on my previous visits: a cellular phone. I commented on it.

John said, "A sign of the times, Harry. Fewer priests, stretched more thinly. The bishop decided he wanted to be able to reach out and touch someone, wherever that someone might be."

I gathered plates and silverware as he cooked. I said, "How long ago did Steven leave?"

"Well over an hour ago. He was headed across the square to the funeral home. This is a terrible, terrible thing he's dealing with."

"What's his plan?"

"The woman's parents and grandparents are all deceased," he said. "No brothers, no sisters. She has an aunt in New York, quite elderly. Steven called her from here. The poor woman was very upset, of course. I spoke with her myself. She asked that Steven decide how matters should be handled. Then he left for the funeral home. He told me Sandra had settled on cremation. It's in her will, apparently, and a copy is being sent over there."

"I didn't realize Catholics do cremation."

"It's permitted. Not too long ago it was hardly ever done, but as each generation ages it becomes more common. I'm comfortable with it."

He drained the pasta and scooped it onto our plates. I held the pot of Ragú and poured sauce over the noodles.

John said, "He's fortunate to have friends in the area." He appeared to be scrutinizing me, wondering how I would respond to conversation about Steven.

"He used to date Veronica, many years ago."

"He told me."

"I'm using 'date' as a euphemism," I said.

"Yes, I know."

"So he's actually her friend, not mine."

"But your relationship with her imposes a certain obligation to be helpful in this situation, yes?"

"I suppose."

"Well, that is as it should be, don't you think?"

I chuckled.

"What is it, Harry?"

"It just occurred to me. If we were married, there would be no question that I would have to try to make her friend my friend."

"Have you considered marriage?"

"We were going back and forth on it. Neither one of us could figure out what we wanted. So we haven't talked about it for a while."

"Does this mean the two of you are uncertain that you want to stay with one another?"

"No, I'm certain I want to. I think she is, too."

"Well, then?"

"I don't know. We never seem to finish a conversation about it. And to tell you the truth, I just don't see that there's any definite point to it. We're together and we'll stay together. I don't see where being married would make a hell of a lot of difference to either one of us. Besides, there's so much else going on right now, I'd hate to make a wrong decision because I wasn't giving it my full consideration."

"These other things that are going on. I assume you mean the murder, and your house guest."

"Yes . . ." My mind drifted to my own more personal concerns.

"Is there more?"

I hadn't planned on telling him about my situation. But it seemed like half of our conversations wound up with me saying things I hadn't planned on saying.

I said, "Something has come up. Something Veronica doesn't know about."

"I see." He was finished asking questions. He was waiting for me to decide how much I wanted him to know. That was how he always played me, and that was how he was playing me again.

"Something no one knows about, except for Bobby Beck."

He tilted his head slightly and nodded. I could read it as an invitation to continue, or an acceptance that I had already said all that I intended to say.

And so the wandering Jew told the Catholic pastor all about his prostate screening and the previous day's biopsy.

John Fitzpatrick listened patiently. He asked me if I was frightened.

"A little."

"And what is it you fear?"

"Melissa growing up without either parent."

"Who will raise her if you die?"

"In my will, it's Bobby and his wife. But I've been thinking this week that I wouldn't want Melissa to lose Veronica. And I wouldn't want Veronica to lose Melissa."

He said, "Veronica is a very strong person."

"Indeed."

"And yet you choose not to share your concerns with her."

"It isn't that I've chosen not to. I just haven't figured out how to do it. She also has a lot on her plate right now, with her friend."

He finished his pasta and pushed his plate away. Leaning

back in his chair, he said, "Tell me, Harry. Would you have waited so long to tell Janet about this?"

"Of course not," I said, surprised at the quickness and sureness in my reply. "She was my wife. She had every right to know."

"I see." He paused. "In other words, being married *does* make a difference."

21

Like most of the town employees, Mildred Smith couldn't afford to live in Concord. And as was the case for most town employees, the wealth of the town and its residents sometimes made Mildred feel envious and just a little resentful.

In the normal course of events, it didn't bother her often, and it didn't bother her all that much. She liked her job in the large first-floor clerical area at Town Hall: handling requests for information, accepting applications for town permits, receiving and processing payments for various town fines and fees.

At least twice a week she managed to attend early morning Mass next door at St. Bernard's on her way to work. She liked the priest; he had an earthy touch that reminded her of her father.

And every Friday she walked over to the Colonial Inn for lunch: something more elegant than the brown-bag sandwiches she brought on the other days.

She had worked there for ten years, her life was pleasant and predictable, she felt valued and trusted in her work, and she was happy. And so she was seldom bothered by the distance between her rung on the social ladder and the rungs occupied by most of the people she came into contact with during the day.

But sometimes . . . Sometimes the condescending attitude, the haughtiness of the town folk, bothered her. Every once in a while it seemed as though someone was going out of his way to belittle or intimidate her, and she felt hurt, and she felt angry, and—for a short while—she hated her job and the town and the people in it. This was one of those days.

At mid-afternoon Mildred handled a phone call from a town resident who inquired about the process for paying fines he owed on five parking tickets.

Mildred gave him the mailing address for Town Hall. "I can save you the trouble of writing it down," she said, "because you can find it on the back of your tickets, way down on the bottom in tiny print. A lot of people miss it."

"I *know* that, lady. I want to take care of this now. I want to pay over the phone with a credit card."

"I'm sorry, sir. We aren't authorized to accept—"

"Oh, that's just *terrific*. Listen, lady, I just learned that there's a goddamn hold on my goddamn driver's license because the goddamn meter maid has nothing better to do with her time. The state won't issue a new license until I clear up these tickets. I need to take care of this today."

"If you want to come in to Town Hall, sir, I'll be happy to—"

"Oh, Christ. That's great. That's really *great*." He slammed the phone down.

Every day she took at least one slightly discourteous call, but this one upset her more than most. It wasn't merely his arrogant attitude, his blaming her for the predicament he had created for himself. She was bothered also by the unpleasant language—the blasphemous words—he hurled at her, a perfect stranger.

She took a bathroom break, drank some water, and counted to fifty. A moment after she returned to her desk, she took another call. This man, like most callers, was pleasant and courteous. "I have some important information that I need you to pass along to the proper party. Do you have a pen handy?"

"Yes, sir."

"Good. Please take down this number."

She transcribed the number he gave her, then repeated it back to make certain she had copied it correctly. She said, "That looks like a Dewey Decimal System number."

"Yes, it is. The number corresponds to a book in the town library. I need you to give that number to the police. Please tell them that they will find important information about Sandra O'Neill in that book. Can you do that for me?"

"I suppose I can, sir, but don't you think you should—"

"Thank you very much. What's your name?"

"Mildred Smith."

"Well, Mildred. Thank you very much for your help. Have a nice afternoon."

"But—"

The man hung up.

Why didn't he simply call the police himself? And who was Sandra O'Neill? Or perhaps he had said Sarah O'Neill; Mildred hadn't gotten a chance to get him to repeat it. No, she was fairly certain he had said "Sandra," so that was the name she jotted next to the number he had dictated to her.

Moments later a man in an obvious hurry walked into the building and approached the clerical area. He barked out the words "Parking tickets" without waiting for someone to serve him at the counter.

Mildred stood and walked to the counter. "I can help you, sir."

"Are you the one I talked to a few minutes ago?"

"I believe so, sir. Are you the gentleman who wanted to clear up some tickets because of a hold on his driver's license?"

"Yes. Five of them." He told Mildred his name and address. She noted to herself that he lived on Nashawtuc Hill, one of the wealthiest parts of the well-to-do town.

Mildred turned to her computer terminal and entered the information. "Our records are showing a total of seven Concord parking tickets, sir."

"*Seven?* That couldn't . . . Oh, hell, I don't have time to argue the point. How much does that come to?"

She entered a command on the keyboard. "The current total due is two hundred and eighty dollars, sir. Would you like me to print out an itemized description?"

"Two hundred and eighty? How the hell could that be? I thought tickets were ten dollars."

"If you mail payment in immediately, parking tickets are ten dollars. But I know how easy it can be sometimes to let things like this slip by." She began to explain the additional costs that had been tacked on: late fees, summons costs, demand notices, notifications of delinquency filed with the state.

"Yeah, yeah, enough already. Let me just pay the damn thing and get a receipt I can fax over to the registry of motor vehicles." He took his checkbook out of his pocket.

"Sir, in order to have your payment credited today, I would need a certified bank check, or—"

"A *certified* check? Why didn't you tell me that over the phone?"

"I'm sorry, sir. I tried to, but you hung up on me."

The man's strident manner had begun to draw the attention of nearby clerks. The one with most seniority walked over. "Mildred, is there anything I can help with?"

"No, I'm fine. This gentleman and I are just reviewing his parking ticket situation."

The older woman eyeballed the man, then said to Mildred, "Well, I'm right over there if you need anything."

The woman left. The man said, "So. Your name is Mildred, huh?"

"Yes, sir."

"Well, *Mil*-dred," he said, drawing out the first syllable of her name, distorting it. "How about cash? You still take *cash* around here, don't you?"

"Yes, sir."

"Well, now. This is *really* my lucky day, isn't it?"

The man reached for his wallet. He counted out the money as he gave it to her. There weren't many people who carried that much cash with them, she knew.

Mildred processed the payment, then printed out a notarized verification slip. To avoid further confrontation, she waived the notary fee without mentioning it to the man. He left in a huff, without a thank-you.

Mildred stepped outside a minute later. She was upset, and she didn't like it when other people in the office saw her that way. It took her a few minutes to calm down. Then she walked inside, took another drink from the water cooler, and returned to her desk.

Another clerk called over to her and pointed to the phone. "You have calls on lines six and eight, Mildred."

She picked up on line six and identified herself.

"Hello, Mildred," he said. "We spoke a little while ago. I'm just checking to make sure you were able to get that information to the police."

"Oh. The library book. I'm sorry, sir, I've been a little tied up. I'll do it in a few minutes, I promise."

"*Now,* Mildred." Civility had vanished from his voice. "Do it now."

For perhaps only the fifth time in her ten years working there, Mildred was tempted to hang up on a caller. She had never done it, and she wouldn't do it now. Besides, he had become only mildly irritating. What right did she have to hang up on him just because someone else had treated her so shabbily?

"Yes, sir. In a few minutes. I just need to take one other call. If you would like the phone number of the police station, I can give—"

The man yelled into the phone. "Don't screw around with me, Mildred. I need *you* to do it. If someone else finds that book before the police do, I'll hold you personally responsible. I've already killed one woman. How would you like to be the second?"

22

"It's four-thirty in the afternoon," Alfred Korvich shouted at me over the phone line. "What the hell do you mean you haven't seen him all day?"

"Which word didn't you understand? I. Haven't. Seen—"

"All right, all right. I get your point." He took a deep breath. "I asked you to do one simple thing."

"You asked me to keep an eye on him. You didn't tell me to be his second skin. He was already gone when you and I talked earlier, and he hasn't returned while I was here."

"Have you been home all day?"

"Most of it. What's got you so riled up, anyway?"

"What's got me riled up, he wants to know." He paused for several seconds. "There's been a development in the murder investigation. I think we may be dealing with a real nut case here. Maybe this is right up your alley. What are you doing now? Can you come over here?"

And so for the second time in less than eight hours, I was the uncomfortable guest of our unhappy police chief in his unappealing Naugahyde palace. I said, "I don't have much time. I need to meet Veronica's train in a little while."

"Worse comes to worst, I send a cruiser to pick her up."

"Not a chance. How would you like to get off the commuter train and find the police waiting for you?"

He started to say something, then apparently thought better of it. He drummed his fingers on his desk for a moment, then said, "About an hour ago a clerk in Town Hall received a phone call. Male caller, he didn't leave his name, she didn't recognize the voice. He asked her to take down this information and give it to the police."

He passed a piece of paper to me. On it I read:

818.3
T391
Copy 4

"Why didn't he call the police himself?"

Korvich replied, "I suppose he didn't want to take a chance on being recorded."

"Why?"

He didn't answer my question. Instead he directed my attention again to the piece of paper. "Any idea what the numbers stand for?"

"It's the Dewey Decimal System. This is the call number for a book in the library."

"Like I said earlier, you're a clever fellow. And now, for the sixty-four-thousand-dollar question, would you care to guess what the book is?"

I glanced at the number again. I shrugged. "I don't know. Nonfiction. Author's last name starts with T. It must be a popular book, since they have at least three other copies."

"A clever fellow, indeed. The number corresponds to a copy of *Walden*. A very special copy."

"What makes it so special?"

"At least three things that I can think of. First, it's probably the only copy in the world that's being checked right now for fingerprints. Second, several of the pages have been ripped out. Third, wedged inside the book, in place of the missing pages, there was an envelope. And inside that envelope were two very interesting items." He paused.

"Go on."

Korvich reached into his desk drawer and pulled out a palm-sized copy of *Walden*. "This is an abridged version. They sell a lot of them at the gift shop by the pond. What? What's so funny?"

"The whole concept," I said, still chuckling. "A book within a book. Like one of those puzzles that kids have, where a box sits within a box within a box . . . you know what I mean."

He wasn't smiling. "A copy just like this one was found near the murder victim. And another copy was inside the envelope in the library book. The small copy is also being checked for fingerprints, as is the other item from the envelope. It was a three-page letter. I have a photocopy you can read." He passed two sheets of paper to me and held on to the third one.

The message was printed in large letters. I read the first page.

BECAUSE

Because . . .

Because I am a true believer.

Because people are more important than pretty things.

Because creation is made with all sorts of people: rich and poor; black, brown, and white.

Because there are those who confuse value with uniqueness.

Because there are those who believe that to keep what they have, they must stop others from getting what they are due.

Because one should be willing to go the distance for a truly worthy cause.

Because the only obligation which I have a right to assume is to do at any time what I think right.

Because those who do not understand this have the same sort of worth only as horses and dogs.

I read from the second page. It consisted of only one sentence.

Because of all of this, I killed Sandra O'Neill.

I looked at Alfred Korvich. He was looking at me, trying to get a read on my reaction. I glanced at the third sheet of paper he was holding. I nodded, and he passed it to me without comment.

And because of all of this, I will kill again.

And again.

And again . . .

. . . until Walden is free, and the people are one.

You may call me —

The True Believer

23

"Wow," I said.

Korvich said, "He must be referring to the development of the Logan tract. The line about people being more important than pretty things, and talking about how Concord should be a place for all sorts of people."

"Maybe this is just a sick prank."

"I don't think so," he replied. "A sick prank is somebody giving poisoned meat to his neighbor's dog, or sending a funeral wreath to someone who isn't dead. But this is different. Look at how many steps he had to go through. Writing the letter. Buying the abridged *Walden*. Going to the library and hollowing out a book. The kicker for me is the way he used the clerk in Town Hall. That shows planning. Also manipulativeness. And she says he sounded pretty agitated the second time he called."

"Why did he call her twice?"

"Once to give her the information, and once to yell at her for not passing it on fast enough to suit him. He was very determined that we get it."

"Wow."

"You're starting to repeat yourself. Read the letter again and tell me what you think of the person who wrote it. Pretend he's the patient of another psychiatrist, and the psychiatrist has come to you with this letter for a consultation on his patient."

I read the message a few times. "I would say he's intelligent, probably well educated. The vocabulary and language read like college level or above. And look at the semicolon in this sentence." I pointed to the first page.

Because creation is made with all sorts of people: rich and poor; black, brown, and white.

"What about it?"

I said, "He uses commas to separate items within a series. 'Black, brown, and white.' Therefore he uses the semicolon to separate that series from the 'rich and poor.' A lot of people wouldn't know to do that."

"What else?"

"This part is unusual. 'The only obligation which I have a right to assume is to do at any time what I think right.' "

"What makes it unusual?"

"He gets a little lost in the sound of the words, the logic slips a little bit, and he comes out at the end presenting himself as the arbiter of what's right and wrong."

"Do you think he's nuts?"

"Well, without dwelling on your inappropriate use of the word 'nuts' to describe a mentally ill person, I'd say there's nothing that suggests a blatant break with reality. But I don't like this next part. It worries me. 'Those who do not understand this have the same sort of worth only as horses and dogs.' "

"Why not?"

"Because that's how killers think when they're getting ready to strike. It's a lot easier to brutalize someone if you tell yourself they're less than fully human. I've seen it with combat veterans I've treated. Also with a gangster I once knew. Killing a *person* is less palatable to the conscience than killing a 'gook,' for example."

He considered that for a few seconds. "Well, at least it tells us one thing. Kay was right. It looks like the killer knew Sandra O'Neill."

"It tells you one other thing," I said. "It means Steven Farr is off the hook."

He raised one eyebrow. "How do you figure that?"

"I don't know if this guy is serious when he says he plans to kill others. But he's telling you that he killed Sandra O'Neill for political reasons, because of her opposition to the development project. You don't have any reason to think that Steven would kill her for a reason like that."

"No. But maybe this letter is a smokescreen. Something to divert our attention away from Farr. You weren't with him today. You don't know that he didn't plant the envelope in the library."

"What are you going to do with the letter?"

"Nothing right now, other than check it out for forensic evidence. Fingerprints, type of paper, stuff like that."

"Aren't you going to take his threat seriously?"

"What do you want me to do—notify everyone in town that their lives are endangered if they oppose the Logan tract project? First of all, that's probably most of the people in town. Second, like I said, at the moment there's no reason to think this is anything more than a smokescreen the killer is sending out to draw attention away from him."

"What does Kay think? Were you able to reach her in New York to tell her about it?"

"Not yet."

"Is she coming back tonight?"

"No. She'll be there until at least tomorrow. There's been an unexpected problem that has kept her tied up most of the day."

"What sort of problem?"

"A shooting."

"A *shooting*?"

"She wasn't hurt badly. And she wasn't the shooter. They hooked her up with a trigger-happy city cop. He shot someone and he accidentally gave Kay a flesh wound, and you have no idea what the paperwork is like on something like that."

"I can imagine. Sort of like filing a response to a malpractice claim. Are you sure she's okay?"

"She sounded fine when I spoke with her. You ever had a malpractice claim filed against you?"

"No. But I've testified in malpractice cases, and I know

people who have been sued. These days, people will sue for just about anything."

"Uh-huh. Like the lady who drank hot coffee while she drove her car, spilled it on herself, and sued the store that sold it to her. She said it was too hot."

I said, "There was a mentally ill man in Philadelphia who tried to commit suicide by jumping in front of a commuter train as it pulled into the station. He didn't die. But he sued the city for the injuries he suffered."

"Yeah," Korvich said, "but my lady with the hot coffee won her suit."

"And so did my fellow in the train station."

"You're kidding me."

"I kid you not." I stood, ready to leave. "Speaking of commuter trains, I need to get over to the depot to meet Veronica."

"Well, just let me know if you hear anything."

"Like, if Steven asks me for a comprehensive list of everyone in town who's opposed to the development project?"

"Something like that. And like I said this morning—I hope you won't say anything about this to him, or even to Veronica."

"I won't say anything to him. I'm not making any promises about Veronica. I'll play it by ear."

I headed for the door, ready to make the short drive to the train depot, which was across the street from the pizza shop. . . .

The pizza shop.

I turned around to face the police chief. "Do you know Robert Kennedy Butler?"

"I know who he is," Korvich replied. "We haven't met. Why?"

"I overheard a conversation between him and Davey Waterstone yesterday. And Butler said something similar to what you have in that letter. He said that people are more important than trees. 'Fucking trees' were his exact words, if I recall correctly."

"Now, *there's* an interesting image for you. 'Fucking trees.' "

"One other thing," I said. "I saw Butler walking along Main

Street this morning. He was coming from the direction of the library."

He thought about that for a moment. "I'll mention it to Kay when she gets back." He leaned back in his chair and yawned.

"No, that's okay—don't get up. I'll see myself out."

I stepped outside and made the short drive from the police station to the depot. The former was on Walden Street; the latter was on Thoreau Street. It all seemed appropriate.

24

Kay Wheaton offered no opinions: only facts. She described again and again—to a series of questioners, one after another—exactly what had happened in the Brooklyn apartment earlier that day.

No, neither she nor Ramirez identified themselves as police officers before the bullets were fired.

No, the man did not make any verbal threats.

Yes, the wounded man pointed his gun at her; and yes, he was moving it toward Ramirez when he was shot.

Kay knew it was like this—and had to be like this—whenever a police officer shot someone. But the delay was irritating. She didn't like big cities anymore, and now she wouldn't get back to Massachusetts until the next day at the earliest.

Her wound had been cleaned and bandaged. She ached, but she refused a codeine-laced drug and stuck with an over-the-counter painkiller. She would have to minimize her walking for at least a week.

Shortly after five o'clock the powers that be were finished with her. They had interrogated Ramirez and her separately, of course, and now Kay saw him for the first time since they arrived back at the police station after the shooting.

"Administrative leave, paid," he said, "until they straighten this thing out."

"You don't look worried."

"Nah." He waved his hand in the air as if he were brushing

away a harmless gnat. "We got him charged with carrying an unlicensed firearm. And two counts of assault on a police officer. One for you, and one for me."

"Oh, that's just great. Now I'll have to come back to testify at a trial."

"Don't sweat it, doll. It'll never come to trial. This guy has two prior assaults, and he's already on probation for the last one. He's got too much to lose if he's convicted again. After the D.A.'s office settles down—they fucking hate it when a cop shoots someone—after they settle down, cooler heads will prevail."

"Meaning exactly what?"

"He agrees not to sue the city or pursue charges against me, we agree not to pursue charges against him. Tie game. No effect in the final standings."

"You act like you've been through this before."

He smiled. "Hey, doll—life in the big city."

"Two things, Ramirez. First, I'm not your doll. Second, where I come from, you shoot someone by accident, it's generally considered polite to apologize."

"Yeah, well . . . you know."

A uniformed officer interrupted them to tell Kay that the Concord police chief was on the phone again. Kay assumed Alfred Korvich wanted a status report on the shooting incident and on her general plan.

She was wrong. He wanted to tell her about a certain phone call to a clerk at Town Hall, and about a certain letter in a mutilated copy of *Walden* at the town library.

"Wow," she said.

"That's exactly what our friend Harry Kline said."

"You told him about this?"

"This morning I asked him to keep an eye on Steven Farr, just like you suggested. I figured if he knew about the letter, that might motivate him a little bit. Besides . . ." He paused.

"What?"

He said, "He's got a kid in that house, and now for all we know he has a killer there. I figured this might persuade him to send her somewhere else until things settle, one way or another."

"I take it, then, that the rumor is false."

"What rumor?"

"The rumor that your heart was surgically replaced at birth with a small engine, and that you have motor oil in your veins instead of blood."

"Oh," Korvich replied. "*That* rumor. I started it myself, Kay. Pass it on. What's next on your agenda?"

"I'm going to interview a close friend of the victim's. A woman named Lisa Downing. I have three more interviews lined up for tonight and tomorrow."

"Well, try to stay out of trouble this time."

"Grout," Lisa Downing said. "It's all because of bathroom grout, detective. Say—are you all right?"

"I'm all right," Kay replied, wincing again. "I injured my leg earlier and it's a little sore. What do you mean, 'bathroom grout'?"

Lisa Downing leaned back in the soft leather couch in her expensive SoHo condominium unit. "Grout," she repeated. "The viscous substance they spread between bathroom tiles. The substance adheres to the tiles and to the wall, and then it hardens. It helps hold the tiles in place."

"I understand that. But I don't understand its relevance to the matter at hand."

"Yes, the matter at hand." Lisa sighed. She looked out the window and nervously twirled the small gold crucifix around her neck. "'The matter at hand.' I suppose that's as suitable a neutral term as any for such a terrible thing." She turned her gaze back toward Kay. "You're looking at me oddly, detective."

"It's your cross. It looks—"

"It looks just like Sandi's cross. I know. She gave it to me for my confirmation, back when we were in junior high school together."

"You knew her for a very long time."

"Yes. We've known each other . . . we knew each other for a very long time." She touched the crucifix again. "I haven't worn this in years. But immediately after you called me this morning with the news, I looked for it until I found it, and I've had it on the whole day."

Kay said, "Why do you say this is all because of grout?"

"Sandi's grandfather struck it rich with some sort of accidental discovery, something that improved the bonding characteristics of tile grout. A large trust fund passed to Sandi when she was twenty-one. Then her parents died a few years ago, and she inherited an enormous amount of grout money. If those things hadn't happened, she'd be living an utterly ordinary life in New Jersey. She'd either be supporting herself in a conventional manner, or—more likely—married to someone who was supporting her in a conventional manner. But instead, she took up with overgrown children, like Steven, and with all those hell-freezes-over people. If she hadn't done that, *Walden* would just be some misanthropic diatribe that we were forced to read in college, and not a place where she would finally . . ." Her voice faded. "Oh, crap. None of this makes any sense. *I'm* not making any sense."

"There was a photograph in her apartment. She was standing between two men, and someone named Glen inscribed 'Hell has frozen over' on the picture."

"Glen Frey. The other man is Don Henley. They're in that rock group, the Eagles. Sandi worked on their reunion tour last year. They called it the Hell Freezes Over tour. I'm sure that at some point I knew why they used that expression, and I'm sure I no longer have any idea." She stood and walked toward the small but well-appointed kitchen. "Can I get you some more coffee, detective?"

"Yes. Thanks."

Lisa Downing went into the kitchen and returned a minute later. "How long will you stay in New York?"

"I have three more of Sandi's friends to meet. I hope to go home tomorrow."

"Where did you get our names?"

"Steven gave me a list." She flipped back to an earlier page in her notepad. "Here—do you recognize these names? I'm going to speak with the first one tonight, and the others tomorrow."

Lisa looked at the other names on the list. She knew them all. Kay asked if there was anyone important missing from the list. "No," Lisa said. "You've got her closest friends, myself included. But I doubt that any of us can help you. Sandi never mentioned to me that she felt frightened or threatened by anyone."

The telephone rang. Lisa walked into the kitchen and answered it. "Hello . . . Yes, I know. She's here now, talking with me about it . . . No, I haven't. I haven't heard from him . . . That's not helpful, Betty. No, that's not helpful at all . . . I'm sure Steven feels as terrible as any of us. No, Betty. That would be extremely inappropriate . . . All right, then. No, that's all right. You're not bothering me . . . Okay. Good-bye."

Lisa returned to the living room. "That was Betty. She's the last name on the list you showed me. She heard from Steven. He's staying with an old girlfriend in Massachusetts while he plans Sandi's funeral service. Betty thinks that's unseemly. She's ready to fly up there tonight and read the riot act to him."

"I'll tell Betty not to worry. I know the woman she's referring to. She lives with another man, and I don't think she's looking to make any changes." She paused. "But what about Sandi? Was she looking to make changes?"

"Changes?"

"Yes," Kay said. "Did Sandi ever talk about getting out of the relationship?"

"No, she never did." Lisa Downing kicked off her shoes and tucked her feet underneath herself on the couch. She leaned against the armrest. "I don't believe I've ever felt quite so tired," she said.

"Did she seem happy?"

"Happy? How many people do you know who are really happy?"

Kay placed her coffee cup down. "I guess your friend Sandi must have been happy enough, or she wouldn't have decided to get married."

Lisa picked her head up. "Married? Who said anything about getting married?"

"Steven did," said Kay. "I think they were almost ready to set a date." She paused. "You look surprised."

"I *am* surprised. That's certainly news to me, detective. Sandi never said anything about getting married."

25

None of us said very much over the dinner table.

I presumed that Melissa's day and Veronica's day had been interesting or boring, frustrating or satisfying, energizing or tiresome, or otherwise worthy of comment. But comments were sparse in the pall cast by the tragedy that had befallen Steven Farr. His somber mood set the tone for my household that evening.

Nor did I have anything to contribute to the conversation. Neither of the two things most on my mind—my medical situation and the possibility, however unlikely, that I was seated across the table from a murderer—seemed appropriate for dinnertime discussion.

Steven told us about his meeting with Father John Fitzpatrick. "Sandi was about as lapsed as you could be and still call yourself Catholic. But I know she would have wanted a memorial Mass. The priest seemed decent enough."

"Are you Catholic?" I asked.

"Hell, I don't know what the fuck I am. Oh . . . sorry, Melissa. Sorry, everybody. I'm just so goddamn sorry for everything. Sorry for everything."

At first I thought his eyes were red from crying. But his speech was slightly slurred and his inhibitions were down. He was probably one and a half sheets to the wind even before he began hitting the dinner chardonnay.

I excused myself and went into the den to make a phone call.

When I was finished, I called my daughter into the room. "I just called Wendy," I said, referring to one of my late wife's best friends. "I asked her to let you stay with her family for the next few days, just until the funeral service. She'll be over in a little while to pick you up."

"Dad," she said in a singsong whine that turned that one syllable into a two-syllable word. "Why? Just because he said the F word?"

"No. Because he's in terrible shape, and I don't want you exposed to all of this. This has turned into a house of mourning. It's not the house I want for you right now."

"But Dad, this is *my* house, too."

"I know, honey."

"You should have asked me first."

"Maybe I should have *told* you first, before I called Wendy, but there was no point in asking. It's not your decision to make. It's mine."

I seldom acted so unilaterally dictatorial in my dealings with her. But when I did, she usually made only a mild protest. Perhaps because I did it rarely, she understood that only something important would cause me to invoke my parental prerogatives so boldly.

"You should go up to your room and pack some things. Do you want me to help you?"

She sighed. "No, I can do it." She started to walk toward the stairs, then stopped and turned to face me. "I can still go to the funeral service, can't I?"

"I didn't know you wanted to."

She shrugged. "Well, he's Veronica's friend. I'm sure she'll go there to be with him. So you and I should go there to be with her."

I couldn't argue with that logic. "Yes, of course you can."

She smiled and headed upstairs to get her belongings.

There was something in her smile that reminded me of her mother. Janet had an expression she used to say to my daughter when she tucked her in at night: *You are beautiful, inside out and outside in.* It was true then; it was true now.

Steven's wineglass had been empty when I left the dining

room. When I returned, he was drinking from it. He set it down on the table, empty again.

The conversation seemed not to have moved forward during my time away. He said, "I'm so fucking sorry, Vee. I just keep thinking that over and over. I didn't mean for any of that to happen, love."

"I know you are, Steven."

I sat at the table. He mumbled his vague apologies a couple of times more, then fell into silence.

I announced that Melissa would be staying with Wendy and her family for a few days. Veronica was surprised. She said, "When did that come about?"

"Just a few minutes ago," I said.

"I didn't hear the phone ring."

"No. I called Wendy."

"Oh, I see," she replied, with a hint of displeasure in her voice. I wondered what bothered her more: Melissa's leaving, or the decision being made without asking Veronica for her opinion.

Steven said, "It's me, Vee. He wants her to leave because of me."

"Don't be ridiculous, Steven."

"No, I'm right, love. He wants to get her away from me."

Veronica turned to me. "Tell him he's being ridiculous."

I said, "I think it's best for her not to be exposed to so much sadness."

Melissa came downstairs with her packed suitcase. A few minutes later Wendy arrived with her daughter, Jennifer. The girl was four years old, with a liveliness that reminded me of how Melissa was when she was that age, just before my wife died. Melissa turned inward after that, and for a long time only traces of that liveliness were seen.

I was glad she was leaving: She had already had enough. As I watched the car disappear down the driveway toward Monument Street, I thought I understood how Londoners felt during World War II: sending their children off to the countryside to keep them safe from the Blitzkrieg.

There was more wine in Steven's glass when I returned to

the dining room. He continued to ruminate about his sorrow and his guilt, and for a moment I wondered if he were about to break down and confess to the murder. And then, after perhaps a dozen professions of his regret, Veronica said, "It was a long time ago, Steven. I don't dwell on it."

And suddenly I realized that it wasn't something recent that Steven was apologizing for, and it didn't have anything to do with Sandi O'Neill. He was talking about the past, and he was talking about Veronica.

He said, "You were never much for dwelling on things, were you, love? Did you ever consider the possibility, all these years, that maybe I dwelled on it?"

"No, I never considered it. I just put it behind me. That's my way of coping, Steven. That's what's always gotten me through difficulty."

"Just like that," he said with a snicker. "Veronica Pace, the iron lady. Well, you should consider it. Consider the possibility that on some eternal plane that I can't understand, where there really is a communion of all souls, where time as we know it doesn't exist, where the past, present, and future are happening at the same time, where God has always existed and will always exist—consider the possibility that God intended a certain young man and a young woman to be together eternally. Consider the possibility that my fall from grace is that I fucked up that godly plan. If you consider that as a possibility, then it makes sense that I would dwell on it, even after all these years."

She glanced at me to gauge my reaction, then said, "You're drunk, Steven. You're just rambling."

"Of course I'm drunk. That's *my* way of coping. I'm a drunken, sinful man who has fallen from grace." He lifted his glass. "Cheers."

Veronica reached toward him and took the glass from him. "Enough, Steven. Everyone has had enough."

"Yes, ma'am," he said with a mock salute. "But one other thing you should consider. For the sinful man, recalling his fall from grace is the only way of reapproaching that grace, even though he fears he will never feel that grace again."

She stood and began collecting the dishes. "I'll take these to the kitchen."

He said, "I'll help." He tried to lift himself off his chair, but he slipped and fell back onto it.

Veronica walked out of the room.

Steven turned to me and said, "She's quite a woman."

"Yes, she is."

"Which makes you a lucky man."

"I know."

"Luck can have a way of running out. You have her now, but maybe you won't keep her. You should never assume anything."

I didn't like his tone. I took what he said as a veiled threat.

"Never assume," he repeated. "About anything."

"I guard my assumptions carefully."

He pondered that for a moment. "What the hell does that mean?"

Veronica returned. "What the hell does *what* mean?"

"Nothing, love. Harry and I were just talking about the nature of luck."

"Well," she said, "I think you should get some rest." She held her arm out for him to grab. "Here—let me help you over to the barn."

I stood. "No. Allow *me*." I gripped his hand and pulled him to a standing position, and I pointed him toward the door. I walked alongside him, step by step, guiding his direction. I draped an arm across his shoulders, steadying him.

We crossed the distance to the barn in the dusk. A small gaggle of Canada geese—a harbinger of the autumn to come—honked overhead as they made their way to the wildlife refuge beyond the field.

The stairway to the barn apartment was narrow. I pushed him ahead of me, bracing myself against the wall in case I needed to spot him if he fell backward.

We crossed through the kitchen and into the modest-size living room. I dropped him onto the couch, perhaps a little harder than was necessary.

I walked into the kitchen, found a shopping bag underneath the sink, and opened the refrigerator. There were two six-pack beer cartons, one of them half empty. I placed them in the shopping bag.

I returned to the living room. "I found beer in the refrigerator. Do you have anything else to drink?"

"Some Jack Daniel's, in the bedroom."

I retrieved the bottle and returned to the living room. "Anything else?"

"No. I thought you don't drink."

"I don't." I put the bottle into the paper bag. "And for as long as you're staying here, you don't drink, either. If I see it, if I smell it, if I even think it, you're out of here."

"Jesus fucking Christ—"

"Don't say that. And there's one more thing."

"What?"

"If you call Veronica 'love' one more time, make certain you have a supply of straws."

"Why?"

"Because you'll have to drink your food. Because if you say that one more time, I'll break your jaw."

"Are you threatening me?"

"Consider it a medical advisory. As a physician, I'm telling you what you need to do in order to remain healthy. I want you to stop sniffing around my woman."

" 'My woman.' That's a tad Neanderthal, don't you think?"

"Fuck you, Steven."

I grabbed the paper bag. I walked down the stairs and opened the door to walk outside. Then I considered the ridiculousness of what I had just said, and I went upstairs again.

"Listen," I said. "What happened to your girlfriend is an awful thing. I know how it affects you. However it happened, why ever it happened, I know it will give you nightmares forever. You're welcome to stay here until the funeral. But that's all you're welcome to."

As I crossed to the house, I heard a glass shatter in the barn apartment.

26

"What's the story between you and Steven?"

Veronica crawled into bed next to me. "There is no story. I left him in the past a long time ago."

"That's the story I'm asking about. Your past relationship."

"Oh." She hesitated. "You've never asked questions about other men before."

I winced internally at the word "men" and the image it conjured: legions of past lovers, each of them with a prior hold on her.

I said, "Maybe that's because I never had one of them in my house before."

"As far as you know."

"What the hell is *that* supposed to mean?"

She turned toward me and touched my chest. "Relax. I was just joking. I didn't mean to upset you. Like I said, what happened between Steven and me was a long time ago. Twelve years."

"I'm twelve years older than you. If twelve years is such a long time, what does that say about the difference in our ages?"

She sighed and rolled onto her back. "Oh, Harry. Please don't be morose. Let's just get through this week and then he'll be gone, and things can get back to normal."

We lay there quietly for a few minutes, and then she said, "He was my first serious boyfriend. We met when I was a sophomore in college. We broke up at the end of my junior year."

"The relationship was sexual, I assume."

"The relationship was definitely sexual." She paused. "Are you sure you want to go there?"

"I don't think I need to hear those details."

"No, and I don't think I want to talk about them. Anyway, you've met him, so you know it wasn't his mind I was attracted to."

"He's not the brightest lamppost on the street."

She laughed. "No, he's not. The attraction was elsewhere. My roommate used to describe him as being 'drop-dead gorgeous.' "

I could resonate with the *drop dead* part of the equation, but I kept that thought to myself.

The geese in the wildlife refuge made a distant, mournful sound.

She said, "You know that I can't have children."

"Of course."

"I don't think I've ever told you why."

"You said your fallopian tubes were scarred from an infection, and that you would never be able to get pregnant."

"But I didn't tell you the story behind that. I did get pregnant once, in the spring of my junior year at Radcliffe . . . with Steven."

"Oh." I didn't know what else to say.

"I wanted the baby. He didn't. We fought about it, over and over. And then he walked out on me. He went to fucking California, or perhaps it would be more accurate to say he went fucking to California. Either way, he left me to deal with it on my own—the pregnancy and the baby. But the baby never came."

She paused for a few seconds. Then she said, "I got an infection. It triggered a miscarriage. And that was the infection that scarred my tubes."

And so Veronica lost one child, and she lost the possibility of ever bearing another one.

"Steven tried to come back to me after I lost the baby. But I knew I would never trust him again, and I didn't let him back in my life. I hung up every time he called, until finally he stopped calling. I never heard from him again until he showed up here two nights ago."

"Did you ever wish you hadn't pushed him away like that?"

"After the initial heartache, I don't recall that I ever gave him more than a moment's thought. It's like you heard me tell him earlier this evening—I cope by putting things that bother me in the past and out of my thoughts. You already know that about me. Why are you asking all of these questions about him?"

"For a couple of reasons, I guess. First of all, I don't like the way he acts around you—flirting with you and touching you and calling you 'love.' "

"It's just an expression."

"Let me finish." I took a deep breath and calmed myself. "Second, Alfred Korvich told me they think he may be responsible for the murder."

"Well, of course."

" 'Of course'? You knew that already?"

She said, "It would be natural for them to focus on him. His story about not being in touch with her for a few days and not worrying about it seemed pretty lame. I noticed that immediately."

"So you suspect him, too?"

"No. But his story makes it sound like he's hiding something. Maybe they were fighting and she decided she wanted to be alone for a few days. And he's afraid to tell that to Kay Wheaton for fear that he'll come under suspicion, so he makes up a ridiculous story that just makes him look all the more suspicious."

I briefed her on my entire conversation with Korvich. She held to the thought that nothing clearly implicated Steven in the murder.

And then I told her about the letter: the message in the library's mutilated copy of *Walden* that promised more killing.

Veronica said, "It's probably a prank. An effort by some save-the-trees weirdo to scare people. In any event, there's no reason in the world why Steven would write a letter like that. If he actually killed his girlfriend, there are only three reasons he could have for writing that letter, and none of them fit the Steven Farr I know."

"What do you mean?"

"First-case scenario. Everything he says in the letter is true. He killed Sandra O'Neill, and he intends to kill others in the name of some nutty social cause. Steven Farr never did anything or took risks for anyone else in his life, unless it was someone he was sleeping with who he was afraid would lose interest in him. He's the last person in the world I would suspect as some guerrilla fighter for a bizarre cause."

She continued. "Second-case scenario. He killed her, and the letter is the smokescreen Korvich said it is, something to divert attention from Steven. Well, Steven runs from his problems. If he had killed Sandi, he wouldn't take the risk of exposing himself with another action like that letter. He'd stick his head in the sand and hope trouble passed him by."

"And what's your third-case scenario?"

"The worst-case scenario. He killed her, *and* he plans to kill others at random to draw attention away from the fact that he killed his lover. Once again, Steven wouldn't take that sort of chance. He's not that clever or indirect. He would just close his eyes and hope no one noticed him."

"So you don't think he would be capable of killing her."

"I didn't say that. Anyone is capable of killing anyone, in the wrong moment, under the wrong circumstances. I'm saying he's not the sort of person to plan it out, or to cover it up with some elaborate scheme."

Everything she said made sense—more sense than the vague justification Korvich had given me for suspecting Steven.

She said, "As far as his behavior toward me is concerned, if you want me to, I'll ask him to go back to the inn."

I sighed. "No, that's not necessary. It's just for a few days. I can deal with it."

"You're *so* mature," she said, laughing. "It's nice for me to be with a man so many, many, many years older than me."

"All right. Let's not push it."

She kissed me lightly on the forehead. "Good night, Harry."

As I lay in the silence, I thought about my idiotic confrontational behavior toward Steven. It was over the line. Perhaps I would apologize in the morning.

I said, "I can only imagine how awful that must be."

"What?"

"To have someone you loved—a girlfriend you had been emotionally and physically intimate with—murdered like that."

"It happened to me once. Well, not exactly. It happened after the fact."

"What do you mean?"

"After the fact of my involvement with the person. Someone I was very serious about while I was in law school. A few years later he was shot to death by a new girlfriend."

"Well, I guess that's one of your former lovers who I don't have to worry about crawling out of the woodwork." I paused. "That was uncalled for. I'm sorry."

She yawned. "Don't be. He was the prick of the century. Incredibly cruel to me. I cut him out of my life when he hurt me, and I never saw him or thought about him again."

"Even so, you must have felt awful when he died that way."

"No, I didn't. The only thing I recall feeling was vindication. I figured someone had given him exactly what he deserved."

"And now?"

"To the extent that I think about it—which is minimal—I suppose I still feel the same way."

"You're kidding me."

"No," she said, "I'm completely serious. Is there a problem with that?"

"I don't know. I just . . . I don't know."

"What? Why do you have a problem with that?"

"I just can't imagine feeling so hateful toward someone I once loved. No matter what she had done to me. Even if I never wanted to see her again."

She sat up. "And I suppose that makes you a better person than me. Is that what you're saying?"

"I didn't say that. I—"

"You can't possibly know what you're talking about. He was so cruel to me, and he treated me so terribly, and now you lie there judging me because I felt no particular sorrow when he died. I suppose if you were in my situation you would have gone to the funeral."

"I suppose I would have."

"I was being sarcastic when I said that."

"And I'm being serious."

"Why the hell would you go to the funeral?"

"I don't know. I suppose I want to believe that some sort of reconciliation is always possible, even after death. That nothing ever really ends."

"You've been spending too much time with your priest friend." She turned away and sat on the edge of the bed. "That's the difference between us. I believe everything ends."

She stood and grabbed her pillow. She said, "Never underestimate the value of hatred, and of the longing for revenge. Growing up, after my mother was killed, I would have been lost without them." She headed for the door.

"Where are you going?"

"I'm going to sleep in Melissa's room. I don't want to be with you right now. Obviously, I'm just not a good enough person for you."

I pushed the covers off and started to get out of bed. "Listen, I never said that. I didn't mean—"

She whirled around. "*Don't* say anything else! And *don't* follow me!" She slammed the door behind her, rattling the bottles of cologne on top of her dresser.

What the hell had just happened?

She had told me about two former lovers: Steven, and her law school boyfriend who was murdered. Both of them hurt her, and both of them she cut out of her life like a surgeon removing a malignancy.

I didn't want to think about surgeons removing malignancies.

I wondered: *If I hurt her, will she walk out on me and never look back?*

I ran the conversation over and over in my mind, trying to decide if I had done anything wrong. But in the final analysis, it didn't matter who was right and who was wrong. Maybe no one was wrong. Maybe we were just two very different people who on this night would sleep in two different beds.

I couldn't fall asleep on my side of the mattress. It was an illusion, I knew, but without Veronica on the other side, the bed felt unbalanced, as if I were in danger of falling off. I moved to the center of the bed and fell into a fitful sleep.

I was awakened shortly after one o'clock by the sound of a car engine. I walked to the bedroom window in time to see the taillights of Veronica's car as it headed down the driveway.

I walked downstairs to the kitchen and looked for a note. None was there. Where the hell had she gone?

I returned upstairs. I noticed that the door to my daughter's room was open. I stepped inside. Veronica was asleep in the bed, covers tossed to the floor. The window was open and the room was chilly. I placed the covers over her.

She stirred and mumbled something. I said, "Shhh. Go back to sleep," and gently touched her shoulder.

I looked out the window of Melissa's bedroom. Veronica's car was gone.

Where was Steven Farr?

27

The True Believer had excellent night vision: good for him, bad for his prey. Nocturnal, like the fox.

He parked a quarter mile away from the target, then walked toward it by cutting through the woods. No reason to park outside the old woman's home; no reason to chance someone taking note of the license plate number of an unfamiliar car on the quiet cul-de-sac.

He traveled light: no need to risk leaving something traceable behind after his mission was completed. In each rear pants pocket a pair of latex gloves: backups for the ones he was already wearing. In his left front pocket, a parting gift for the old woman. In the right pocket, a gravity knife, brand new, no prints. The knife was his contingency plan: messier but quicker than the preferred course of action. Prior planning prevents piss-poor performance.

The thin crescent of the moon gave enough illumination for passage through the woods. What was that line about the moon? Something spoken by the gimpy woman in a play by that faggot, Tennessee Williams. "A little silver sliver of a moon." Yes, that was it. A little silver sliver. The fox needs no more than that to light his way.

Even a visitor to Concord might learn a great deal about the woman without difficulty, for she was one of those figures everyone in town either knew or knew about. Adjectives abounded: feisty, indomitable, strong-willed. But what it came down to, he knew, was this: a stubborn old woman about ninety years old who had outlived her husband and her own children because she simply refused to die. Too pigheaded to move into an assisted living setting, or even into an apartment or smaller house. Daily maid service, but no company or protection at night.

Add "foolish" to the list of adjectives: It was the middle of the night, yet her sliding patio door was unlocked. No need for forced entry. No noise to rouse the old woman or anyone in the nearby houses.

He had killed before, of course, but not with such planning and premeditation. He had expected more reaction from his autonomic nervous system. But he had a higher purpose, and this had a calming effect. And so his skin was cool: no sweat. His pulse was a steady seventy-two: no fear.

There was a wall phone in the kitchen; he lifted the handset from the hook and let it dangle.

In the corner of the kitchen was a staircase leading to the second floor. When he reached the foot of the stairs, he heard a man's voice in the distance. He leaned forward: straining, listening, deciphering. A television newscaster intoning a recap of the day's O.J. events. Did Orenthal James use a gravity knife? Quick, but messy.

He ascended. The voice grew louder. Faint light from the television screen spilled into the hallway through the cracked-open bedroom door. If she was sleeping, Plan A. If she was awake, the knife might be necessary. He pulled it out of his pocket but didn't release the blade. He hoped she was sleeping; he preferred inflicting a merciful death.

He pushed open the door: slowly, slowly. The old woman lay on her back, mouth wide open. A line of spittle extended from her mouth to her chin, reflecting the television light.

She was still—so still he wondered if nature had already finished her off. That wouldn't do: If she was already dead, he would have to butcher her and hope the coroner didn't tease out the fact that she expired before the blade cut into her. He smiled at the thought: Many a killer had no doubt tried to make their handiwork look like an act of God. But if the old woman was already dead, he might be the first person in history intent on making a natural death look like murder. Because that was the whole idea: To kill. And to kill again. And to keep on killing, until his objective was gained.

He leaned close to her, looking for signs of life. He picked up the remote control and pressed the mute button. The moment the sound ceased, the woman's eyes snapped wide open: unfocused, not comprehending. "Rex," she whispered. "What is it, boy?"

No time to waste. He dropped the knife on the floor. He grabbed her neck with both hands, pushing both thumbs into the depression just above her chest bone. A brief, tiny gurgling sound, then silence: no air could pass in or out.

And now she focused, and in her final moment there was a look of . . . of what? Fear? Recognition? Gratitude? And then there was no look at all.

She emitted a small flatulent blast, with accompanying fetid odor. Her final statement in this life: a multimedia gastrointestinal farewell.

It was done.

The True Believer had excellent night vision. He also had excellent peripheral vision. He saw the dark mass leap from the floor near the foot of the bed.

He fell to his knees and reached for the gravity knife.

The Doberman pinscher crouched on the bed directly next to him. Hot breath and drool pouring from a snarling mouth. Shoulder muscles tensing, waiting to spring: a slab of sinewy, pulsating meat.

Click: release of blade.

"Easy, Rex. Good boy, Rex."

The dog growled. The dog pounced. The dog was impaled in midair by the blade that was thrust into his underside.

Man and dog toppled to the floor in one heap. The knife remained jammed into the animal. The man grabbed the knife with both hands and sliced through the dog's abdomen. Warm liquid spreading over his hands. The smell of innards hitting the air, becoming oxygenated. Yelping and more yelping, perhaps loud enough to alert the neighbors.

He yanked the knife from the animal's gut. Then he rammed the blade into its chest, and again, and again, and again. Thrashing gave way to spasms. Spasms gave way to quivering. And quivering gave way at last to stillness. The dog lay inert and eviscerated, pieces of inner tissue hanging loosely from its body.

He stood and surveyed the carnage. Bloodshed was not part of the plan. Sweat pouring now; pulse racing now. He looked at the stupid fucking woman and her stupid fucking dog. She should have had the good grace to die a long time ago.

Two minutes earlier, mercy had been his intent. But no longer. Now he plunged the knife into her belly: twisting, pulling, slicing.

Off in the distance, another dog barked.

It was time to leave.

Down the steps, across the kitchen, out the sliding patio door. He could feel the blood rushing through the veins of his temples.

Twenty or thirty yards into the woods he realized he had forgotten something: not something he left behind, but something he failed to leave there.

He ran back into the house, up the stairs, into the bedroom.

It felt ten degrees hotter than it had moments before. The air reeked, saturated with the odor of stinking viscera.

The True Believer reached into his pocket and pulled out his gift: a palm-sized book. He dropped it on the woman's body. Streaks of her blood washed across the one-word title on the cover: *Walden*.

28

Veronica shook me by the shoulder until I awoke. "What are you doing down there?"

I glanced around. I was lying on the floor of my daughter's bedroom. "I guess I fell asleep."

"I figured that part out. How long have you been there?"

"Since a little after one o'clock. What time is it?"

"Six-thirty. I've got to get moving. I have my regular Wednesday morning staff meeting first thing." She watched me stand and walk toward the window. "What are you looking at?"

"Just checking outside to see if your car is there."

"Why wouldn't it be there?"

"Steven went somewhere at around one o'clock. That's what woke me up. I came in here, covered you up, and I guess I stayed. I wanted to be with you."

"Then why aren't you in bed with me?"

"I didn't want to wake you up. And I was afraid you would tell me to get out. Besides, that's my *daughter's* bed. I think I would feel very weird lying there with you." I paused. "Well, would you have?"

"Would I have what?"

"Would you have kicked me out?"

She sighed. "I don't know. Probably not."

"You were right about last night. I had no business judging you like that. I guess I just got worried."

"Worried about what?"

"I got worried that if I were to disappoint you, you would just cut me out of your life and never look back, like you did with Steven and that other person you told me about."

"I'm not going to leave you, Harry. You're my last chance. If I don't get it right this time, I don't know what I'll do. Well? Is my car there?"

"It's there. I wonder where he went."

29

At ten o'clock Wednesday morning, approximately thirty-six hours after Sandra O'Neill's body was identified in the Boston morgue, Kay Wheaton finished interviewing the fourth and last of the murdered woman's friends on her list.

This much seemed certain: If Sandi O'Neill and Steven Farr had planned to marry, they were apparently the only two persons who knew it. None of Sandi's friends were aware of it. Three were surprised in the extreme, and one of the three said she would have been less surprised to learn that Sandi had decided to end the relationship. Roy Stamis, the recording studio assistant winged the previous day by Joseph Ramirez, also knew nothing of any planned marriage.

Of course, keeping wedding plans secret wasn't a crime. Nor was pretending to be engaged when one really wasn't. But if Steven was pretending to be on more solid footing with Sandi than he really was, perhaps it was because he was trying to hide something more sinister.

Kay used her final interviewee's telephone to call NYNEX. A billing and records supervisor who had given her a hard time the previous day had actually come through with a result. It was news that came as a surprise to Kay, because it seemed to lend support to Steven's version of events. At seven-thirty the previous Thursday evening, Sandi O'Neill had, indeed, used her cellular phone to call her own home phone number.

"A four minute call," said the NYNEX records supervisor.

"Four minutes exactly?"

"No, of course not. The account holder was billed for four minutes. The actual call was ... let me see ... it looks like three minutes and thirty-five seconds."

"Three minutes and thirty-five seconds," Kay repeated. "And your company rounded that up to the next minute," Kay said.

"Of course. It's so much more convenient that way."

Kay couldn't tell whether or not the woman on the other end of the line was being sarcastic. Clearly, the technology existed for breaking a minute into increments and billing accordingly. Just as clearly, NYNEX had decided it was more "convenient" to simply bilk its customers for unused time.

Kay called for a cab and headed toward the airport and the shuttle flight to Boston. As the cab crossed the 59th Street Bridge, Kay tried to imagine what that last conversation between Sandi and Steven was like. A lot could be said in three minutes and thirty-five seconds.

She remembered reading that the average husband and wife spend eight minutes in conversation with one another each day. She liked that statistic: It made her think she wasn't missing much by being single.

She remembered a segment in the movie *Yellow Submarine*: As the Beatles sang "When I'm Sixty-Four" in the background, sixty animations—one per second—were displayed in an effort to show the viewer that a minute was a very, very long time. Sandi and Steven had talked for 215 seconds.

Kay mulled over these thoughts and recollections as the cab moved along Northern Boulevard. And before she was even certain why she was doing it, she pulled out her cellular phone and called the home phone of Steven and Sandi.

The phone rang five, ten, a dozen times. Kay hung up.

She thought that odd: no answering machine. She remembered that Sandi's office phone had an answering machine, but she couldn't remember seeing one linked to the phone in the bedroom the previous day. Of course, she hadn't spent much time in the bedroom before all hell broke loose.

Kay told the driver to turn around and head to Brooklyn.

* * *

On the way to the apartment, Kay had the taxi driver stop at a Radio Shack store. She went inside and purchased two answering machine tapes—a standard-size cassette and a microcassette. If there were an answering machine in the apartment, one of those tapes would probably fit.

Outside the apartment, Kay struck a deal with the driver: He turned the meter off while she was inside in return for her promise that she would still use his cab to get to the airport. They agreed he would start the meter again if she stayed inside longer than fifteen minutes.

The town of Concord would reimburse her for the cab fare, and there was really no reason for her to quibble with the driver over the meter. But the phone conversation with the NYNEX supervisor had rubbed her the wrong way. Kay felt as if she were trying to even things out with the universe: Sandi O'Neill had been billed for empty time, so now she was taking some of that time back.

Once again Kay opened the three dead-bolt locks, each with its own key. And once again she unlocked and opened the door that led to the staircase. This time she took the steps much more slowly, favoring her injured leg as she climbed.

The bedroom phone was attached to an AT&T answering machine with dual microcassettes: one for the outgoing announcement, the other for incoming messages. She removed the tape for messages and replaced it with the newly purchased blank one.

She walked into Sandi's office and dialed the bedroom phone. Once again she let it ring a dozen times before hanging up; the answering machine didn't engage.

She returned to the bedroom and examined the answering machine. It was switched off. She switched it on, returned to Sandi's office, and called again.

Steven's voice came on the line with a typical answering machine greeting. After his message, a beep sounded. Kay glanced at the second hand on her watch and began timing.

The machine disengaged and a dial tone sounded after less

than ten seconds. She tried again, and again the machine disconnected quickly. *Voice activated,* she thought.

She dialed the bedroom phone once more. This time she began talking at the sound of the beep, reciting children's nursery rhymes, then counting forward and backward in English and Spanish, just to keep the machine from disconnecting at the sound of silence.

Just as she suspected, the machine—like most answering machines—had a ceiling for each individual message. Eventually it cut off.

Kay repeated the process two more times. Each time, the answering machine cut off after exactly the same interval.

She returned to the bedroom. She left the newly purchased tape in the unit and pocketed the one that was in it previously. She considered turning the machine off, since Steven had left it that way, but decided against that.

Before she locked up, Kay watered the plants in the second-story apartment—something she hadn't thought of doing the day before. It seemed at once like both a stupid and an important thing to do.

"I gave you an extra five minutes," the cabdriver said. "I guess it don't hurt to do a favor for the local police."

"I'm not local," Kay replied.

"Even so," he said. "You never know. What goes around comes around." He started the engine and they were off to the airport.

Kay said, "Do you have an answering machine at home?"

"Who, me? What I want something like that for? Too many people trying to reach out and touch me already. Thank you very much, uh-uh, forget it, no way, ma'am."

She smiled. "Maybe someday you'll change your mind. They can come in quite handy if you're expecting an important call. You can say a lot in three minutes and thirty-five seconds."

"Say, what?"

"Three minutes and thirty-five seconds. That's how long a message you can leave on the answering machine in that Brooklyn apartment."

30

There were two notarized copies of my will: one in my safe deposit box, and one in Bobby Beck's law office. I kept a photocopy in my desk; I reviewed it as I ate lunch.

It was comforting to know that Melissa would be well provided for if I died. Paradoxically, I owed much of that good fortune to Nathan Jacobs, my former father-in-law, with whom I shared a ripened sense of mutual disregard.

When Janet and I got married, Nathan purchased a million-dollar life insurance policy on me, along with an annuity that would cover the premium until I was in my late fifties. He did this without asking us first. He thought it was a wonderful gift: a guarantee that his daughter and his unborn grandchildren would be secure if I were to die. But I recognized the gesture for what it was: at best, a subtly stated belief that I would be incapable of providing for my own family's welfare; at worst, an unconscious expression of his wish that I would drop dead at the earliest convenient moment.

Janet resented her father's implication that my life was somehow more valuable than hers. She insisted that we purchase an identical policy on her. It was ironic: Were it not for her father's purchase of the policy on me, we never would have bought the policy on her. And now the million-dollar principal from the payment on her policy was still intact. If I were to die, another amount equal to that would come Melissa's way.

Bobby was named as my executor. And as the will currently stood, he and his wife would become Melissa's guardians.

The will was written before I met Veronica. She was well-off in her own right, far wealthier than me, so there was no reason to worry about making financial provisions for her. But the thought of her and Melissa no longer living together was gnawing at me.

The issue of who Melissa would live with would be moot if Veronica and I were married. And we had talked about marriage, in fits and starts, now and again. But the conversation always seemed to putter to a stop short of any conclusion.

The last discussion of the matter—if one could call such brief mention a discussion—occurred about six weeks earlier. We had the house to ourselves while my daughter was at a slumber party. It was late at night, and we had just enjoyed an unexpected course of bone-jangling sex on the chaise lounge on the screened-in rear porch.

There was a full summer moon, and the distant chorus of night animal sounds from the wildlife refuge. We lay there naked, her head resting on my chest. I said, "I think I just saw a falling star."

She nuzzled against me. "Make a wish."

I thought for a moment. "Do you know what I wish?"

"What's that, darling?"

"I wish that your face is the first thing I see in the morning, and last thing I see at night, for the rest of my life."

She wrapped her arm around me. "I second that emotion."

"Do you understand what I'm asking?"

"I heard a wish. I didn't hear a question."

"I'm asking you to . . . I want us to be married."

She was quiet for a moment. Then she looked at me, smiled, and said, "I had forgotten whose turn it was."

"I don't understand."

"I had forgotten whose turn it was to bring that topic up, and whose turn it was to say, 'Let's leave well-enough alone for now.' "

"And is that what you want to do? Leave well-enough alone for now?"

She sighed. "Oh, Harry. Will you please just shut up and make love to me again?"

And I did shut up, and we did make love again, and it wasn't the worst way in the world of changing the subject.

Afterward she said, "The next time I guess it'll be *my* turn to bring it up. And then *you* can say we should leave well-enough alone."

"What if I don't say that? What if you bring it up, and I simply say yes?"

"Well, I suppose that will present us with a very interesting situation."

31

Kay Wheaton's flight to Boston left La Guardia shortly before noon.

The man sitting next to her had a microcassette recorder. Kay borrowed it and listened to the incoming message tape she had removed from Steven Farr's answering machine.

The AT&T automated voice announced that the first message on the tape had been received at nine-thirty on Saturday morning. It was a brief message from a friend who wanted Steven to call back. A second brief message from that same friend came through two hours later.

The tape continued. Kay listened to the final portion of an earlier message, the beginning of which presumably had been erased by the two messages she had already heard. A man said he was returning Steven's call about a Martin guitar on sale. At the end of the message he said he was calling at four o'clock on Friday afternoon.

Then came the final message, received on Friday evening at seven-thirty. It was from a woman who apologized for dialing the wrong number. Kay smiled: She never would have guessed that anyone in New York would be polite enough to leave an apology on a stranger's answering machine reached by mistake, rather than simply hang up. *Maybe there's hope for the world, after all,* she thought.

The hiss of blank, unused tape followed that fourth message. Kay rewound the tape, then played it again. This time she used her watch's second hand to time it. From the beginning of the time stamp on the first message until the end of the fourth and final message on the tape, exactly one minute and fifty seconds passed.

Kay leaned back, closed her eyes, and constructed a chronology that was part fact, part supposition.

The previous Thursday at seven-thirty in the evening, a call was placed from Sandi O'Neill's cell phone to her home phone number. That call lasted three minutes and thirty-five seconds, the precise time length of the maximum allowable message permitted by the answering machine. Sandi O'Neill was murdered shortly thereafter.

At least two messages were left on the answering machine on Friday: the call regarding the guitar, and the wrong number apology.

Steven played the Friday messages, then rewound the tape to its beginning.

Two messages were recorded on Saturday. They were brief: not long enough to erase all of the material from the previous day.

Steven listened to the Saturday messages, then rewound the tape once again.

On Sunday, Steven left Brooklyn for Concord, ostensibly to rendezvous with Sandi and then journey with her to the White Mountains. When he left his home, he either forgot to switch the answering machine on or decided not to bother with it.

Did Steven put a new tape in the machine on Friday, the day after Sandi O'Neill was killed? If he did, then what was on the old tape? Did the old tape hold a three-minute-thirty-five-second message from Steven to his own answering machine, placed with Sandi's cell phone? Kay wondered: If she found the tape, would she hear Steven's voice reciting children's nursery rhymes and counting forward and backward in English and Spanish?

32

Nancy Talbot couldn't smell a thing. Her late August conifer allergies had kicked in, clogging her head. Just one more aggravation in a long list of irritants.

Nancy Talbot's life sucked. She knew it; she assumed everyone else did, too. The fact that everyone else knew made it suck all the more.

Twenty-eight years old, with two college degrees and only a dissertation standing between her and a doctorate—and here she was, living with her parents and working as a part-time housekeeper.

No man in her life. No desire for a man in her life. A three-year-old child left behind by the previous man in her life, who at last accounting was living somewhere in Oregon. Well, good riddance to him.

At least the old woman paid well. And the part-time hours were flexible, making child care arrangements easier. At some point, she told herself, she would complete her dissertation and do something with her life. She figured if she kept telling herself that, she might eventually come to believe it.

And so on this Wednesday, just like almost every other workday for the past two years, Nancy Talbot left her parents' West Concord ranch house early in the afternoon and drove two miles to the stately home on Simon Willard Road. She parked on the quiet cul-de-sac and used her key to enter through the front door.

All was quiet. The old lady must have managed to switch her television off before drifting into her midday nap. That was unusual. Nancy often said the woman held the North American record in the speed event: fastest time falling asleep with the television sound blaring and the remote control clicker in her hand.

Even Rex, the gaseous four-legged beast, was quiet. That was unusual, too. Well, let them both sleep. Easier to do her chores without any interruption.

At first glance, everything in the kitchen seemed normal. The previous night's dinner dishes were still on the table, waiting for Nancy to clear and wash them. But why was the phone off the hook, dangling from the wall-set cord? Nancy replaced it, then lifted it again to make certain the line was in order. She heard the dial tone and then placed the phone on the hook once more.

She opened the dishwasher and began to load it. On her first trip between the table and the dishwasher, she glanced at the sliding door that led to the patio. It was unlocked and open, a foot-wide gap leaving plenty of room for the Doberman pinscher to pass through. Once before, about a year earlier, the old woman left the patio door open, and Rex got out, and Nancy spent more than an hour looking for him, and she finished her chores late, and she was late picking her son up from day care, and . . . oh, crap. Not this again. Better to look first inside the house for the aging hound.

She walked over to the door. As she shut it, she saw the smear of dried liquid on the patio. It almost looked like a footprint, leading away from the door. Yes, it was a footprint. No, that was ridiculous, it couldn't be a footprint. She had obviously spent too much time watching the O.J. trial: tales of the legendary bloodstained Bruno Magli shoes.

"Rex?" She made a smacking sound with her lips, trying to summon the dog. "Rex—come here, boy." She tried to call loud enough to wake the dog, but not so loud as to wake the woman.

She circled the first floor, through the dining room and living room, and then stood at the bottom of the front staircase that led from the foyer to the second floor. She began to climb upstairs.

As she ascended, a foreign, pungent odor began to penetrate her clogged nostrils. Perhaps Rex had had another accident. She sure as hell hoped the old woman hadn't reached the point of soiling herself. Job or no job, Nancy Talbot was prepared to draw the line at bedpans.

But it wasn't a fecal odor, or any other odor familiar to her. By the time she reached the second-floor landing it was almost overpowering, and for once she was glad she had allergies.

The woman's bedroom door was partially open. She walked slowly toward it. "Rex? Ma'am? Hello?"

The television glow from the darkened room bounced off the hallway wall. Still all was silent.

"Hello?" She knocked on the door. She waited a few seconds, then pushed it open.

She stepped inside.

She screamed.

She vomited.

She passed out into a pile of entrails.

33

I was walking along Walden Street, near the post office when Kay Wheaton drove by. She stopped when she saw me. "Need a lift, Harry?"

"I'm heading home."

"I'm going to your house, too. Hop in."

I opened the door and got inside. "Why are you going to my house?"

"I want to talk with Steven about some things I learned in New York."

"Are you just getting back?"

She nodded. "My plane landed about an hour ago. I drove straight to the police station to talk with the chief, and to look at the letter from the fellow claiming responsibility for killing Sandi O'Neill."

"What did you think?"

She shrugged. "I don't know what to think. But someone went to a great deal of effort to write it and deliver it. So it's hard to dismiss."

"I heard about the shooting. How is your leg?"

"It's a superficial injury. The front muscle quadrant of my left thigh. I won't be running any marathons for a while, but I'm all right. It could have been a lot worse, considering the situation."

Kay told me about her adventure with the urban cowboy, New York detective Joseph Ramirez. She said, "I've seen shooting victims before, but this was the first time I was actually present when someone was shot, or was shot myself. Pretty scary stuff."

"I know. I was shot once, too."

"You were?"

"A couple of years ago, before you came to town. There was a murder that was made to look like a hit-and-run accident. I wound up getting in the way of the killer."

"The chief told me about that case. He said you helped solve it. He didn't mention that you got shot."

"I guess he only thinks about the part that was important to him."

We were alongside the grassy ellipse in the center of town, heading toward the Colonial Inn and just about to turn onto Monument Street, when a call came over the portable police radio that was resting on the seat between us. "Detective, I have the state police on the line. They're getting a signal from your murder victim's cell phone."

"Patch them through." Kay quickly pulled to a stop next to the curb by Town Hall.

Another voice came on the line. A state police dispatcher reported that someone was, indeed, using Sandra O'Neill's cellular phone. "We picked it up from Norwood a little while ago. Now he's in the Dedham area, coming toward Newton. We only get him for a couple of minutes at a time. He must be making several short calls."

Kay said, "He's moving at a pretty decent clip."

"Hard to measure exactly, but based on the distance between telecommunication poles, I'd guess anywhere from forty to sixty miles an hour."

"He must be coming up the highway. Route 128."

"Must be. Northbound lanes."

"Let's keep this line open," Kay said.

"Roger."

Kay pulled away from the curb. She bypassed the turnoff to Monument Street and my house, and she drove around the ellipse until she was heading east on Lexington Road. "Hold tight, Harry. We're going for a ride."

The First Parish Church was on our right, next to the town square. As soon as we passed it, Kay accelerated quickly. Concord's history passed before us in a blur: the houses where Louisa May Alcott and Nathaniel Hawthorne once lived, and then the small patch of green that two centuries ago was the site of the Battle at Meriam's Corner.

Route 128, the beltway that encircles the greater Boston area and cuts through the town of Lexington, was about four miles farther down the road.

Kay spoke to the state police dispatcher. "Where is he now?"

"Still in Newton, heading toward Waltham. If he stays on the phone long enough, there's a chance we can triangulate the signal and pinpoint his location a little better."

"Do you have any cruisers on that part of Route 128?"

"Northbound, we have a guy a few miles behind. He's picking up some speed, trying to catch up without using his siren. We're not looking to force a high-speed chase. We have another guy coming southbound who's gonna turn around at the Burlington exit, then get on the road when the signal reaches that area, if it gets that far. Our guys have the description of the murder victim's missing automobile."

"I doubt the killer would be stupid enough to be driving it."

"Well," said the dispatcher, "there's lots of stupid people out there. Let's hope this guy is one of them."

We crossed into the northernmost sliver of Lincoln, and then almost immediately entered Lexington. Kay asked me if I knew where Steven was.

"He was at my place when I left there, about twenty-five minutes ago."

"That's not enough time to drive to Norwood and then partway back. It's not him in that car. If the person using the phone is our murderer, then your friend Steven may be off the hook."

"He's not my friend."

"No, I suppose he's not."

We passed the Minuteman National Park visitors' center. I

said, "When I use my cellular phone, I have to punch in a personal code. Someone who steals it wouldn't know the code, and wouldn't be able to use it."

"They have phone hackers, just like they have computer hackers. People you can pay to figure out the identification code, or to reprogram it with a new code."

The state police dispatcher cut in. "We lost him again. He must have hung up. I'll let you know if he comes back on line."

Kay reached Route 128 and turned onto the entrance ramp to the northbound lane. At the end of the ramp she pulled into the breakdown lane and glided to a stop with her motor running.

The dispatcher said, "We've got him again. He's heading into Lexington."

Kay reached across me, opened the glove compartment, and pulled out a small pair of binoculars. She leaned out her open window and watched the cars coming from our rear. She yelled out so I could hear her over the hum of the highway traffic. "I feel lucky today. Do you feel lucky, Harry?"

"Not particularly. Why?"

"Because we're going to follow the first person I see talking on a car phone, regardless of the type of car he's driving. And if we're lucky, we'll have the person who's using Sandi O'Neill's phone."

A minute or two later she spun around, tossed the binoculars into my lap, and hit the gas pedal. "Bingo," she said. "That red car that just passed by—over there."

Her acceleration was swift, but she was melting into a stream of cars going fifty and more miles per hour. By the time she became part of that stream, the vehicle she had spotted was at least a hundred yards ahead of us.

She said, "He's in the center lane. I'm going to move up on him in the right lane, where he's less likely to spot me. See if you can read the license plate."

I stared into the binoculars for several seconds. "It's some sort of Chevy, Massachusetts plates, 410-THN."

Kay relayed that information to the dispatcher as she gained slowly on her target.

We passed the exit for Bedford. Kay pulled even with the

Chevy just in time for us to see the driver snap the cell phone shut and place it on the seat next to him.

Kay spoke to the dispatcher. "You just lost the signal again, right?"

"No, he's still going strong. Crossing over from a Lexington tower to one in Bedford."

"That couldn't be. He just . . ." She smacked her steering wheel in frustration. "Damn it, we're following the wrong guy."

Kay eased up on her accelerator. Cars in the left and center lanes began to pass us. We proceeded along the highway toward Bedford, the silence broken only by the dispatcher's occasional notice that the cell phone signal was still moving northward in our approximate area.

I turned around and used the binoculars to scan the cars behind us. Kay looked as best she could at the cars around and ahead of us, but most of her attention was focused on keeping up with traffic on the busy expressway.

Suddenly, a brown car in the center lane cut sharply and without warning into the right lane, directly ahead of us, forcing Kay to hit her brakes.

I said, "He's an asshole."

"Yes," Kay replied, "he's an asshole. But take a look. What else do you see?"

She pointed toward the driver. I leaned to one side to get a clearer view of him. I said, "He's an asshole with a cell phone in his hand."

She smiled. "I told you I felt lucky today. Maybe, just maybe . . ."

Kay gave the car's description and license plate number to the state police dispatcher.

We were approaching the Burlington exit. At the entrance ramp beyond it, a state police cruiser was supposed to be waiting to pick up the chase and pull the brown car over. But we never reached that point: With another sudden movement, the brown car veered off the highway at the exit.

Kay followed suit. Both cars slowed down as they traveled

along the exit ramp, then came to a stop when they reached the traffic light at the ramp's end.

The state police dispatcher's voice crackled through the static on Kay's portable police radio. "The cell phone signal isn't moving as quickly. It may even be stationary."

"I know," Kay answered. "We're off the highway now. I think this is our guy."

The light turned green, and the car we were following turned right toward Burlington Mall. The driver placed the cellular phone out of our view, and he placed both hands on his steering wheel. Almost immediately the dispatcher said, "We've lost him again."

Kay replied, "No, we haven't. He's right in front of me, and I saw him stop using the phone. This is *definitely* our guy."

The brown car was moving slowly along the avenue beside the shopping mall.

"Detective," the dispatcher said, "the car you're following was reported stolen this morning. Registered to a Geraldine Hindermuth in Bedford."

"He's turning into the Burlington Mall parking lot."

"We'll notify the Burlington police."

Kay followed the brown car into the lot. The driver parked about fifty yards from the mall entrance next to the Johnny Rocket's restaurant. Kay parked one row over from him, farther from the entrance.

The driver stepped out of the brown car. He looked no more than twenty years old. He was white, average height, slender but strongly muscled, with light brown hair and deeply tanned face and arms. He wore denim jeans and a bright green sleeveless T-shirt. The cell phone was clipped onto his belt.

Kay radioed the man's description to the dispatcher.

The dispatcher said, "Burlington says they can have three cruisers there in less than five minutes. Best to take him when he comes out again, rather than cause chaos inside the mall. Do you know how many entrances there are to that mall?"

"More than three."

"Is your radio portable or stationary?"

"Portable."

"Can you follow him inside and track his position so we know when and where he's about to exit?"

"He's already halfway to the entrance, and I have an injured leg, but I'll do my best."

"All right. I'll keep this line open."

I said, "What's the big deal? You won't lose him. He has to come back to get his car."

"He stole it, Harry. Maybe he's abandoning it here. Shopping mall lots are often used for that." She unbuckled her seat belt and opened her car door. "You stay here. Ouch—God, my leg hurts."

She reached for her portable police radio, but I grabbed it first.

"What are you doing?" she asked.

"Show me how to use this."

"I can't let you—"

"He's almost to the entrance. How do you use this damn thing?"

She hesitated for a moment. "It's in listening mode. Depress this switch to talk. Volume control over here."

I identified myself to the state police dispatcher, then headed for the mall just as my target stepped through the entrance doorway. When he disappeared from view, I began running, hoping to close the gap between us.

The entrance opened into one of the corridors that run perpendicular to the mall's main concourse. Coming in from the mid-afternoon sun, it took a moment for my eyes to adjust to the reduced light inside the mall.

Green T-shirt was standing at the Fanny Farmer cookie stand halfway down the corridor. I walked at a casual pace, thinking I would look less conspicuous than if I stood in one place until he began to move again. When I was only a few yards away from him he glanced around. Our eyes met for an instant. I looked away and kept moving past him, toward the main concourse.

I heard him order a large fresh-baked chocolate chip cookie.

I came to the main concourse. I sat on a bench near the Crabtree & Evelyn store and waited for him. He reached my position a minute or two later. He stood a few yards away and finished munching on his cookie. Then he walked past me and into Lauriat's bookstore.

Green T-shirt didn't look like a book reader to me, so I wasn't surprised when he emerged empty-handed a short while later. He turned to his right and strolled slowly along the main concourse toward its north end. Foot traffic was light. It was easy for me to keep him in sight without having to risk giving myself away by getting too close to him.

He looked in store windows on both sides of the concourse, checked out the kiosks in the center, and took his own sweet time progressing down the length of the mall. He was particularly slowed by the items on display through the window of Victoria's Secret. I followed at a distance of about twenty-five yards.

Eventually he walked into Crate & Barrel. I sat on a bench next to the water fountain. I could see him inside the store, engaged in conversation with a clerk. I took that opportunity to report my position into the portable radio.

The dispatcher told me that there were nine separate entrances to the mall—three of them directly into one of the concourses, and the rest of them into one of the anchor stores: Sears, Filene's, Macy's, and Lord & Taylor. Within a few minutes there would be three cruisers in place; with sufficient warning from me when the subject was about to exit, they should be able to cover the situation.

Two toddlers were tossing pennies into the nearby fountain. The water was shut off every November, and the area for Santa Claus was constructed over the dry fountain. Nine Decembers earlier, on what was to be our last visit to the mall as a family, Janet and I brought our daughter there to see Santa. Melissa was four years old, and it was just a couple of weeks before Janet fell ill.

As Janet and I walked along the crowded concourse that evening, we turned to look at a window display, each thinking that the other had hold of our daughter's hand. When we turned away from the window a half minute later, Melissa was gone. It took ten terrifying minutes to find her. I still got anxious thinking about it.

Less than two months later, Janet was gone.

I peered into Crate & Barrel. I couldn't see Green T-shirt. I was certain he couldn't have exited without my seeing him. I stood and walked slowly toward the open doorway. Where the hell was he?

And then I focused on something I should have remembered earlier: That store, which is at the corner of the main concourse and another corridor, is L-shaped. And it has a second doorway that opens onto the other corridor.

I entered the store. I walked until I reached its center: the joining point of the two legs of the L. I turned left and looked into the area that had been hidden from my view in the main concourse. The tall, thin young man with the dark tan and sleeveless shirt wasn't there. He had entered the store through one door and, apparently, exited through the other.

I walked briskly toward that second doorway and stepped into the corridor.

I heard the smack and felt the force of a hand falling hard on my shoulder. "You looking for someone, mister?"

He spun me around. Green T-shirt stared at me through hollow-looking eyes that were so dark I couldn't distinguish between their irises and their pupils.

"Do you know me, mister?"

"No."

"Then why the fuck you following me?"

"Following you? Why would I be following you?"

He looked confused, then angry. "Well, if you—hey! *I'm* the one asking *you* why the fuck you following me. Well, why the fuck you following me?"

"Like I said, I don't even know who you are."

And then, with the most atrocious timing imaginable, the dispatcher's announcement crackled over the police radio. "The suspect's name is Michael Hindermuth. The car belongs to his mother, who reported that he took it without permission.

Prior charge of breaking and entering, continued without a finding, placed on pretrial probation for a year."

The muscles in his neck tensed. His face—glaring at me from a distance of a foot—turned bright red. "You some kind of cop?"

"No."

He paused for a moment, then said, "Good."

In the next moment I was on the ground. My ears were ringing, my head was hot with pain, and my face no doubt bore knuckle imprints from the punch I never saw coming.

From my prone position I saw Michael Hindermuth dash the short distance back to the main concourse, then turn and run in the direction we had come from.

I stood as quickly as I could. I steadied myself, and I took off after him.

I was a little dizzy, and he had a head start and the advantage of youth. But he also had the hormones of youth, and they helped do him in. Passing by Victoria's Secret once again, he proved constitutionally incapable of refraining from glancing reflexively at the displays of lingerie and the photos of tawny-skinned women with bared, flat stomachs and nearly bared, hilly, and well-cleaved chests.

In the instant that he looked away, he bounced off a bench. He remained on his feet and moving, but he lost several steps from his lead over me.

He turned into the corridor leading to our point of entry into the mall. As he ran its length, he looked back at me once, twice, and then a third time. And each time he looked back, he lost another step.

Nearing the exit now, and with only a couple of yards separating us, I lunged forward headfirst, bringing him down with a perfect shoulder block to his lower back. He tumbled forward, and I heard the squealing sound his cheek made as he slid on the tiled floor.

I hit the floor at the same time. I lay on my back just a few feet from him. I saw him raise himself to his knees. He made a slight motion toward me.

Suddenly a gun appeared in my field of vision, its barrel

aimed directly at Michael Hindermuth's head. The gun was in a hand, the hand was attached to an arm, and at the end of the arm was Kay Wheaton: bending awkwardly, favoring her injured leg.

She said, "Don't even *think* of moving."

She was flanked by two uniformed Burlington police officers. One of them grabbed the suspect's arms and handcuffed him behind his back. Then the other cop pulled the young man into a sitting position and leaned him against a nearby wall.

Kay said, "You have the right to keep your fucking mouth shut. If you do *not* keep your fucking mouth shut, everything you say can and will be used against you in a court of law." She finished telling him about this right and that right and his right to give up his rights. And then she said, "Now, please, *please*, tell me you're at least seventeen years old."

"I'm nineteen."

"Good. You automatically get tried as an adult. How does a life sentence at Walpole sound to you?"

"Walpole?"

"Maximum security, you idiot."

"I *know* what Walpole is. Since when does taking your mother's car get you sent to Walpole?"

"You're forgetting the phone, Michael. You stole it."

"You can't prove that."

"And then there's the woman you stole it from. The woman you murdered."

It took a few seconds for her words to filter through his confusion. Then, with either real or manufactured astonishment, he said, "*Murder?!* Lady, what the *fuck* are you talking about?"

34

"I didn't kill no one," Michael Hindermuth said.

"Then how did you get this phone?" Kay asked.

He leaned his head against the wall and sighed. He looked up at Kay and asked, "You gonna tell my mother about this?"

"Listen, you jerk—your mother is the least of your problems if you don't start answering my questions. Now, how did you get that phone?"

He glanced up at me and the two Burlington police officers. He turned toward Kay and said, "It's *my* phone. I bought it myself."

"Is that the best you can come up with? Because that's total bullshit, Michael. Every cell phone sends out its own specific signal when it's being used, and they can be automatically traced. I'll bet the guy you paid to reprogram the phone after you stole it didn't tell you about that, did he?"

He looked away from her and stared at the ground. "I didn't kill *nobody*, and that's all I'm saying."

"Let me make this simple for you, Michael. A woman was murdered last Thursday evening. She had a cell phone that turned up missing. You have her cell phone. Without anything else to go on, I have to assume you stole the phone, and you killed her."

"I ain't talking to you without a lawyer."

Kay turned to the two police officers. "You heard him. He wants to see a lawyer first. You have enough evidence to charge him with receiving stolen property and unauthorized use of a motor vehicle. I'll work up the murder charge and be in touch in a couple of hours." She looked down at Michael Hindermuth, who was wriggling uncomfortably from the handcuffs. "You made a smart decision."

"I did?"

"Of course. If you killed that woman, the smartest thing for you to do is lawyer yourself up, shut the hell up, and refuse to talk with me. But let me tell you something. If you really *didn't* kill her, then right now is the time to help yourself. Tell me everything there is to know about how you got that phone, with no bullshit, and maybe we can do something about the stolen car charge."

He looked at me for several seconds. "You lied to me when you said you wasn't following me."

"Obviously."

"And you lied when you said you're not a cop."

"No, that was the truth. I'm a psychiatrist."

His eyes widened. "A psychiatrist? Man, *you're* the crazy one, running through the mall like that at your age. How old are you?"

"Forty-four."

"You run pretty good for an old guy."

"Maybe you should lay off the chocolate chip cookies."

He smiled when I said that, but the smile faded quickly. He looked up at Kay and said, "I took the phone. I'll show you where I got it. But I don't know nothing about no murder."

Michael Hindermuth and his mother lived in an apartment in Bedford, the town that lies between Burlington and Concord. He took us to an office park near his apartment complex. Michael rode as the manacled guest of the Burlington police; Kay and I followed in her car.

Kay radioed ahead to the Bedford Police Department, and one of their cruisers was waiting for us when we pulled into the complex.

The office park consisted of a half-dozen large, modern buildings, each one six stories tall. Michael led us to a parking lot behind one of those buildings. The seven of us—two Burlington officers, two Bedford officers, Kay, Michael, and I—stepped out of our respective vehicles. The police removed Michael's handcuffs.

Michael led us down one of the rows of cars. As we walked I noticed a work site next to this particular building, where another building was in the early stages of construction. Various pickup trucks, forklifts, and earth-moving machines dotted the area. A few workmen were milling about, not engaged in any obviously useful activity.

"Here it is," Michael said, and he pointed to a white four-door Honda Accord. "I stole the phone out of this car."

Kay walked to the rear of the vehicle and looked down at the license plate. Then she looked at me and nodded, and I knew we were standing alongside Sandi O'Neill's car.

She said, "The doors are locked. How did you get in?"

"They weren't locked before."

"What do you mean?"

"My mother and I live over there." Michael pointed to an apartment complex just beyond the grove of trees that lined the parking lot. Then he pointed in the opposite direction and said, "One of my buddies lives over that way. Saturday afternoon I cut through the lot on my way to his house. That's when I saw the car. I probably wouldn't have noticed it, except it had New York plates. We partied pretty late and I stayed on his couch. Sunday morning I was crossing back through the lot and the car was still here. I thought that was a strange thing, so I decided to take a look. That's when I saw the phone."

"Where was it?" Kay asked.

Michael pointed through the car window. "Right there, on the floor, the passenger side. And then I noticed the door on the driver's side wasn't locked. So I walked around to that side and . . . well, you know."

"You opened the door and stole the phone."

He sighed and said nothing.

"What else did you take?"

"Nothing. There wasn't nothing else to take."

"In other words, you looked, but couldn't find anything else to steal."

He shrugged his shoulders and looked down at the ground.

"Do you want to think about that question for a minute or two? Because these fellows over here"—Kay pointed to the Bedford officers—"they're going to be searching your mother's apartment and your friend's apartment. And if they find *anything* else that came from this car, and you don't tell me about it now, then you will be standing in a pile of enormously deep shit."

"Nothing!" he said. "I swear, the phone was the only thing there. I took it, and then I left."

"How did the door get locked?"

"I locked it when I left."

"Why?"

"I don't know. Force of habit, maybe. I always lock car doors."

Kay thought for a moment. "Has the car been here ever since?"

"As far as I know. I don't come through here every day, but I did see it this morning. Looks like it's in the same parking space."

Kay turned to one of the Bedford officers. "Can you have this car towed in? I'll arrange for the state police to send a forensics person to inspect it."

"You got it," he replied.

Kay said, "I want your friend's name, Michael. The one you partied with Saturday night. And his address and phone number."

He gave her the information, reluctantly.

"And I need to know who reprogrammed the cell phone so you could use it."

"My friend knows a guy. It cost me fifty bucks. I just got it back yesterday. Today is the first time I used it."

"And finally, Michael—where were you last Thursday evening and Thursday night, if you weren't at Walden Pond killing the woman who owned this car?"

"Florida, visiting my father. I been there for two weeks, just come back on Friday. That's why my mother's so pissed at me. She hates him. I didn't steal her fucking car. We argued, she smacked me, I grabbed her keys and left."

"Do you have the stub from your plane ticket, or some other way of proving you were in Florida?"

He nodded. "It's at my mother's place."

"All right." Kay turned to the police officers from the two different towns. "If his alibi holds out, Concord has nothing to charge him with. It's up to you fellows whether you want to go after him for taking his mother's car or stealing the phone." She handed Michael one of her business cards. "Call me if you want me to talk to your mother, help smooth things out. I'll tell her about your cooperative attitude, and maybe she'll agree to drop the charge."

The Burlington police officers placed the handcuffs back on the young man and led him away. The Bedford policemen radioed the car's location to their dispatcher, then left.

Kay and I returned to her car. She placed the key in the ignition. Just as she was about to start her car she said, "Wait a second. I just realized something." She rummaged through her pocketbook and pulled out another key chain. "These are Steven's." She inspected the various keys, selected one, and said, "I wonder."

She stepped out of her car again, and I followed her. She placed the key in the trunk and turned it. The trunk popped open, revealing three pieces of luggage and a woman's pocketbook. Sandi O'Neill's name was visible on the luggage tag of the suitcase on top.

Kay went to her car for a moment, then returned wearing latex gloves and carrying a small plastic bag. She released the latch on Sandi O'Neill's pocketbook. A wallet was in plain view. Kay removed it carefully and gave it a cursory inspection. She said, "A substantial amount of money, and several credit cards. And you know what this is, don't you?"

I looked at the reddish brown smear on the wallet. "Blood?"

"Most likely." She placed the wallet in the plastic bag. "Anyway, it looks like our friend Michael Hindermuth was telling the truth."

"What do you mean?"

"If he killed Sandi, then used her car to give himself a lift home, you'd expect him to clean out her wallet, at least take her cash. I'll be surprised if his alibi for the time of the murder doesn't check out."

We returned to Kay's car. She drove past the construction site and exited the office park.

I said, "I wonder why the car was dumped here."

"I don't know. I'll add that to the list of questions I have for Steven Farr. I think it's time for me to have a friendly chat with him."

The street we were on connected to Route 62. We followed that road through the center of Bedford and into Concord. We passed Sleepy Hollow Cemetery, where my wife lay buried.

The Concord police dispatcher's voice came over Kay's radio. "Detective Wheaton, are you there?"

"I'm here. Coming into Concord center."

"The chief is waiting for you at 307 Simon Willard Road. Wants you there as soon as possible. We have another murder, and it looks very, very ugly."

35

I didn't recognize the young woman whose blouse was covered with blood. She was conscious, with rapid, shallow breathing and a glazed look in her eyes. She was sitting in a chair on the front porch. A policewoman stood next to her, a hand on her shoulder. A paramedic was taking her vital signs.

Alfred Korvich was standing on the lawn in front of the house. Kay parked on the cul-de-sac and we both walked up to the police chief.

Kay pointed to the blood-splattered woman and said, "Was she injured badly?"

"She isn't a victim. She's the housekeeper. Says she discovered the body when she arrived around two o'clock. Fainted dead away, came to a while later—and here's the kicker. She was so upset and confused that she actually tried to straighten up the murder scene before she called us. Like it would reflect badly on her if she left things the way she found them."

"Perhaps she was trying to cover something up."

"Well, you'll talk to her yourself. But I doubt it. Her story sounds pretty genuine to me."

"Who was the victim?"

"One Abigail Claymore-Whitley, age ninety-one. And her dog."

"Her *dog*?"

"Her dog," he repeated. "It's not a pretty sight."

Kay headed toward the front door. I followed.

Korvich called after me. "Yo, Harry—who deputized *you*?
You can't go in there."

"Oh. Right. Sorry." I stood next to him as Kay went inside
the house.

"Besides, like I said, it isn't pretty."

"I've seen homicide scenes before."

"Not like *this* one, you haven't. And even if you had, you've
never been at one that had a smell like this."

"What sort of smell?"

"Take blood, vomit, excrement, and rotting innards, mix
them all together. Let it ferment for several hours in the August
heat. Except for the vomit, which was the housekeeper's con-
tribution when she got here and discovered the rest."

"Rotting innards?"

"Think 'disembowelment.' "

"Geez," I said. "Which one—the woman or the dog?"

"Both."

"What a terrible way to go."

"Yes," he agreed. "A hell of a way."

I had never met Abigail Claymore-Whitley, but I knew of
her. A couple of years earlier the Concord selectmen designated
her as the town's Honored Citizen. Sometimes that annual
honor was based on good works; other times, on longevity. In
her case, it was probably more the latter than the former, although she was known to give hefty sums to conservation and
preservation causes, including the Walden Woods project.

"Chief Korvich? Chief Alfred Korvich?"

I turned in the direction of the voice. A young black man
with dreadlocks, shorts, and sandals, looking very much out of
place in this wealthy and conservative enclave, was approaching us.

Korvich said, "This street's blocked off, buddy. Who the hell
are you?"

The man identified himself as a reporter for the *Middlesex
News*. He said, "Chief, this is the second Concord murder in
less than a week. Isn't that unusual?"

"Unusual?" I could see him struggle to contain his anger.
"Hell, no. It's not unusual at all. In fact, it's a little lighter than

usual this week. The only thing unusual is, ordinarily we do a better job of keeping it secret, so as not to alarm the tourists." He paused. "Jesus Christ, man. I can't believe you're writing that down. What the hell is wrong with you?"

The reporter noticed the bloodied housekeeper. "Is that the killer?" he asked.

"Listen, buddy. I don't know how you got here, but I want you behind that barrier, down that way. We'll have a statement for the press when we finish the preliminary investigation of the murder scene."

"The public has a right to know, Chief."

"Yeah, yeah, right." He waved the reporter away with a dismissive gesture, and the man returned to the entrance of the cul-de-sac.

I said, "I see you've been working on your technique for media relations."

"Don't give me a hard time, Harry. I'm not in the mood. And don't be causing me any more problems. You've already done enough for one day, according to the Burlington police chief."

"What are you talking about?"

"Your little stunt at the mall, trying to play hero."

"Seems to me I helped capture someone we thought might be a killer."

"He was running straight into the police when you tackled him. Seems to *me* the only thing you did was cause chaos in the mall, expose yourself and other civilians to danger."

He walked over to one of the uniformed officers and began talking to him. I stood by myself for several minutes. I had never seen so many Concord police officers in one place. There were five cruisers, a police wagon, and an ambulance. Thanks to the police barricade, only a few people were in the area: probably neighbors watching from their own front lawns and doorsteps. I couldn't see what was happening on the other side of the barricade.

The housekeeper was still seated on the porch. Either she or someone else had removed her blouse, perhaps to hold it for forensic analysis, and for a minute or two she sat in only her

jeans and bra, her arms folded across her chest in embarrass-
ment. Then a paramedic threw a blanket around her shoulders.

Two other paramedics emerged from the house, coughing
and carrying a small stretcher. On it was a cloth-covered object, which I presumed to be the dog's remains.

A few minutes later Kay stepped outside. She, too, was
coughing. She was holding a plastic bag that contained a small
item I couldn't identify from where I stood.

Kay walked over to the housekeeper and showed her the
small item. I couldn't hear what they were saying, but the
woman was shaking her head as if to say no.

Kay walked across the lawn toward the police chief. I followed her. Her back was toward me as she showed the item to
Korvich. At first I still couldn't see it. She said, "This looks
new to me. Unopened and unread. The housekeeper says she's
certain she never saw it here before. I think our killer left a
calling card."

"Holy shit," Korvich said. "Holy fucking shit."

I took a step closer.

Inside the plastic bag was a small book, streaked with blood.
I had seen an identical item the day before in Korvich's office
when he showed me the letter from the man who claimed responsibility for killing Sandi O'Neill. And an identical one had
been found nearby Sandi's corpse.

Inside Kay's plastic bag was another copy of the palm-sized,
abridged version of *Walden*.

36

HAVE MERCY ON US

"That's the worst I've ever seen," Kay said as she drove past the police barricade. "The medical examiner says it happened at least twelve hours before the call came into the station. I feel like the smell is still on me."

"It is," I said.

On the other side of the barricade were about two dozen by-standers. I knew that at least one of them—the man Alfred Korvich had spoken with—was a reporter. As we drove along, a car with the Channel 7 news logo passed us, heading toward Abigail Claymore-Whitley's cul-de-sac.

She said, "The medical examiner says she was strangled *and* eviscerated, presumably in that order. And the dog . . . God, it was like a slaughterhouse."

"Korvich says the housekeeper moved things around before the police came."

Kay nodded. "I think she was embarrassed about throwing up. Also, she apparently fainted on top of the dog. That's why she had blood on her."

"Why did they take her blouse?"

"If the dog managed to bite or claw the killer, some of the killer's blood may be mixed in. And we may be able to type it."

I thought about the O.J. trial, where certain blood samples were revealed to have a mixture of his DNA and his victims' DNA.

"It's strange," she continued. "The inconsistency in the

killer's behavior. On one hand, he seems quite controlled and planful. The letter he left in the library. The telephone call to the clerk at Town Hall to bring the letter to our attention. Bringing copies of the book to leave as a calling card. But on the other hand, the killings themselves look so chaotic and out of control."

"I would guess that the more out of control he is, the more likely it is he'll slip up."

"This second murder was especially messy. Whoever did it probably left with blood all over him, maybe fibers and other things to tie him to that house. And he left a pretty good bloody footprint on the deck behind the house. We'll get a shoe size from that, and maybe even the type of shoe."

"Are you going to tell the press that both murders were committed by the same person?"

She thought about that for several seconds. "I don't know. I'm inclined not to."

"Why?"

"Generally speaking, we have two possibilities here. Either Steven is the killer, or someone other than Steven is the killer."

"I'd say that covers it."

"If it's Steven, he's probably finished killing. The murder of his girlfriend, either planned or impulsive—and then one more as a smokescreen to throw us off the trail. He would have no reason to risk exposure by continuing the killing. And so I have nothing to gain by alarming people about a serial killer."

"And what if it isn't Steven?"

"If it's not Steven, then he *wants* me to tell the press, because he wants to publicize whatever the hell crusade it is that he's carrying out. If I don't do that, if I frustrate him, then he may try to get the word out himself. Letters to the media, maybe even phone calls. The more of that he does, the greater the chance he'll slip up and reveal himself. Hell, I don't know, Harry. It's a crapshoot, either way."

Kay drove past the high school on Thoreau Street and headed toward Walden Pond.

I said, "This isn't the way to my house."

"There's something else I want to check out before I question your friend Steven. I know, I know—he's not your friend."

We crossed Route 2 and passed the town landfill. I said, "Steven left my house in the middle of the night. Around one in the morning. He went for a ride in Veronica's car."

"How long was he gone?"

"I don't know."

A short distance past Route 2, Kay turned into the lot of the small gift shop, directly across the road from the pond.

A middle-aged woman in a floral print sundress was seated behind the cash register. She recognized Kay. "You're the one who was here last Friday, looking into the murder."

"Yes, that's right. And when I was here I noticed that you sell an abridged version of *Walden*. A green cover, small enough to fit in my hand."

"Yes, certainly. Shambhala Publications puts it out."

"I wonder if you know how many you've sold recently."

"Well, we're not computerized, so normally I probably wouldn't be able to give you an accurate answer. But someone called on the phone yesterday morning about that very same item. He asked me how many were in stock. I counted thirteen, which I probably remember because I'm a little superstitious."

"Did the caller come in and purchase any?"

"No. That's the odd part. From the way he was talking, I assumed he wanted to buy several right away. But I only sold one copy yesterday, to a very nice family from Scotland."

"And today?"

"I haven't sold any copies."

"Perhaps another clerk sold them."

"Well, there's only me and Peter."

She called the other clerk to the register. She asked him if he had sold any copies of that edition of *Walden* during the previous few days.

"Definitely not," the second clerk said. "And I would remember if I had, because whenever someone brings it to the register to buy it, I try to persuade them to buy a copy of the entire text instead. The abridged version you're talking about cuts out too much of the good stuff."

The second clerk returned to the other side of the small shop.

Kay said, "I'd like to purchase one myself. Where are they?"

The woman behind the register directed Kay to a small wicker basket on top of a counter in the corner of the shop. Kay walked over there and looked into the basket. Instead of removing a book, she carried the entire basket to the register.

Kay said, "If you started with thirteen and sold one, you should have twelve left in the basket. I wonder how you explain this."

The clerk and I looked in the basket. There were only two copies of the book.

"Oh, dear," the clerk said. "I believe we've been robbed."

37

Viewed as a tableau, we could have been four friends gathered around the table for an early evening game of bridge. Kay Wheaton and Steven Farr were north and south partners, seated across from one another at my kitchen table. They were flanked by Veronica and myself.

But there were no cards, refreshments, or small talk. It was just past five o'clock on the last Wednesday in August, and murder was the topic of the day.

Kay said to Steven, "Before we talk about Sandi, let's talk about Roy Stamis."

He looked surprised. "My studio engineer? What about him?"

"You said he had the week off, but he was at your place when I got there."

"He was? I did tell him to take the week off. But if he decided to come by the studio, what's the big deal?"

"The big deal is the bullet he took in his arm. At least, it seemed like a pretty big deal to him."

"You *shot* him?!"

"I was there with a New York detective. Stamis surprised us with a gun. He thought we were intruders. The New York detective shot him."

"Is he okay?"

"Yes, he's okay. And I'm glad he was there, because it turns

184

out he had some important information. He said you stayed behind to work on an album when Sandi left for Massachusetts."

"Right, like I told you Monday night."

"So you did." Kay paused. "He said you worked on the album alone for a couple of days because you suggested that he take some time off."

"Uh-huh. He's been wound up pretty tight lately, which is probably why he gave you a problem. I thought if he took some time off it would take some pressure off."

"So he didn't actually see you last Thursday, the day Sandi came to Massachusetts, the day she died."

He pondered that for a moment. "I guess not. I think we talked on the phone, though."

"I asked him that. He says you didn't. And you already told me you didn't see or talk to anyone else that day."

Steven looked at Kay blankly for a few seconds. Then, with open eyes reflecting sudden awareness, he said, "Wait a *second.* This is about *me,* isn't it? I can't give you an alibi, so you're thinking I came to Massachusetts and killed her." He turned to Veronica. "Can you believe this?"

"It's all right, Steven. This is how she has to do her job."

That seemed to calm him down a little. He said to Kay, "Well, go ahead. I don't have any secrets. And even if I did, I'm a lousy secret keeper."

"Actually, it sounds like you're a pretty good secret keeper."

"What are you talking about?"

"Your engagement to Sandi. None of her friends knew anything about it. Two seemed pretty shocked, including one who said that whoever told me that was full of crap. She said Sandi was more likely to dump you than get married to you."

"Yeah, well, what the hell do they know? We hadn't told anyone, that's all. We only decided a little while ago to get married, hadn't even picked a date. Sandi wanted to keep things quiet until we had more of the details set."

"Why?"

He shrugged his shoulders. "I don't know. I figured it was a woman's thing. I didn't care."

"When she has good news like that, a woman wants her

friends to know all about it. Unless, of course, she's not so sure things are going to work out."

"She was sure. We both were."

"If she was sure, then why was she so concerned about keeping the news secret?"

He was quiet for a few seconds. "I don't know. You'd have to ask her."

"Well, that's going to be a little difficult, don't you think?"

He pushed his chair back from the table and stood. "I don't need to put up with this shit."

Veronica grabbed his wrist. "Sit down, Steven."

He looked at her, perplexed. "What?"

"Sit down. Let her do her job. Get it over with now."

He sat again, with obvious reluctance, and he glared at Kay. She said, "We've located Sandi's car in a parking lot in Bedford."

"Where's Bedford?"

"The next town over."

"How did it get there?"

"I assume her killer drove it there after he left her at Walden Pond. He parked it in a place where a car left overnight might not draw attention immediately."

"Why would he do that?"

"Do you have any ideas?"

"How would I know? I'm not a cop. Besides, how do you know she didn't drive there, meet someone, then drive with that person to Walden?"

"Because her luggage was in the trunk, even though she had already checked into the Colonial Inn."

"Maybe she never got a chance to take her bags into the inn."

"No, she took them in," Kay said. "The bellhop at the inn recalls helping her. He said he remembers her because she was pretty."

Steven nodded. "People always remembered her."

"Was that a problem for you?"

"What are you talking about?"

"Did it bother you that other men found her attractive? You

know the old saying—if you want to be happy all of your life, don't make a pretty woman your wife."

Steven sighed and shook his head slowly. "You don't have any idea what you're talking about." He glanced at her hand. "You're not married, are you? Do you have a man? You seem a little tough to me. Do you even *like* men?"

Caught unprepared by that, Kay was quiet for a moment.

He sneered. "Like I said, you don't know what you're talking about."

"Her luggage was in the trunk of her car," Kay said, getting the conversation back on track. "I think whoever killed her went to her room afterward, gathered her things, and wrote a note for the maid in Sandi's name saying she was checking out early."

"What for?"

"For the same reason he made sure there was no identification on her body, and for the same reason he put the car somewhere it might not be noticed for a few days. He was trying to buy time by making it hard for us to identify her."

He shrugged. "I still don't get it. What's the purpose of that?"

"Indeed. What *is* the purpose of that?"

I remembered what Alfred Korvich told me, and so I knew what Kay was thinking: If the police had found Sandi's body and identified her immediately, they would have called Steven to notify him. And if he couldn't be found, that might draw suspicion upon him.

Veronica and I sat quietly while Kay questioned Steven. I was silent because I had nothing to say. But Veronica, former prosecuting attorney that she was, knew all about building a criminal case against someone. She was watching and listening, no doubt wondering whether there was a case to be made against her former lover.

Kay continued. "Do you know Max Rothman?"

"The name sounds familiar." He thought for a moment, then turned to me. "Didn't you mention his name to me the other night?"

I said, "Steven told me Sandi came to Concord to meet with

a developer about a project near Walden. I mentioned Roth-man's name." I turned to Steven. "You said you didn't recognize it."

"I didn't. I only recognize it now because you mentioned it the other night." He thought for a moment. Then his eyes widened and his voice grew louder. He turned to Kay. "Wait a minute. Who the hell is this guy? Does he have something to do with all this? Is he the one she went to see last Thursday?"

"How do you know she planned to see someone?"

"She told me. She said it was just that one business meeting before the start of a vacation. Something about trying to buy out a developer."

"Had she ever met him before?"

"I have no idea."

"Did she say anything else about him?"

"I don't think so. Not that I would remember." He paused. "Have you talked to him? If he was the last person to see her, maybe he knows something."

"We don't know that he was the last person to see her, or that he even saw her at all."

"Well, don't you think it would be a pretty damn good idea to find out?"

Kay reached for her pocketbook and pulled out an appointment book.

Steven said, "That's Sandi's."

"Yes. It was."

He groaned softly. "Did you find that in her car?"

"No. Interestingly enough, I found it in Brooklyn, which I find a little odd. Why would someone go on a trip and leave her appointment book behind?"

"I don't know. Except for that one meeting, this was going to be a vacation for her. For both of us. Maybe she figured she didn't need it."

"Maybe." Kay returned the appointment book to her handbag. "You neglected to leave your answering machine on in your apartment."

Steven looked confused. "Oh. I guess I forgot. I do that sometimes."

"You forgot to turn it on when you left to come to Massachusetts on Sunday, yet you had it working on Friday and Saturday. I know, because I listened to your messages."

He said, "You played my answering machine?"

"Yes." She waited to see how he would respond to that. When he said nothing, she continued. "You told me Sandi called you after she arrived in Concord last Thursday. Did you talk with her, or did she leave a message on your answering machine."

"We talked."

"You're certain of that?"

"Yes."

"How long did you and she talk?"

"I don't know. A couple of minutes, I guess." He paused. "Oh, hell."

"What?"

He sighed. "It was the last time we ever talked." A tear welled in his left eye. "The last thing she said was to ask me to bring her Hell Freezes Over sweatshirt in case she got cold at the campground."

"How long have you had that particular answering machine?"

"How long . . ." The sudden shift in conversation had him confused. "I'm not sure. Sometime last year. Why?"

"Have you ever put in a new tape for incoming calls, or does it still have the tape it came with?"

"I don't know. The same tape, I think." He rubbed his hands together. "Why are you asking me all these stupid questions?"

Kay reached into her pocketbook again and pulled out a microcassette. She placed it on the table, midway between her and Steven. "I took this out of your answering machine this morning. It's a Radio Shack tape. You can't buy them anywhere other than a Radio Shack store, like the one in your neighborhood. The answering machines that Radio Shack makes probably come with Radio Shack tapes, but your answering machine is manufactured by AT&T."

He stared at the tape and furrowed his brow. "Hell, I don't know. A while back Sandi complained that the tape clarity was beginning to fade. Maybe she put a new tape in."

"How long ago did she complain about that?"

"Maybe a month ago. Really—what the hell difference does it make?"

"Less than two minutes of the tape were ever used. In other words, no single batch of messages ever totaled more than two minutes. If you had been using the tape for any significant period of time, I would expect that at one point or another you and Sandi would have accumulated more than that."

He pushed the tape back toward her side of the table. "Honestly, I have no idea about the answering machine. And I have no idea what any of this has to do with catching Sandi's killer."

Kay placed the tape in her pocketbook. She stood and walked to the wall phone. She lifted the handset and dialed a number, then handed it to me. "I'm calling Steven's apartment. Leave a message on the answering machine. It's voice-activated, so keep talking until you hear the beep that lets you know you've run out of time. Veronica, would you please time Harry to see how long he talks?"

Steven's recorded voice instructed me to leave a message, and then a tone sounded. I counted up to ten a couple of times. Bored with that, I started to recite the Gettysburg Address. I didn't know why Kay wanted me to do this, but I was a little chagrined to realize that I could no longer completely recall the speech I once knew by heart. I'm sure I transposed a phrase here and there, probably left some things out, and might even have repeated sections of the speech. Just as I reached the part about not perishing from the earth, the tape ran out. I heard a short beep, and then dead air.

"Done," I said, and handed the phone back to Kay.

Veronica said, "About three and a half minutes."

Kay returned the phone to the base on the wall. "Actually, it was three minutes and thirty-five seconds."

"How do you know that?" I asked.

"That was Steven's machine. I timed it three times while I was in his apartment. That particular unit has a ceiling of three minutes and thirty-five seconds per message."

Steven said, "I don't get it."

Kay said, "At around seven-thirty last Thursday evening, a call was made from Sandi's cell phone to your home phone."

"I told you she called me."

"Yes, and you were quite clear that you actually spoke with her. You said she didn't leave a message on the machine."

"Right. So?"

"I find it interesting that the phone call last Thursday lasted exactly three minutes and thirty-five seconds, the maximum amount of time you can use to leave a message."

Steven furrowed his brow and scratched the side of his head. He appeared to have no idea what Kay was implying. I wasn't sure I knew where she was heading.

Veronica, of course, knew exactly what was going on. "Steven," she said. "Kay thinks it's possible that the phone call was made to your answering machine. That you didn't talk with Sandi over the phone."

He stared at her blankly.

Veronica continued. "Kay is suggesting—" She looked at Kay as she spoke. "I think Kay is wondering if it's possible that *you* made the call from Sandi's phone."

"That I made . . . but what . . . huh?"

Suddenly it clicked for me, and I blurted it out. "To establish an alibi."

"An alibi?"

"You come to Massachusetts with Sandi," I said. "No one else knows you're not home. You wind up killing her. You panic. You figure out what to do with her belongings and her car, and you figure out another way to get back to Brooklyn. But you need some way of proving you were in Brooklyn the whole time, that you never came to Massachusetts in the first place. So you create a record with her cell phone to make it look like you were using your phone in Brooklyn."

It took a few seconds for that to sink in. Then he glared at Kay and snarled, "This is unbelievable. Is that what you think?" He looked at Veronica and said, more softly, "Is that what *you* think?"

"I didn't say that, Steven."

"Vee, I loved Sandi. I did *not* kill her." He thought for a moment. "Do I need a lawyer?"

Veronica glanced at Kay, then said, "I don't think you need one at the moment. But I don't know that there's any particular advantage that would come to you by continuing this conversation."

Kay said, "I don't have anything else to ask right now. Oh—I almost forgot. What size shoe do you wear, Steven?"

"Ten and a half. Why?"

"Another murder victim was found this afternoon on Simon Willard Road." Veronica and Steven snapped to attention. "I think that murder and Sandi's murder are related. And there was a footprint in blood at this afternoon's site. I don't know what size it is yet."

Steven stood and smacked his hand against the tabletop. "That's enough! First you accuse me of killing Sandi, and now you think I killed some guy I don't even know. Well, I was here all afternoon. But you'll be glad to know I don't have anyone to vouch for that."

"First of all, it was a woman who was killed. Second, the murder occurred sometime between midnight and dawn."

"Well, I was over in the barn all night. I drank too much wine at dinner, had words with Harry when he helped me back to the barn, and then I slept it off."

I knew different. Kay and Veronica knew different, too, because I had told them about seeing Steven drive off at one in the morning. None of us spoke.

He grimaced. "Oh, shit. I forgot. I woke up in the middle of the night. I couldn't stand being by myself over there, so I went for a ride."

"How long were you gone?"

"I don't know. Maybe an hour. Maybe more."

"Where did you go?"

"I'm not sure. I don't know this area. I just drove in circles until I found my way back."

"Whose car did you use?"

"Veronica's."

Kay thought for a few seconds. "Harry, I'd like to look in the barn apartment, if that's all right with you."

"Hey," Steven said. "I didn't say you could look through my stuff. You need a warrant for that. Doesn't she need a warrant to do that, Vee?"

Kay said, "I would need a warrant to go through your things without your permission, Steven." She turned to me. "I would need a warrant to go through the barn without *your* permission, and, frankly, I doubt that I have enough evidence to get one."

Steven said, "You don't have *any* evidence."

Kay continued. "May I look in the barn, Harry?"

"Of course."

"Veronica," she said, "have you used your car since Steven went for a ride last night?"

"No. I got a ride to and from the train station so I could leave the car for Steven to use if he needed it."

"Well, I'd like to look in your car, if I may."

Veronica hesitated for just a second. She glanced at Steven, who I thought gave a slight nod in her direction. "Yes," she said, "you can look in my car."

We all walked outside. Veronica's car was parked next to the barn. Kay opened the driver's door and looked around without getting inside. Then she closed the door. "If I want to bring your car to the state police forensic lab, will that be all right with you?"

This time Veronica answered affirmatively without looking at Steven.

We proceeded into the barn and up the stairs to the apartment. We walked through the living area and into the bedroom.

Everything was in its proper place. The bed was made. Steven's suitcase lay empty and open in a corner of the bedroom, his clothes and toiletries apparently unpacked into the closet and the dresser.

The dresser drawers were closed. The closet door was shut. It was my dresser and it was my closet, but any reasonable person would know they contained Steven's belongings, and Kay no doubt would need a warrant or Steven's permission to open them. She said nothing. Instead, she walked from room to room, visible to us the entire time through the open bedroom door, looking for who knew what.

When Kay reached the kitchen, temporarily out of earshot, Veronica spoke quietly. "Let her look through your things, Steven. If you're in trouble, I'll help you. But if you have nothing to do with any of this, this is the best time to show it."

Kay returned to the bedroom. "Why did you and Harry argue last night?"

Steven said, "He took exception to my friendship with Veronica. I think his exact words were, 'Stop sniffing around my woman.' "

Kay and Veronica scowled and turned toward me at the same time, like members of a synchronized feminist marching brigade. I was glad that I was the closest one to the door. I shrugged my shoulders and turned my palms upward: the universally recognized sign of submission for those who know they're fighting a losing cause.

Kay said, "There was a substantial amount of blood at the murder scene on Simon Willard Road. I don't suppose you'd be willing to let me search through your belongings, would you?"

Steven frowned at her for several seconds. Then, in an eerie instant, he broke into a broad smile. He walked over to the closet and opened the door, then pulled out the drawers of the dresser.

Kay spent the next several minutes sifting through Steven's possessions. I doubted that she seriously expected to find bloody clothing squirreled away. More likely she was looking for copies of the palm-sized abridged version of *Walden*.

"Thank you, Steven," she said when she was finished.

"Yeah, right. You didn't find anything, did you?"

"Sometimes you don't know what you have the first time you find it. For example, what should I make of the fact that you have this?"

She reached into the still-open bottom dresser drawer and pulled out a bulky olive-green sweatshirt. She unfolded it, clearly revealing the words *Hell Freezes Over*, in large block letters. Underneath those words, in smaller print, it said: *Eagles Reunion Tour, 1994.*

"That was Sandi's," Steven said. "It's the sweatshirt she asked me to bring the last time we talked."

"I notice that it's an extra large. Sandi was on the petite side."

"She liked to wear bulky—ah, why the hell am I trying to explain things to you? You're wasting my time. You're wasting *your* time. Go find whoever it is who killed Sandi. And if you have a couple of minutes to spare, you can also go fuck yourself."

Steven Farr grabbed the sweatshirt. He walked out of the room and down the stairs, and he stepped outside and under the darkening sky of the late August evening.

38

I looked out the bedroom window. The kitchen in the barn, previously dark, was lit. "Steven is back," I said.

"I know," Veronica replied as she loosened her skirt and stepped out of it. "I just noticed. The police probably know, too."

"The police?"

"No doubt there's a cruiser posted at the end of the driveway. With all of those books missing from the gift shop, I'm sure Kay is taking the possibility seriously that the killer still has plans. And I'm sure she's made arrangements to keep an eye on Steven."

"It's ten o'clock," I said. "I wonder where he was for the last four hours on foot."

"Speaking of 'on foot,' I have a feeling I'm going to be without a car for a few days."

"Kay didn't say she definitely wanted it."

"I'm sure she wants it. I would want it if I were in her situation. She was just extending me a courtesy by raising the issue tentatively, hoping I would agree without making her play hardball."

"How could she play hardball? You heard her say she doesn't have enough evidence to get a warrant."

"She could play hardball by calling the Bureau. She could create an awkward situation for me by telling Martin that I'm being less than fully cooperative with the local police in a murder investigation."

Martin Baines was Veronica's supervisor: Special Agent in Charge of the FBI office in Boston.

I said, "If she were sure she wanted it, she would have said so more directly. What makes you think she's extending you a courtesy? Just because you're both women?"

She paused in her disrobing and stared at me.

"Sorry," I said. "That was out of line."

"Yes, it was. And you're already skating on thin ice for your comment about Steven sniffing around me. That was *way* out of line. I didn't like that at all."

"You're right. I shouldn't have said that."

"You shouldn't have even *thought* that. I'm not an animal secreting some sort of mating scent. And if Steven were to present a problem—which he doesn't—then I could handle it."

"Point well taken."

"And noted?"

"Yes," I said. "And noted."

"Good." She smiled slightly. "Perhaps there's hope for you yet, my caveman." She gathered up her discarded clothing and placed them in the hamper.

I said, "Do you think Steven killed Sandra O'Neill and Abigail Claymore-Whitley?"

"No. I admit that I can imagine him striking out impulsively at Sandi, although I don't think he would ever beat anyone as ferociously as the killer beat her. But I certainly don't see him engaging in the sort of homicidal premeditation that was involved with the second killing. I don't see Steven being that planful about such a thing. He's never been very planful about anything."

"You haven't seen him in a long time. People can change."

"That's what you always say. Perhaps that's why you became a psychiatrist. But I don't think people change as much as you think they can."

"I know. That's what *you* always say."

She said, "Under the right circumstances, with more evidence than the wild speculations Kay has, I would be willing to consider Steven striking out in anger. But not premeditating the second murder."

"Under the right circumstances, I'd be willing to consider *anyone* striking out in anger. People can do some incredibly stupid things on impulse."

"Did you know the woman who was murdered?"

"Only by reputation," I replied.

"I wonder why she was killed."

"She gave a lot of money to preserve Walden Woods. Maybe that's the connection, given what the killer wrote in his letter."

"I wonder if Sandi O'Neill ever met her."

"I assume Kay will try to figure that out."

Veronica grabbed her robe. "I'm taking a shower." She headed for the bathroom, then turned around and spoke again. "I didn't want to say this while Kay was still here because I didn't want to embarrass you. But what you did at the mall today was reckless. You should have let the police handle the whole thing."

"I was afraid a killer might get away. That's why I followed the kid inside."

"And if he really had been a killer, you could be dead right now."

"I guess I didn't take the time to think about that."

"Well, like you said—people do incredibly stupid things on impulse." She smiled again. "I need you to stay around. Melissa needs you to stay around. I don't want you to run off playing the hero again." She walked over to me, kissed my cheek, and walked into the bathroom.

I heard the Canada geese once more: a reminder that there were only a few weeks left until autumn. Sandi's memorial Mass was three days away. Melissa's birthday party would come a week later. I thought about the dead woman I had never met, and I thought about the soon-to-be young woman who still needed me around. I wondered how long I would be around for her and for Veronica.

I need you to stay around. I couldn't put it off any longer: I had to tell her about my worries.

In the distance, the sound of a jet came from the direction of the Air Force base in the next town. They weren't supposed to fly out that late at night, but people don't always do what they're supposed to do. The low rumble got louder and drowned out the sound of the geese.

I looked out the window one more time. The rooms in the barn apartment all were dark.

39

The True Believer stood outside the house and listened to the hum of the late-night jet. Then the distant roar receded—replaced not by the staccato burst of automatic gunfire but by the atonal honking of the Canada geese.

He saw the man look out the window, but the True Believer had no fear of being seen. Blending had always been his secret strength. No one fears the tree—until the tree springs swiftly from the shadows to cut its enemy down.

He had been standing outside the house for an hour: circling, waiting, planning. Soon he would be inside. He had been there before. He knew the layout.

And he knew the people. The man was his target; he hoped to spare the woman. But like the poet wrote, the best laid schemes of mice and men . . . etcetera, etcetera, and so forth.

He hoped there would be no blood this time. The blood always gave him nightmares. Last night was no exception: Scar tissue of old wounds being ripped open, viscera exposed and ready to spill. Images of gnarled crones and masticating dogs, slit bellies, hot lava blood washing over him, drowning him . . .

Well, now: At least there would be no pets to worry about this time. Just the man and woman. So intent was he on his goal, the man was already dead in his mind. But the woman was alive. He hoped he could keep her that way. If she stayed out of the way, he would let her be.

He approached the house, honing in on the weak point he had selected for his attack: a screened section of the porch that would easily give way to his gravity knife. He was prepared to wait inside the house all night for a chance to take his target without hurting the woman. But if need be, then need be.

The True Believer pushed the tip of his blade into the screen and pulled sharply down. As he sliced quickly through the screen filaments, the ping of metal on metal made a joyous sound.

40

The Canada geese flew over my house and headed toward the wildlife refuge. Their plaintive sound faded, leaving me unexpectedly forlorn. They would likely rest nearby for a night or more, then continue southward. And then the autumn would come.

I remembered the fall of my senior year at Tufts. Bobby and I drove up to New Hampshire one weekend and climbed Mount Kearsarge. We watched the trees with their autumnal colors shining in the late afternoon sun. I said, "This is the most beautiful thing I've ever seen."

Bobby replied, "It's humbling if you stop to think about it. All of this was here ages before us, and all of it will remain ages after we're gone."

"I'm just glad we got to see it. It would be nice to come back every year. Something to be thankful for, seeing it again."

"That's the whole idea behind the *shehekiyanu*."

"The *what*?"

"You know," he said. "The prayer that gets said on holidays." He recited a few lines in Hebrew. "Loosely translated, it means, 'Thank you, God, for letting me stick around long enough to see this time of year once again.' "

Two weeks later Bobby was with me when I met an attractive first-year student from Connecticut named Janet who eventually became my wife.

Two months after that, unbeknownst to me at the time, Veronica witnessed the murder of her mother. She was nine years old. And now I wondered, as I had wondered so many times, what it would be like to grow up with such a tragedy woven so tightly into the fabric of one's life.

I lay alone in bed, waiting for Veronica. I glanced around at the bedroom we shared. Before she came into my life, I slept alone. Before that, the room belonged to my wife and me. Before that, and before that, and before that, men and women I never knew had shared this space. I wondered what would happen there after Veronica and I were gone. And I wondered if we would get to see another year there together. I resolved that if I should be so fortunate as to share another August 30 with her, I would recite the *shehekiyanu*.

The impermanence of everything weighed on me. I felt a need for connection, for anchoring, lest I be cut off and fall into an abyss.

I heard the shower running. I tossed off the covers and walked into the bathroom. "I'm in here," I said.

"All right," Veronica replied from the other side of the shower curtain.

I opened the curtain partway. "I want to watch you."

"That might be fun." She held out a tube of foaming gel for me to grab.

"*Watch* you," I repeated. "Not 'wash you.' I want to watch you."

"Oh." She paused. "Well, that might be fun, too."

She rubbed the gel between her hands, working it into a thick lather. I watched the water drizzle down on her, beading on her skin, slipping down along the contour of her body.

She said, "You're making me self-conscious."

"Don't be. I just needed to see you. I didn't want to wait."

She began to spread the gel over her shoulders and arms. She moved quickly at first. But then, as she watched me watching her, she began to take her time. "Is that what you want?"

"Yes. I like that very much."

"You're easily pleased."

"You please me," I said. "You always have."

She coated her stomach with lather, then her back and legs.

She left her breasts for last. Finally she touched the creamy white froth to them, her nipples growing taut beneath her lingering caress.

She smiled and nodded at the hardening mass at the bottom of my groin. "I see I have your attention," she said.

"Absolutely and completely." I stepped into the shower. "Turn around."

She did as I asked. I stood behind her and whispered, "I could never get enough of you."

"I don't want you to get enough of me," she answered. "I want you to always want more of me."

I reached my arms around her and began to slide my hands along her breasts. "I'll take over from here."

"You've never done this to me in the shower."

"I know."

I pulled on one of her nipples. She shuddered, then leaned against the wall to steady herself. "Oh" was all she said.

I pressed against her. "I need you," I said.

I moved my hands from her breasts, over her shoulders, along her arms: slowly, slowly, slowly—and then back to her breasts. I cupped them with my hands and twisted the nipples gently with my fingertips.

She had difficulty maintaining her balance and leaned against the wall for support. She said, "You're making it hard for me to stand up."

"You're making it hard, too," I replied, leaning against her to emphasize the full double-entendre meaning of my words.

She moaned softly.

I ran my hands from her chest to her stomach, then across the thatch of curls, down to her sweet and salty center. One finger disappeared into her darkness, then a second, then a third.

She moaned again. She pushed down on my fingers with her body. "God, yes."

I felt a compelling ache to be in her, to be part of her, to bury myself within her being. If I could melt into her, no dark force would ever be able to take me away from her.

I reclaimed by fingers, slick with her wetness, and placed the tip of my cock against her opening. I pushed forward, inching myself inside.

She shuddered again, she spasmed, she grew weak and fell backward toward me. I leaned forward and caught her against my body, trapping her between my chest and the wall.

Like a racer entering a stream of fast-moving traffic, I picked up the pace as quickly as I could, moving into high gear in a matter of seconds. I hurled myself into her: pounding her, pinning her, controlling her movements with my weight and my forcefulness.

I dug my fingers into her thighs and pulled myself into her as completely as I could go. My thrusts were long, quick, deep. She grimaced and groaned each time I hit the end point. The sight and sound of her arousal keyed mine all the more.

Every cell in my body cried for release. I lifted her a few inches off the shower floor and pushed full force against her, jamming her against the wall, driving into her like a rapid-firing piston.

I reached between her legs with my fingers as I pushed my cock into her. I found her swollen clit and rubbed against it. Her groans grew louder, echoing off the tiles, rocking the room like thunder.

She called my name over and over.

I wanted to reach every part of her soul: the little girl I had never known; the old woman she would one day be, whom I might never know. I wanted somehow to touch her in a way she had never been touched before. And I wanted her to remember me until the end of time.

I held on for dear life, and then I spilled into her. I imagined it flowing into her deepest recesses: a reminder of me to stay within her forever.

And then it was over.

I pressed my lips to the back of her neck and kissed her gently.

"Wow," she said. "That was unreal." And then she began to laugh.

"Why are you laughing?"

"Because I'm thinking—I know what just got into me, so to speak, but what in the world got into *you*?"

She turned around. She stopped laughing as soon as she saw my face. "Oh, God, Harry—why are you crying?"

"Because I don't want to leave you."

The alarm in her voice was instant. "*Leave* me? What are you saying?"

I began to sob. "I'm saying that I love you, and I'm afraid I'm going to die."

41

Veronica turned the spigot to stop the water flow. "Harry, tell me what's wrong."

My eyes still wet, I opened the shower curtain and reached for our towels.

"No," she said, pulling my hand back. "Sit down right here. Tell me right now. Please."

And so I told her. As we sat in the shower—our bodies glistening with water, the air filled with steam and the most intimate of scents—I told her everything: the abnormal reading on my recent blood test, the appointment with Jamie Ray five days earlier, the biopsy on the day before yesterday. I had been keeping the secret for only a little more than a week, but it felt like eternity.

"Did the biopsy hurt?" she asked.

"Very much."

"Good. You deserve it." She saw me wince, and she said, "I'm sorry. That wasn't fair. But I'm angry at you for keeping all of this secret."

"No," I replied. "*I'm* sorry. I should have told you. Bobby said so, and John Fitzpatrick said so—"

"Bobby? Father John? Really, now—is there anyone else in town other than me who you *didn't* tell?"

We looked at each other for several seconds. Then her eyes welled with tears. "Oh God, Harry—I don't want this to be happening."

"I know."

She forced back her tears. "This is *not* happening."

Veronica stepped out of the shower and wrapped herself in a towel. "I *refuse* to let this be happening. Do you understand me? You will *not* die on me. I refuse to lose you." She strode into the bedroom, slamming the door shut behind her.

I stayed behind for a minute or two, not knowing what to say.

The bedroom lights were off when I entered the room. Veronica had thrown the curtains open. She lay naked on her back, her silhouette visible in the pale light of the small slice of August moon.

I lay next to her.

She said, "You should have told me sooner."

"I know."

"It hurts me to think you didn't trust me enough to tell me."

"I'm sorry." I touched her hand lightly.

"When you hurt me, I get so angry. And then I don't want to be with you. And then the thought of not being with you makes me feel so alone. It goes away, and then everything is all right again. But I hate it so much, the thought of being alone without you. I remember how terrible I felt after I left you."

Two years earlier, when things were rocky between us, I made things exponentially worse by sleeping with Marjorie Morris. It was my intention to keep the brief affair secret, but I didn't have any experience with sexual duplicity, and I covered my tracks poorly. When Veronica discovered the truth she walked out on me. And I was in despair: not just for having lost her, but for having hurt her—and for having hurt Melissa, who knew instinctively that I was at fault for Veronica leaving. I had never before inflicted such hurt on someone I loved.

She said, "I want to ask you something, and I need you to be as honest as you can." She paused. "Do you still think of other women?"

"What do you mean?"

"Janet, Marjorie—do you sometimes think about them, think about . . . being with them?"

"Sometimes."

"Do you sometimes fantasize about women you meet, imagine knowing them, being with them?"

"Sometimes."

"Do you think you'll ever reach the point where you don't have those sorts of thoughts about other women?"

I hesitated, pondering her question. "No," I finally replied. "Not completely."

"Do you think you'll ever act on those thoughts? Do you think you might be unfaithful to me someday?"

Now there was no hesitation. "Definitely not."

"How can you be so sure?"

"Because I couldn't . . ." I felt myself choking up. "I know how much I hurt you and Melissa when I was unfaithful before. It was an awful feeling. I promised myself I would never be the instrument of such hurt again."

"I'm sorry," she said. "I didn't mean to make you cry again."

I closed my eyes. I felt a tear trickle down my cheek. And then I felt her lips on my cheek.

"It's okay, darling," she said, leaning over me. "It's okay. We're such children sometimes. But we really are something, aren't we?"

"I don't know what we are."

"What we are," she said, "are lovers until the end of time."

She lay on her back again and held my hand. "When do you expect to have the biopsy results?"

"Maybe by the end of next week," I answered.

"Are you afraid?"

"Yes, I'm afraid."

"Well, perhaps it will be easier to wait now that you're not waiting alone."

"Yes."

We were quiet for several seconds. Then she said, "I want you to do something for me."

"What is it?"

"I want you to repeat these words. 'I love you.' "

"I love you."

" 'I will not lie to you.' "

"I will not lie to you."

" 'I will not hide the truth from you.' "

"I will not hide the truth from you."

" 'No matter how much I think the truth will hurt you.' "

"No matter how much I think the truth will hurt you."

" 'Ever again.' "

"Ever again."

She sighed. "Do you mean that?"

"Yes, my love. I mean that."

"Will you ever betray me?" she asked.

"I will never betray you."

"And will you ever leave me?"

"I will never, ever leave you."

"All right, then." She covered my hand with hers, then pulled it to her breast. "I think about your wife sometimes, too."

"Why do *you* think about her?"

"Because of how she must have felt. I know how hard it was for you and Melissa to lose her. But sometimes I can't help but think how hard it was for Janet. How sad she must have been to leave the two of you."

"She had this expression she used with Melissa. 'You are beautiful, inside out and outside in.' Sometimes she would start the sentence, and Melissa would finish it. I wonder if Melissa remembers that."

I rolled onto my side, facing her. "Bobby and his wife are supposed to take care of Melissa if anything happens to me. It's all spelled out in my will."

"I know."

"I want to change it. I want Melissa to be with you. Here, in this old house."

"What do you suppose Bobby will say about that?"

"Bobby will want whatever I want. He's my true friend."

"Even if I wanted to raise her as an Episcopalian?"

I laughed. "You wouldn't be able to raise Melissa as an Episcopalian—or as anything else—unless she wanted you to."

"Now, *that's* for sure. She may be the most single-minded person I know. Where does she get it? You obsess about things, look at every side of an issue over and over. And from the way you talk about Janet, I don't think Melissa's stubbornness comes from her."

"You're joking, right?"

"What do you mean?"

I said, "Don't you know who she gets her strong will from?"

"Who?"

"From you."

"No. She was strong when I met her."

"She's stronger now because of you."

She paused. "Oh."

"I thought you knew that."

She lay in silence for a few minutes. Finally she said, "I'll take care of your daughter if you die, and I will love her as my own." Then she stood and walked toward the door.

"Where are you going?"

"I'll be right back."

She returned a minute later holding something in her hand. She sat next to me and switched on the lamp by her side of the bed. She said, "This was my mother's Bible. Melissa saw it on my shelf several months ago and asked if she could borrow it. She says you didn't have a Bible in the house before I moved in."

"She's right."

"She reads from it sometimes when you're not around. Shows me passages that catch her interest. Not long ago she found one she really likes, and it turned out to be one I really liked when I was a girl. May I read it to you?"

"Of course."

"It's from Ruth, who was another very strong-willed woman." She placed one hand on my chest and read. " 'Entreat me not to leave thee, or to return from following after thee. For whither thou goest, I will go. And where thou lodgest, I will lodge. Thy people shall be my people, and thy God my God. Where thou diest, will I die, and there will I be buried. The Lord do so to me, and more also, if ought but death part thee and me.' "

"That's very nice."

She switched off the lamp and lay next to me again. "Yes," she said, "that's very nice."

She rolled onto her stomach. I stroked her back for several minutes, until the pattern of her breathing told me she was asleep.

I was bone-weary tired, but images of the day's events kept me awake: the chase at the mall, the events at the murder scene, Kay's ungentle interrogation of Steven. I thought watching late-night TV might take the edge off, but I didn't want to wake Veronica.

I left her side, where I felt safe, and walked downstairs.

42

Lurking in a corner of the darkened den, the True Believer listened to the footsteps on the stairs: slow, plodding, almost certainly male. He heard his unsuspecting host yawn—definitely male—and approach the den.

The man entered, picked up the remote control, clicked the television on, then headed out of the room. A moment later, sounds of a refrigerator opening and closing. Footsteps again, then once again into the den carrying a glass of milk. He sat on the couch and began to surf channels with the clicker.

The True Believer drew the cord from his pocket and pulled it taut. For an hour he had wondered if he would get an opportunity to take the man while sparing the woman. This was his chance. He stepped slowly and quietly toward the couch.

The man clicked from one late-night local news program to another. A reporter stood in front of a familiar-looking home. "The murdered woman, Abigail Claymore-Whitley, was a lifelong Concord resident."

The man jumped up from the couch. "Oh my God!" He stepped to the doorway and yelled upstairs. "Yvette! Come here! Hurry!" He reached for the switch on the wall, and the room was bathed in light.

The two men stood facing each other, just a few feet apart.

Alex Mason stared at his unexpected guest, more annoyed than frightened. "What the hell are *you* doing here?"

"I have a present for you, Alex."

213

"What sort of present?"

The True Believer reached into his pocket, removed an object, and held it out to the other man.

Alex Mason said, "*Walden*? What the hell do I want another copy of *Walden* for? What's with the latex gloves—are you a proctologist all of a sudden? And who the hell said you could come here uninvited?"

Mason was so full of himself—as usual—that he was oblivious to the obvious threat the circumstances posed.

"Alex, you're an insufferable idiot. That's not why I'm doing this, but it certainly makes the job a lot easier."

"What the fuck are you talking about? You never make any sense, you know that?"

Movement upstairs: Yvette Mason opening her bedroom door and heading toward the stairwell. From the top of the stairs she yelled, "What do you want? I'm in my nightgown. Is there someone else there? Who are you talking to?"

"I'm talking to—"

The True Believer clutched Mason by the throat and stifled him. "You moron. Are you trying to get her killed, too?"

"Alex," the woman shouted again, "who's there with you?"

And then, from the television: "Concord police won't say whether they think this latest murder is related to the recent murder of a New York woman at Walden Pond last week. But both victims were active in the fight against development of land near Walden. And Seven News has learned that police received information suggesting that both victims may have been killed because of those efforts."

A look of understanding—too little, too late—appeared on Alex Mason's face.

Footsteps coming down the stairs; no time left to waste.

The True Believer held his quarry against the wall with one hand and reached for his knife with the other. A deep slash, ear-to-ear, through sinew and flesh.

He ran from the den seconds before the dead man's wife entered through the other doorway.

Outside again, the humid air almost sucked his breath away. The still night was rocked by a woman's ear-piercing wail.

43

Nothing focuses the mind quite like the sight of flashing police lights coming up the driveway.

Within minutes after sitting in front of the television in the den, I slipped into a dream that was set in my childhood home. In gross violation of the household rules, Veronica and I were in my bedroom, carnally engaged. Suddenly we heard sirens. I looked out my bedroom window. Police cruisers and neighbors surrounded the house. Jamie Ray, ace urologist, was there with a megaphone. She said, "We know you have a girl in there. Come out with your hands up." And there were flashing lights everywhere . . .

The flashing police lights woke me from the dream. They proceeded past the house. The cruiser came to a halt outside the barn.

I walked outside in my robe and slippers. A police officer stepped from the cruiser and knocked loudly on the door to the barn apartment.

I said, "Can I help you, officer?"

Before he could answer, the door opened. Steven was in pajamas, barefoot. His hair was tousled. His pajamas looked slept in. There was a crease on his cheek: an impression that came from lying in the same position for a long time. He shielded his eyes from the flashing lights. "What? What is it?"

"Steven Farr?"

"Yes." Steven saw me. "What's this all about, Harry? Why did you call the police?"

I started to reply, but the police officer spoke first. He said, "Just getting back home, sir?"

"It's not my home. And does it *look* like I'm just getting back?"

"How long have you been here, sir?"

"Since Monday evening."

"I mean, what time did you last come in here?"

"Christ, I don't know. I went for a walk. Got back maybe nine or ten o'clock. What time is it now?"

"It's almost eleven-thirty, sir."

I said, "This is my house, officer. Is there something I can help you with?"

He turned and nodded. "Are you Dr. Kline?"

"I am."

"Detective Wheaton should be here in a few minutes. She asked me to ascertain the whereabouts of Mr. Farr."

"Is there some sort of problem?" I asked.

"I'm sure Detective Wheaton will explain when she gets here. In the meantime, Mr. Farr, if you would be good enough to step outside, it would be appreciated."

"I'm in my pajamas, for chrissake." He paused. "All right, I'll go get my robe." He turned away and muttered something under his breath.

The police officer clasped a hand around Steven's arm, preventing him from walking inside. "It would be better if you didn't go inside, sir. You can wait in the cruiser if you're chilly."

"Uh-uh. I'm not getting in the cruiser. I'll wait here. Harry, do you have an extra robe I can borrow?"

I looked at the police officer. "Any problem with that?"

He shrugged. "No problem."

I glanced at Steven. He looked perplexed, or frightened, or both.

I went into the house and walked upstairs. I got a robe for Steven. I awoke Veronica, told her what was going on, and asked her to come outside.

Kay drove up the driveway shortly after Veronica and I reached the barn. She parked by the house and stepped out of her car. She touched the hoods of our cars, then walked toward the barn. She stopped midway and asked Veronica and me to walk to where she stood.

Steven said, "I don't know what's going on, but I don't like it."

As we walked toward Kay, I said, "I don't know what's going on, either, but I'm glad Melissa isn't here."

Veronica said, "What's going on is that there's been another murder."

"How in the world do you know that?"

"She just checked the cars to see if they've been driven recently. What else would bring her out to do that so late at night?"

We stood with Kay between the house and the barn. She said, "That police officer saw Steven walk up the driveway from Monument Street at about nine-fifteen. Were the two of you home then?"

"Yes," Veronica said. She had been right; the police were keeping tabs on Steven's whereabouts.

"Did either of you talk to him?"

I said, "Not until a couple of minutes before you got here, when I came outside to see why there was a police cruiser in my driveway."

"You haven't gone out, have you, Harry?"

"No. Why?"

"Just checking." She turned to Veronica. "You'll vouch for him on that?"

"Yes. Why? Who was killed this time?"

"It was Alex Mason."

If you've never been told that someone you knew was murdered, there's no way to make you understand what it feels like. I didn't like the man. In my private thoughts I had wished him unpleasantness. But this was real life, and it jarred me.

Kay said, "I know you and he had what one might call strained relations."

"Damn it, Kay. Half of Concord had strained relationships with him. *You* had strained relations with him."

She nodded.

I said, "How did it happen?"

"I don't know the details. His wife was in bed. She heard him talking with someone in their den. Mason yelled for her. When she got there, he was bleeding to death. And he was holding one of those copies of *Walden*."

"When did it happen?"

She checked her watch. "Yvette Mason called for an ambulance about twenty-five minutes ago. I just got word a few minutes ago, on my way here, that he died."

Kay walked toward the barn. Veronica and I followed her.

"Hello again, Steven."

"Hello, Kay."

"What have you been up to since you walked out on us before?"

"Walking around. Crying for Sandi. Being pissed off at you. Then I came back here and went to sleep."

"You were pretty angry at me a few hours ago."

"You needn't use the past tense."

"If you say so." She turned toward me. "I'd like to look through the apartment again."

"Go ahead," I replied, "but you won't find anything. He's not the one you're looking for."

"What do you mean, I'm not the one she's looking for? What the hell is going on?"

Veronica said, "Relax, Steven."

"I *am* relaxed," he replied, sounding anything but that.

Kay went inside.

Veronica said, "There was another murder tonight."

"You've got to be kidding."

"It looks like the work of the same person who killed Sandi and the other woman."

"I saw something on the news about the other woman being involved in preserving Walden."

"Yes," Veronica replied.

"What's the story with this one?"

I said, "His name was Alex Mason. He had his own reasons for wanting to keep things the way they are. He didn't like the idea of lower income housing in his town. I'm willing to bet he gave a lot of money to the Walden Woods project."

Kay returned after a few minutes. She addressed the uniformed officer. "You said you saw him return on foot at nine-fifteen."

"Yes, detective."

"No cars came on or off the property between then and now."

"No. And nobody on foot, either, at least not along the driveway."

"When did he answer your knock on the door?"

"Between eleven twenty-five and eleven-thirty. I drove in here as soon as you gave instructions to do it."

"That's between eighteen and twenty-three minutes after the ambulance was called. Add a minute or two for Mason's wife to discover the body and place the call. A total of twenty-five minutes at most between the murder and you making contact with Mr. Farr."

"Sounds about right, detective."

Kay turned to me. "Where is Mason's house?"

"On top of Fairhaven Hill."

"That's a pretty hard hill to get down, with or without a vehicle, especially at night."

"Yes," I said. "And it's way over on the other side of Route 2. From the foot of the hill to here it's about three miles."

Kay turned everything over in her mind. She looked at Steven, then at the uniformed policeman, and then at Veronica and me. "Not possible," she said.

"Not possible," I agreed.

"What?" said Steven. "What are you talking about?"

Veronica said, "Without a car to take you door-to-door, there's no chance someone could kill Alex Mason and then, twenty-five minutes later, be standing here in his pajamas." She touched his arm. "You're in the clear, Steven. Kay knows you couldn't possibly be the killer."

Steven exhaled, long and loud. He leaned against the door to the apartment, eyes closed.

"Anyway," said Kay, "when I looked through your belongings before, I verified that you wear a ten and a half shoe. A couple of hours ago I was informed that the bloody footprint at the Claymore-Whitley house was a size nine."

Steven opened his eyes and glared at the detective. "Are you going to leave me alone now?"

"I'm hoping that if we talk some more about Sandi, I might learn something that will help me find her killer."

"Yeah, well, if you think of something specific to ask me, you can call. Until then, please let me be." He opened the door to the apartment.

"Steven," Kay said. "Wait."

"What?"

"I just want you to know I'm sorry for your loss. I don't think I said that before."

"No, you didn't."

"I got a good feeling about her when I was in your place in Brooklyn. And when I was talking to her friends. I'm very sorry."

He turned around without replying and closed the door in her face.

Kay sighed and said, "Well, I think things are going very well, don't you? I've been shot, I have three dead bodies on my hands, I have every reason to expect more, and I've been wasting my time trying to extract a confession from the wrong guy. Yes, things are going *very* well, indeed."

44

A small cluster of reporters and photographers, perhaps a half-dozen people in all, rushed over to me when I appeared at the end of my long winding driveway to retrieve the Thursday morning *Boston Globe*. There was one television news van, and it was situated as close to the driveway entrance as it could possibly be without blocking it.

A microphone was thrust into my face. Questions abounded from all sides. "Mr. Farr, did your fiancée know either of the other murder victims?" "Have the police questioned you?" "Are you Steven Farr?" "Do the police have any idea who might be responsible for this?"

I wondered how they knew Steven was staying at my place. I said, "The answers to your questions, in random order, are no, yes, how the hell do I know, and none of your damn business."

"Jesus Christ," someone muttered. "Lighten up, fella. Grab some coffee or something."

I walked back to the house.

Abigail Claymore-Whitley's murder made the front page, below the fold. There were no details about the method of death, and no mention of the dog. There was a brief "why would anyone want to harm such a lovely old lady" statement from a neighbor, and a couple of paragraphs about the victim and the family members she had outlived. Near the end of the article was a recap about Sandi O'Neill's murder, finishing with a statement that this was the first time in Concord history when two murders had been recorded in the same month. There was no speculation regarding a connection between the two cases. And—newspaper deadlines being what they are—there was no mention of Alex Mason's murder.

Channel 7's six o'clock morning news—the more tabloidlike of the local programs—regaled viewers with graphic descriptions of both new murders, and the slaying of Abigail Claymore-Whitley's Doberman pinscher. Citing "a source close to the investigation," the talking-head newscaster made unspecific reference to evidence that linked all three unsolved murders to one another. She concluded her hyperbolic remarks thus: "And so the peaceful village of Concord, Massachusetts—where Minutemen fired the shot heard 'round the world to repel the British invaders—is once again in a state of alarm, on full-scale alert."

On the surface, the peaceful village of Concord, Massachusetts, looked no different than usual—no more alarmed or alerted—when I walked to the Colonial Inn for an early breakfast with Bobby.

But you could see it on people's faces when they passed strangers on the street: a moment of sustained eye contact, longer than one would normally make, as if searching the other person's intentions; and then a quick turning away.

The Colonial Inn dining room was almost empty. A lot of the local regulars were on vacation, and we were still a couple of weeks away from the initial influx of fall foliage tourists. Our waitress took our order and filled Bobby's coffee cup.

Bobby said, "This is beginning to sound like something out of a mystery novel."

"No one in his right mind would set a mystery novel in Concord."

"Maybe not," he replied. "But with three homicides and one Fidocide—"

"Fidocide?"

"Fidocide. The killing of Fido. Look it up in the dictionary. With three homicides and one Fidocide, Alfred Korvich must be going crazy." He mixed cream into his coffee. "Have you told Veronica about your biopsy yet?"

"Last night. She said she refuses to let me die."

"Perhaps the reach of the FBI is longer than I realized."

"It would be nice to think so. She's pretty stubborn about something once she sets her mind to it."

"Well, sometimes pigheadedness can be a virtue," Bobby said. "Are you going to tell Melissa?"

"Not yet. I'll wait for the biopsy results, then figure out where to go from there."

"She's a good kid."

"Yes, she is." I remembered Veronica's comments about my daughter's stubbornness. I said, "I want to change my will, Bobby. I want Melissa to live with Veronica if anything happens to me."

"For Melissa's sake, or for Veronica's?"

"Both."

"I can do the paperwork tomorrow."

"Thanks. Veronica thought you might have a problem with that. I told her you would want whatever I want."

"Am I that transparent?"

"Always. That's why I like playing poker with you. You're the world's worst bluffer."

"And proud of it," he replied.

"I know. You're strange that way." I paused. "You know, this will sound pretty illogical, but if I die, I'll really miss you."

Our waitress brought our meals. Bobby buttered a slice of toast and said, "How are things with your houseguest?"

"He'll be gone by the end of the weekend, I hope. Tomorrow morning there's going to be a memorial Mass at St. Bernard's for Sandi O'Neill, and then cremation."

"The news this morning says all three murders might be related."

"Kay Wheaton told me that she has suspicions in that direction." I hesitated. "Actually, she has more than suspicions, Bobby. I'd appreciate your keeping this quiet, because I doubt she wants me to be repeating this to anyone. But they have physical evidence to link all three murder scenes." I told him about the copies of *Walden*. "And they have one other thing."

"What's that?"

"The killer sent a letter to the police. Korvich showed it to me. The writer claimed responsibility for murdering Sandi O'Neill. He said that more killings would follow. By the time the police could decide whether or not to take the letter seriously, there were two more bodies to deal with."

"Did he say why he's killing people?"

"Well, he was a little vague, and he rambled a bit. As best as I can tell, he's angry at people who are trying to stop the development of the Logan tract. So *he's* trying to stop *them*."

"Alex Mason and Mrs. Claymore-Whitley both gave a lot of money to help preserve the woods."

"Right," I said. "And Sandi O'Neill was an organizer and fund-raiser for the effort."

"A lot of people in town have spoken out against developing that land. Including yours truly. I wonder if he has specific victims already chosen."

"If he does," I said, "he didn't reveal that in the letter. He only said that there would be more."

Bobby pondered that for a moment. "Well, so far he seems to be a man of his word."

45

The True Believer was on a reconnoitering mission: inspecting the effects of his handiwork. He sat on a bench in the center of town and watched the people as they readied themselves for the new day.

He was among them, but not of them. So it always had been.

He recalled something that had happened more than thirty years earlier. The president was dead, his head exploded under the impact of a sniper's bullet. His parents sent him out to buy a special-edition evening newspaper. He walked to the local store. On his way there he passed several people, each one walking singly. Some he knew; some he didn't. He spoke to no one; no one spoke to him. But with strangers and acquaintances alike, there was a moment: A meeting of the eyes. A silent acknowledgment that both parties in the interaction were thinking about the same thing. One thing that overshadowed considerations of any other event on that long ago November evening.

And so it was today. People weren't talking. But he knew what they were thinking about. One thing overshadowing all other considerations.

He was tired. Killing took a toll. A lesson relearned. He needed rest, because the night would be on him again almost before he knew it. And he needed a plan: He knew what he intended to do when night fell, but not where or to whom. The overall plan had come to him only recently, a serendipitous thing. What happened with the woman from New York was unfortunate. Alex Mason and the old widow were choices. Now what?

The lawyer was walking toward him from the direction of the Colonial Inn. He stopped in front of the bench. "Hell of a thing," the lawyer said. One consideration overshadowing all others.

"Yes, a hell of a thing," the True Believer replied.

The lawyer sighed, looked around at the town, then said, "My wife and kid are visiting her sister in Maine. I hope the police settle this thing before they get back."

The True Believer paused for a moment. He believed in serendipity: A plan hatched. He said, "It's the kind of thing that makes you think about your own mortality. You handle estate planning, don't you?"

"Yes."

"Would you be willing to look over some documents for me, give me some advice?"

"Sure. You can mail them to my office." He reached into his wallet for a business card.

"Well, the truth is, I'm supposed to get them back to my lawyer by Monday. I guess I'm looking for a second opinion, just a quick going over. I was wondering — could I stop by your house this evening, maybe around seven-thirty? Just a half hour is probably all I need."

The lawyer thought for a moment. "I suppose so. Do you know where I live?"

"No."

The lawyer wrote out his home address on the back of a business card, handed it to the man, and said good-bye.

The True Believer knew that every war has casualties. Some are clearly justified. Others are not as justified but are necessary, or at least unavoidable, in the larger scheme of things.

He knew the lawyer was opposed to the development of the Logan tract. And he knew the lawyer to be a decent man. But sometimes decent men have to be sacrificed: like civilians who live near strategic bombing targets. And so this summer night, a sacrifice would be made.

Bobby Beck would die.

46

When I returned home, Kay Wheaton was sitting at the kitchen table drinking coffee and eating a bagel.

Kay said, "I got here about fifteen minutes ago. Veronica just left for work. She told me it was all right for me to wait in the house for you. She said you'd be back at around this time."

Just then the phone rang. It was my daughter, calling from Wendy's house to check in. I missed her, and I told her so. And she said the same to me.

"When can I come home, Dad?"

The night before last, I had told her I wanted her out of the house because of the sadness that would be present while Steven was there. And that was true, as far as it went. But Alfred Korvich's warning about harboring a murder suspect was part of the decision, too. And now Steven was no longer a suspect.

I said, "You can come home whenever you want to."

"Just a second. Let me ask Wendy." A minute later she came back on the line. "We're going to the beach today, and they have a cookout planned after we get back. I'll come home after that. Okay?"

"More than okay."

I hung up the phone and turned to face Kay. "What are you smiling at?" I asked.

"You. Did you know that you glow when you talk to your daughter?"

"Well, she's my daughter," I replied, not knowing what else to say. Embarrassed by the unexpected focus on that part of me, I deflected it. "Do you want children?"

She took a few moments to formulate a reply. "I don't think a single, unpartnered woman who works this kind of job should be thinking about parenthood. Maybe later. There's still plenty of time."

I thought about something my father used to say: Time is the greatest teacher, but eventually it kills all of its students.

Kay said, "I came here because I'd like you to take a look at this."

She handed me a piece of paper. It was a photocopy of something printed in large letters, like the letter the police had retrieved from the library's mutilated copy of *Walden* two days earlier. She said, "We're checking the original for prints. I doubt that we'll find any."

LOBSTERS

Lobsters are innately stupid, and lobsters are instinctively aggressive, and this is not a happy combination.

The thick rubber bands that get placed on their pincers are not for the protection of people. They are for the protection of the lobsters, who tend to rip their own bodies and those of their confreres to shreds.

And men are innately stupid, and men are instinctively aggressive, and again this is not a happy combination.

But a man needs to know but little more than a lobster in order to catch him in his traps.

I have caught three so far: soldiers in an army aligned with the land and the past, and against the people and the future. I would prefer to stop. But I am willing to continue, and con-

*tinue I will: until Concord awakens to the spirit of the people
once again.*

I believe this will happen.

The True Believer

Kay said, "He placed the letter in an envelope, addressed it
to the police, taped it to a rock, and tossed it through a window
of Middlesex Savings before dawn. That got our attention.
What do you think of it?"

"I don't know what to think."

"I was hoping you would come with me today while I look
into this."

"Why?"

"Because I still can't run fast." She paused. "That was a
joke, Harry."

"Oh."

"In fact, Veronica made me promise not to let you engage in
any more heroics."

"She thinks I'm an idiot for running after Michael Hindermuth at the mall."

"Well, so do I." She smiled. "But I appreciated it very much,
nonetheless. By the way, his alibi checks out. He was in
Florida, just like he said he was, when Sandi O'Neill was killed
and her car was stolen."

"I'm not surprised."

"Neither am I. Also, he wears a size ten shoe, too big for the
footprint at Mrs. Claymore-Whitley's house. Anyway, I'd like
you to help me out, because now that we know it wasn't Steven
throwing a smokescreen with these letters, I'm assuming the
writer—the killer—is a head case. I'm going to talk with some
people who have been vocal on the side of developing the
Logan tract. I'll start with Max Rothman and that Butler fellow.
You've met them. I haven't. Maybe you can help me figure out
if either one of them could be our killer. But before we do that,
I want you to come with me to see Davey Waterstone."

"Why do you want to see him?"

"When I spoke with him last week, I didn't even know the identity of the first victim, and I certainly didn't know anything about the reason for her murder. A lot has happened since then. Perhaps our so-called Lord of Walden will have some notions about who is killing off the friends of Walden."

The phone rang again. I answered it and heard my daughter's voice. "Dad—I almost forgot. I left a bracelet at Uncle Bobby's house last week. I'll ask Wendy to take me to Uncle Bobby's after dinner, and then I'll be home."

47

The expansive lawn of Davey Waterstone's multiacre estate was well-tended, but there were no other marks of a landscaper's care: no flower beds or sculpted shrubbery. The wraparound porch of the large house had no outdoor summer furniture.

Kay said, "It almost looks like no one lives here."

"No one does."

"What do you mean?"

"You mentioned it yourself when we were at the North Bridge on Sunday. Davey lives in a trailer behind the house. I'm sure he pays to have someone keep the place up, but he doesn't use it."

"Oh, right. But he said I should come to the house, not the trailer."

"I suspect the trailer tends toward mild squalor. Maybe he's embarrassed to entertain there."

Davey greeted us at the front door and led us into a spacious tile foyer. The foyer rose to the three-story height of the house, and sunlight poured through a skylight that ran its entire length and width.

He was dressed in denim pants and a work shirt. His long hair, normally pulled back into a ponytail, was parted in the middle and hung down to his shoulders. He offered us coffee, but neither one of us wanted any.

"I didn't know I'd be seeing you today, Harry. I can't recall the last time I had two visitors at the same time."

He brought us into a library that was two stories high and fifty feet square. Oak bookcases, filled to near capacity, lined the walls.

Kay said, "I asked Harry to help me sift through certain aspects of this case because I think a psychiatrist might have a useful perspective. And I'm here to ask for your help, because of what you know about Walden."

Davey waited until we sat, then took his place on an over-stuffed easy chair. " 'I had three chairs in my house. One for solitude, two for friendship, three for society.' " He paused. "That's from *Walden*."

"I was referring to Walden Pond, not the book."

"Oh. How can I help you?"

"The police department has received two letters from the killer. It seems pretty clear that his motives are political, for want of a better word. Not personal."

"I heard them say on the news that the killer is some sort of fanatical antipreservation nut. Makes sense, given the obvious common theme in the victims he picked."

"Did you know them?"

"I never met the young woman. What was her name again?"

"Sandra O'Neill."

"I knew the others, of course. They lived here all their lives, like me. Abby was an acquaintance of my parents' when I was a boy. And Alex was a year or two behind me at Groton."

"Did you like them?"

"I didn't know her well enough to like or dislike. And as for Alex, well, Harry can tell you that he wasn't the kind of man one could easily like. Still, hard not to feel bad for him, with his son serving time over at the local prison."

"Do you think Sandra O'Neill knew the other victims?"

He shrugged. "I have no idea. I've never been a part of any organized effort to save the woods. My involvement has been more personal. They've been a haven for me, like Estabrook Woods on the other side of my property. I spend time at Walden, sometimes teach people about it. But as you might have heard, I'm not much for keeping company or being a part of things."

Kay glanced around the room. "I would get lost in here."

"I *have* gotten lost in here. Many a time."

"You know, Davey—may I call you Davey?"

"Of course."

"It seems to me that you could be at risk if the killer continues to target enemies of the development project."

"I doubt that I would make anyone's list. I'm not a lightning rod for people's beliefs. I keep to myself. What's that saying? 'One man's terrorist is another man's patriot'? Well, you can count me out. I've had enough of that in my life. I don't need it anymore." He paused. "Well, I guess none of that is relevant to the matter at hand. What is it you want to know?"

"Have you ever heard of anyone threatening to use violence over Walden Woods?"

"I've heard people on the preservation side talk about strapping themselves to trees, or sabotaging bulldozers. But I've never heard anyone on either side talking about hurting anyone. Of course, if you really thought it, you probably wouldn't say it."

"Do you know Max Rothman?"

"The developer? No. Why? Do you think he might have something to do with it?"

"I'm just looking for somewhere to begin thinking about this."

"Well, I'm old rich, and he's new rich. We old rich folks are prepared to believe just about anything about the new rich. But I don't know anything specific about that person."

"How about Robert Kennedy Butler?"

Davey glanced at me. "We saw him at the pizza shop a few days ago, remember?"

"I remember."

He scowled and made a dismissive gesture with his hand. "He's an irritating young man, but I doubt he would have the stomach for something like this. Mostly, he's an inadequate, spoiled child who will never live up to his legacy."

Kay said, "Are you referring to his father?"

He nodded. "His father worked for Robert Kennedy and gave all that money to civil rights organizations. So now he runs that silly little group—if you want to call something that small a group—that lobbies for affordable housing."

"He's made some controversial statements, writing letters accusing people of racism. Angry stuff."

"Well, what he says is true, at least as it applies to some people in town. But like I said, he's not the one you're looking for. Hell, even old Abigail Claymore-Whitley probably could have pounded the living crap out of him. He doesn't compare to his father, or the ones who came before."

I remembered something odd that Butler had said at the pizza shop. "He said his grandmother was a prostitute."

Davey looked puzzled. "He said what?"

"When you and he were trading insults on Monday. He said his family goes back in Concord just as far as yours does. Then you called his grandmother a prostitute. He agreed with you, and he even seemed proud of it."

He thought for a moment, then broke into broad laughter. "*Now* I get it. You think you heard me call his grandmother a whore."

"Yes."

"His grandmother was a Hoar, spelled H-O-A-R. The Hoars had deep roots here, although I don't think any of them remain here. In his own way, I suppose he's trying to carry on that part of the family tradition, too."

"What do you mean?" Kay asked.

"Are you familiar with King Philip's War?"

Kay and I looked at each other, equally ignorant.

Davey said, "Perhaps you know who Massasoit was."

"The Indian," Kay said.

I said, "Plymouth Plantation. The treaty with the pilgrims."

Davey nodded. "That's correct, class. He was chief of the Wampanoag Indians, although perhaps we should consider using the term 'Native Americans.' Anyway, his son, Meta-comet, became known as King Philip. Metacomet led an uprising in the 1670s that became known as King Philip's War. Should I continue?"

We both said, "Yes."

"The English executed three Wampanoags for murder, and one thing led to another, and the next thing you know there was a war that involved several tribes and all of the New England colonies. Sort of like World War One, where some Serbian nationalist assassinated an Austrian archduke, and the next thing you know practically every country in the world is pissed off at someone."

He paused. "Once upon a time I wanted to be a history teacher." He sighed. "But I digress. Anyway, it was a terrible and bloody time, with atrocities on both sides. By the time they killed Metacomet and impaled his head on a pole, the war had practically ended the Indian presence in Massachusetts."

He continued. "Concord lost many men. There was a regrettable lust for revenge. Several years earlier Concord had developed a village for Indians who wanted to become Christians. They were called the Praying Indians. There were about sixty of them. The Praying Indians were peaceful. They caused no harm during the war, and probably helped shield Concord from more harm just by being present here. But they were Indians, and I guess all Indians looked the same to the colonists. So an armed party rode out to the village to arrest them. One man spoke out against this. John Hoar, our friend Butler's forefather. He thought the town folk were merely using the war as an excuse to rid themselves of the Praying Indians, that racial prejudice was the real reason."

I said, "That sounds like Alex Mason. I've always assumed he wasn't so much interested in saving the woods as he was in keeping certain kinds of people out of Concord."

"Well, our friend Butler would agree with you on that point. Anyway, all of the Praying Indians were arrested and put into prison or slavery. End of history lesson." He paused. "At that particular moment John Hoar was a lone voice against racism in Concord. And Robert Kennedy Butler's grandmother was a Hoar."

Kay said, "Do you have any suggestions regarding whom I

should question about the murders, other than Rothman and Butler?"

"I don't know. Money is always a powerful motivator. I guess I would look at anyone who has a financial stake in avoiding delays in the Logan tract project. Rothman's banker, any other investors. The Logan family probably won't get all their money until the project is under way, so they would likely have an interest in keeping things moving forward. Other than that, I don't know."

Kay said, "If you think of anything, please call me."

"I will. I hope you solve this very soon. This is a terrible cloud for the town to live under. Too many funerals. I suppose I'll attend the services for Abby and Alex. I didn't know the young woman, and I suppose her family will be burying her in New York or wherever it is they're from."

I said, "Actually, she has no family to speak of." I told him about Steven staying at my place, and about his plans for a memorial Mass the next morning. "On Saturday, around sunrise, Veronica and I will help him spread the ashes at Walden. He says that's what Sandi would have wanted."

Kay stood to leave, and I followed suit. Then she turned to Davey and said, "The stories you heard in the news about the police having evidence to link the murders is true. I planted the story, without giving any details, because I thought it would help control wild speculation. I didn't tell the press about the letters, and I would appreciate it if you would keep that knowledge secret for now."

"Of course." He stood. "I'll show you out."

We returned through the tiled foyer to the front entrance. Davey Waterstone said, "As long as I already know about the letters, would you like me to read them? Maybe I'll see something you've overlooked."

Kay hesitated for a moment. "I don't see why not." She took the photocopies out of her purse and handed them to Davey.

He read the first one, then the second, and then said, "Well, he certainly has a sense of irony, doesn't he?"

"What do you mean?"

"The quotations he used." He paused. "Oh. I assumed you recognized them."

Kay and I exchanged a confused glance.

Davey said. "These are photocopies. May I circle some passages?"

"Okay."

He made marks on the letters with his pen, then held the pages in front of us for our inspection. These words from the first letter were circled:

Because the only obligation which I have a right to assume is to do at any time what I think right.

Because those who do not understand this have the same sort of worth only as horses and dogs.

He had selected this sentence on the second letter.

But a man needs to know but little more than a lobster in order to catch him in his traps.

Kay said, "What's the significance of the words you've marked off?"

"They were written by Thoreau. The line about the lobster is from *Cape Cod.* The others are from *Civil Disobedience.* Perhaps I was too quick to dismiss Mr. Butler from consideration."

"Why do you say that?"

"*Civil Disobedience* is the Bible for nonviolent protest movements. Gandhi cited it. So did Martin Luther King. The two of you, my friends, may not have read it. But I bet Robert Kennedy Butler has."

48

"She never showed up," Max Rothman said.

"She never showed up?" repeated Kay Wheaton.

"Is there an echo in here? The woman never showed up. Which was fine with me."

"If she didn't come here—"

The phone on his desk rang. He answered it without offering us an excuse or apology. "What? . . . Yeah . . . Yeah . . . No fucking way! That is un-fucking acceptable. Tell him that . . . Well, put the stupid son of a bitch on and I'll tell him myself. I'll wait." He grabbed a pen and began to write a note on the pad next to the phone.

Max Rothman Enterprises occupied half of the top floor of an office building in North Cambridge, near the Arlington and Somerville town lines. From his window I could see the multi-level parking lot for the Alewife subway station. Alewife marked the northernmost end of the Red Line, which went under five Cambridge squares—Davis, Porter, Harvard, Central, and Kendall—then through Boston and all the way to Braintree. There at the southernmost end, seventy-five years earlier, another murder case with political overtones began, when Nicola Sacco and Bartolomeo Vanzetti were arrested for the slayings of a shoe factory paymaster and guard. There was worldwide outrage when they were convicted. In 1977, Governor Dukakis signed a document that proclaimed their innocence. Sacco and Vanzetti, having been executed fifty years earlier, were unavailable for comment.

Rothman slammed the phone onto the receiver. "I'm tired of waiting. The schmuck can call me back. This was one shitty day even before the two of you got here. Where were we?"

Kay said, "You were saying that Sandra O'Neill didn't meet with you last Thursday."

"She didn't come. She didn't call. I didn't care."

"She had you marked down in her appointment book for four in the afternoon, a week ago today."

"Look. She called me maybe two or three days before then. Told me who she was—"

"You never met her before?"

"No. She told me who she was and said she wanted to meet with me. I said I was busy. She kept bugging me. I told her I might be free late in the afternoon but that she should call ahead because things change. Look." He moved some papers aside on his desk, revealing a monthly blotter calendar. He pointed to the date in question, August 24. "Do you see anything written down for four o'clock?"

"No."

"And here." He opened a personal-size appointment book. "What do you see?"

"Nothing."

"Right. And over there." He pointed to a three-month project board that took up most of the wall to our left. "Do you see her name?"

"No."

"Exactly. That's how interested I was in seeing her; I didn't even write her name down. Didn't even remember she had called until I saw her name in the paper the day before yesterday, after they finally identified her body."

"Why didn't you call the police at that point?"

"To say what? That some woman I don't know didn't make it to an appointment I never wanted in the first place on account of she was dead, which you already knew? Come on, lady. I didn't give it a second thought."

I was still looking at the wall where the project board hung.

There were large photographs of several construction sites hanging next to the project board. One in particular caught my eye.

Kay said, "Mr. Rothman, would you be this unpleasant, unhelpful, and disrespectful if you were talking to a *male* police detective?"

"Absolutely. Ask Kline over here. Kline, am I a pleasant person?"

"I don't know you that well."

"As far as you know, am I a pleasant person?"

"No, as far as I know, you're not a pleasant person."

"And am I a helpful person? Again, as far as you know."

"No, you're not a helpful person, as far as I know."

"And am I—what was that third one? Am I a respectful person?"

"I'd say you're a perfect oh-for-three."

He turned toward Kay. "There. I rest my case. You being a woman has nothing to do with it."

I pointed toward the wall and said, "Are those pictures of your current projects?"

"Yep."

"Mind if I take a look?"

"Nope."

I walked over to the wall.

He said, "Listen, detective. Nothing personal here. But I can't help you, and I'm dealing with some serious shit."

The phone rang. He picked it up. *"What now?! . . .* I'll call him back." He slammed the phone down again. "I would be grateful if you would leave here and go out and find the asshole who's screwing around with my project."

"Excuse me?"

"That was my primary lender's office calling. Ever since the news broke that someone is trying to kill off people who oppose my Walden project, they're getting very nervous. Bankers don't like controversy. They don't even like their names mentioned. Whoever this murderer is, if he thinks he's doing this project a favor, he's got another think coming."

"What time did you leave your office last Thursday, Mr. Rothman?"

"Hell, I don't know. Five-thirty, six."

"Where were you last night at eleven?"

"Home."

"And the night before, say, around midnight?"

"Home."

"And your wife was there, I suppose?"

"You can suppose again. She's at one of her goddamn spas for the week. Two thousand dollars so she can come home six ounces lighter, with herbal vitamin supplements and bottles of special cream that run the bill up another three hundred. Why are you asking? You want to know if *I* killed the old lady and the creep?"

"The question did pass through my mind."

"Listen. Max Rothman plays by the rules. If I don't like them, I try to get them changed. But I play by them. Twenty-five years in this business, dealing with business scum and labor scum and any kind of scum you can think of, and no one has ever had cause to question the way I do things. Check it out. You'll find it's so."

"What size shoe do you wear?"

"Nine, nine and a half. Depends. Why? You got a footprint?" He laughed. "Hey, maybe it was O.J. with those Bruno Maglis."

I looked closely at one of the photographs. "This construction site is in Bedford, isn't it?"

"Yep. You know it?"

"I was there yesterday. So were you, Kay. Take a look."

She walked to the wall and studied the picture. "Well, I'll be damned." She pointed her finger at the parking lot, which was empty in the photo, and brought it to rest precisely where we had found Sandi O'Neill's car the day before.

She turned around and faced Rothman. "I want the names of everyone who has worked on this site in the past two weeks. You see, maybe you'll get a chance to be helpful, after all."

49

The Committee for Affordable Concord Housing—CACH for short—had its office above a dry cleaner in West Concord, where rents were lower than in the center of town. The office consisted of two small rooms that were separated by an archway without a door.

In one room there was a photocopy machine, along with some flyers waiting on a table to be folded. The other room had a computer and a single phone. That was where we found Robert Kennedy Butler.

He was alone in the office. I suspected that was a relatively common state of affairs. It looked very much like a one-person operation, with occasional help from an idealistic volunteer; I wondered if there had ever been more than three people in the office at any one time.

Robert Butler was sitting on a frayed couch, looking out the window. He turned to greet us, didn't stand up, and returned his gaze to the window. There was a day's worth of stubble on his youthful face, and his clothes were wrinkled.

He was expecting Kay, but he was surprised to see me. "I remember you. You're Waterstone's friend." He laughed: a bitter, mirthless laugh. "*He* must be feeling pretty good right about now."

"Why do you say that?" Kay asked.

"The irony of the whole thing. Some moron goes around killing people who are opposed to the Logan tract development—

or at least that's what the news reports are saying. But the up-shot is probably going to be more publicity and support for the people trying to stop that development." He sighed. "I'd offer you coffee, but I haven't made any."

"Did you sleep here?"

"Yes." He yawned. "What time is it?"

"Noon."

"I just got up a little while ago. Sorry."

His manner was deflated, almost depressed: a far cry from the angry, arrogant young man I had seen two times earlier that week.

"Why did you sleep here last night?"

"I live by myself in Cambridge. Sometimes it's just as easy to stay here."

"Do you drive here from Cambridge?"

"Sometimes. Usually I walk up to Porter Square and take the outbound commuter train that stops down the block from here."

"Is that what you did yesterday?"

"Yes."

"How about the night before? Tuesday night. Did you sleep here?"

"No. I was at my mother's house in Brookline. My sister and her family are visiting from San Francisco. We went out to dinner, and I slept over. Why do you ask?"

Kay didn't reply immediately to his question. After a few seconds he said, "Wait a minute. Are you trying to see if I have an alibi? You can't be serious. Well, call my mother if you want to, ask her about Tuesday night. I don't have anything for last night."

"How about last Thursday evening, when the woman was murdered at Walden Pond?"

Robert Butler thought for a moment. "I was with my father. He came up from Hartford to see my sister's family. On Thursday evening he took me out to dinner and then to the Red Sox game. I suppose he's trying, belatedly, to bond with me. Unfortunately, I hate Mexican food, and I hate baseball."

"Where did you eat?" Kay asked.

"Sol Aztec, something like that."

"Sol Azteca," I said. "What did you have to eat?"

"What does that have to do with anything?"

"Nothing," I replied. "I was just curious. I eat there all the time."

"Oh. I don't know what they called it. Some sort of shrimp entrée with a green sauce that wasn't too spicy for me."

"Camarones al cilantro," I said. "Grilled shrimp in a sauce made with coriander."

"If you say so." He turned to Kay. "You can call my father, too." He gave her his parents' separate phone numbers.

She said, "Have you ever read anything by Thoreau?"

"Just *Walden*, which I forced myself to read last year. I didn't like it."

"Why not?"

"Well, for one thing, I think it's hypocritical to write about living close to nature when your cabin is right next to a train track you can use as a path to the center of town, less than a mile away. I hear that when he finally saw *real* wilderness, up near Mount Katahdin in Maine, he couldn't handle it." He paused. "But there was something else I didn't like."

"What was that?"

"He went to Walden when he was twenty-eight, just a year older than I am now. He wrote the book a few years later. I didn't like his attitude. Condescending. Conceited. So sure that he knew more about important things than everyone else, no matter how much more experience they may have had. And if he didn't know about it, then it couldn't have been important. In short, he sounded like the sort of man who no sensible person would want as a friend. Regrettably, he reminded me of myself."

Kay interviewed him for another fifteen minutes or so. None of her questions implied a supposition that he might have been involved in the killings, so I assumed she was satisfied that his alibis would check out. She was interested in knowing who else was active or vocal in the effort to turn the Logan tract into a housing development. With apparent reluctance, he named some people.

"Most of them are students," he said. "Some high school, some college. A lot of them are Concord kids who are slumming. Working for social change from a position of comfort and privilege. Well, that's not their fault, I guess."

"Who funds this committee?" she asked.

"Max Rothman has chipped in, for obvious reasons. A few scattered checks for small amounts of money from some other people. But for the most part, it's me. Thank goodness for the Hoar and Butler generation-skipping trust funds."

He turned toward me. "In the pizza shop the other day, you heard me criticize your friend for not having a job, not doing anything constructive. The truth is, at least he once did something, or so I've heard. But me—what have I done? I write a few letters, I get some people riled up, three people are killed, and I'll probably wind up closing this so-called committee down. Not much to show for a life, is it?"

"You're still young," I replied.

"Well, they say it creeps up on you. One day all you're worried about is your sex life, then before you know it you're worried about dying. Or as my father so inelegantly puts it, 'Pussy today, prostate tomorrow.' " He looked at me, eyes questioning, and said, "Is that really the way it is?"

50

The moment we left Robert Butler's office, Kay used her

The moment we left Robert Butler's office, Kay used her
cell phone to call his mother's number. The woman confirmed
what Butler told us about his whereabouts on the night of Abigail Claymore-Whitley's murder. She also confirmed, secondhand, Butler's account of his visit with his father at the time
Sandi O'Neill was killed.

We stopped for a late lunch at the pizza shop on Thoreau
Street, where Davey Waterstone and I had sat together three
days earlier. There were no other customers there.

I said, "Robert Butler was a lot different when I saw him here
on Monday. Feisty. Confrontational. Not the subdued, introspective guy we just talked to. What? Why are you laughing?"

"I'm sorry," she said, "It's just that word. 'Feisty.' I don't
think I've ever heard it used regarding a man before. People
use it to describe a woman who's assertive or combative."

"Like you."

"Is that how you see me?"

"If I were in a tight spot, I would want you on my side." I
paused. "Now what?"

She bit lightly on her lower lip: a contemplative pose.
"That's a nice thing to say about someone. I'm not used to re-
ceiving compliments from men who aren't trying to hit on me.
I feel like I need to reciprocate."

"I was making a statement of fact. You're not obligated to
say anything in return."

The counter clerk called out. "Pizza's ready."

"I'll get it," Kay said.

She paid the clerk for our large pepper-and-onion pizza and brought it to the table.

"I owe you," I said.

"You can get it the next time."

Two young women walked in, paid for a take-out order, and left briskly without a word to one another or a glance at anyone else.

Kay said, "Everyone is very quiet today."

"Yes. I noticed it in town this morning. It's always quiet in Concord during the last week of August, but it seems unusually so today."

She uncapped her Diet Pepsi and pulled a pizza slice onto her paper plate. "I'm not surprised Butler's alibis check out."

"Me neither. I don't think he's cutthroat enough to be the True Believer."

"Cutthroat. An interesting choice of words, given the situation."

"What do you mean?"

"That's how Alex Mason met his end. Ear-to-ear, and deep. One step shy of decapitation."

"Do you want the entire pizza to yourself? Is that why you choose this particular moment to regale me with the details?"

"Oh. Sorry. Shop talk. I forgot you work in a different shop. Anyway, I agree with you about Butler. I don't think he's our killer."

"What do you think of Rothman?"

She thought for a few seconds. "I think he's very, very clever. Too clever to abandon Sandi's car at one of his own construction sites. Maybe it's just a coincidence that the car wound up where it did. Or maybe he paid someone less clever than him to kill her, someone who works at that site. That's a long shot, but I wouldn't discount the possibility without checking into some of the people who work there. Maybe someone saw something. Maybe someone heard something. But like I say, it's a long shot."

"Remember I told you on our way there that he and I played tennis last Sunday?"

Kay nodded.

"He did something that was pretty striking at the time, maybe even more so in retrospect."

I told her about the wager: his two hundred dollars versus a hamburger. And I described the end of the match: Rothman called my winning shot in play when he had the perfect opportunity to call it out-of-bounds.

"He was pissed as hell," I said. "Cursed at me and stormed off the court, two hundred dollars poorer. But he called it as he saw it, even when it worked against him. He played by the rules, just like he said he does."

"What are you saying—that just because he played honorably in some male-versus-male war dance, he wouldn't be involved in murder?"

"I'm just saying it's something to consider."

We finished our lunch and drove toward my house. Kay didn't need my help anymore that day, and that was fine with me.

It was one of those late summer afternoons that reveal Concord in all its beauty: flower beds outside the colonial homes on Main Street, tasteful displays in the gift shop windows. A few bicyclists had paused for a break in the shade of a tree on the grassy ellipse in the center of town.

Kay drove up the long gravel driveway to my house. Steven was standing outside the door to the barn apartment. With him was a muscular black man whose right arm was in a sling. I had no idea who he was. Kay said, "Well, I'll be damned," and stepped out of the car.

I walked with her toward the two men. She looked at the stranger and said, "I didn't expect to see *you* again."

"Me either," came his reply.

She turned to me and said, "This is the man who got me shot."

"And you're the lady that got *me* shot." He pointed toward her leg with his left hand. "You okay?"

"Better than you, from the looks of things. How is your arm?"

"Interesting doing with your left hand the things you do with your right hand your whole life."

Steven introduced me to Roy Stamis, his studio engineer. "Roy took the train up for Sandi's memorial Mass. I'm hoping it's all right with you if he stays with me in the barn. We'll probably leave after we spread the ashes on Saturday."

"Of course."

"Thanks." He turned to Kay. "Any luck?"

"I'm working on it, Steven."

"I'm sorry I was so curt with you last night. Anything you want to know, just ask."

"I will. Thanks."

Steven and Roy went inside. I walked Kay to her car.

A soft breeze blew through the trees and scattered a few early turning leaves. She said, "Alfred Korvich told me that the prettiest trees in autumn are actually the weakest ones, the ones that are likely to die sooner."

"Food for thought."

"Yes."

I looked around at the picture-perfect scene: high pines on the left, maple trees on the right, the rolling field behind the house, the woods and wildlife refuge beyond the field.

I said, "Some things happen in Concord the same as they happen elsewhere. Child abuse. Spouse battering. Racism. Substance abuse. They're not obvious, but they exist. I hear about them from my patients. You probably hear about them, too. Things like that cut across boundaries. There aren't any armed sentries to turn them away at the town line just because Emerson and Thoreau once lived here. Hell, I know for a fact that one of the largest new homes in town was built with co-caine money. But this is not the sort of place where terrible murders occur, one after another."

"Harry, my deluded friend," said Detective Kay Wheaton. "Obviously, you are very, very wrong."

51

Roy Stamis was a gourmet cook. He surveyed the ingredients on hand in the kitchen, sent Steven to the supermarket for some other items, and—even though limited to using only one arm—whipped up a delicious summer seafood dinner for the four of us.

We learned that Roy knew Sandi before Steven had met her. As Veronica and I cleared the dishes, Roy talked about some of his happy memories of Sandi. He was garrulous and friendly, easy to like, and he was on a one-man mission to help Steven through the memorial Mass and the dispersion of Sandi's ashes.

Melissa called from Wendy's house to tell me they were getting ready to leave. She was going to stop at Bobby's house to pick up her bracelet, then come home.

After dinner Steven borrowed my portable steamer; he returned to the barn to work the creases out of the suit that Roy had packed and brought up from Brooklyn. Veronica took Roy on a sunset drive around town. I stayed behind; I wanted to be at home when my daughter returned.

Melissa called again a short while later. She was crying. "Oh, Daddy. It's just terrible. I think he's going to die."

"*What?!* Where are you? What are you talking about?"

Now Wendy's voice was on the other end of the line. "It's a cat, Harry. We're outside your friend Bobby's house, and the kids found a badly injured cat. I just called the police on my cell phone, but I think the animal will die by the time they get here."

They had arrived a few minutes earlier. They found a note on the front door from Bobby; he had taken his dog for a walk and would be back shortly. While they were waiting for him, Melissa and Wendy's young daughter, Jennifer, played in the yard and came upon the cat.

The sight of any dead or injured animal always made Melissa frantic. She wasn't that way as a very young child. It started sometime after her mother died. I remembered offering to get a dog or cat for her sixth or seventh birthday, thinking it might be good for her to have a pet for a companion. But she refused. "Pets die," she said.

I asked Wendy to put Melissa back on the line. She was still sobbing. I said, "Come home now, sweetheart. You can get your bracelet from Uncle Bobby some other time. There's nothing you can do to help the cat, and it's just making you upset."

"Wait, Dad. I think I hear Uncle Bobby walking up the driveway. Maybe he can help."

52

Twilight descending. The time of the fox: *Vulpes fulva*.

The True Believer walked toward the lawyer's house. He saw the girl. She was probably about twelve years old. She was talking on a cellular phone. And she was weeping.

A much younger girl clung to a woman, apprehensive. The woman was stroking the little girl's hair.

This was unexpected: That morning the lawyer said his family was out of town. Now what should he do?

The crying girl put the phone down and called out to him. "Uncle Bobby, there's a . . . Oh. I thought you were my uncle Bobby."

Had she not seen him, he would have retreated. Too late for that now: It would only arouse suspicion. He approached them.

The younger girl looked very much like her mother. Not so the older girl. Coloring and features very different. Adopted, perhaps, or just favoring her father more than the younger girl did. Or maybe not the woman's daughter.

"Mr. Beck is expecting me. We have a short business meeting scheduled."

The woman said, "He'll be back in a few minutes."

"Is there something wrong?"

"Yes," the woman replied. "Obviously." She paused. "I'm sorry. This is just a little unnerving."

"What seems to be the problem?"

The older girl's voice quavered when she spoke. "Can you

come look? We found a cat. He's been hurt really bad. Maybe you can do something. Over there, by that tree. Please." She headed toward the tree, about thirty yards away.

He looked at the woman. "Shall I take a look?"

"If you wouldn't mind. I'm afraid I don't have the stomach for it."

He walked over to the older girl. She pointed to a spot about five yards away, trying to avoid looking. She closed her eyes and forced herself to breathe deeply, trying to remain in control.

He was never much for cats. They all looked the same to him. This was one of those nondescript gray house cats that—until now—had likely been destined, sooner or later, to make the close and fatal acquaintance of the wheel on a moving motor vehicle. But no longer. Its body was limp and mangled. Eyes lifeless and unfocused. Rich, warm froth bubbled from its mouth: internal bleeding, impossible to stanch. He did not know the cause; he was certain of the prognosis.

He stood and faced the girl. "What's your name?"

She continued to avoid looking at the animal. "Melissa."

He moved a step to his left, blocking her view of the cat. "Melissa, this cat won't survive. It's suffering badly. It would be inhumane to let it live any longer like this."

"You don't know that."

"I *do* know that. I've seen such things many times before. The proper thing for me to do is to kill it now. Quickly."

"Even if you're right about it dying, that doesn't make it right for you to kill it. You're not God."

"No, I'm not. But this is the order of things. This is what is proper."

Odd, he thought, yet touching: her caring for this anonymous animal. Had she not been there, he would have killed it in an instant. Or maybe not, since the cat's suffering was of no consequence to him. In any event, her being there—and her tears for the creature—made things different. Doing things properly took on momentary importance.

He said, "I won't kill it if you don't want me to."

She stood there quietly for several seconds.

"How old are you, Melissa?"

"Almost thirteen."

"Long ago, in some cultures, a person was considered to be an adult at that age."

"I'm not an adult. I never want to be an adult."

"You're an adult for now, Melissa. For this moment and for this decision. The cat will either suffer more and die soon, or suffer no more and die now. This is your call."

She turned away from him, facing the woman and young child who stood clinging to one another near the house. "Kill him," she said. "Please kill him for me."

"Don't look."

The True Believer wielded his knife like a surgeon. With one deft move he sliced completely through to the ground, severing the cat's head.

"Done," he said.

"Oh, God." The girl began to cry again, and she ran back to the others.

He walked to the side of the house. There he found a box of plastic trash bags and a large trash barrel. He grabbed a bag and walked back to the cat's carcass. With his knife he speared the head and dropped it into the bag, and then followed suit with the torso. He tied the ends of the bag, returned to the house, and tossed the bag into the trash barrel. He washed the blood from his knife with a hose.

He returned to the front of the house. The woman had one arm around each child, and they were all seated on a long patio couch.

A thought occurred to him. Not exactly a voice. More like a self-exhortation: *Take them all.* Unsuspecting. Defenseless. Take them all, and then take the lawyer. The houses in the neighborhood were set far apart, and it was getting dark enough to avoid being spotted by anyone else in the vicinity.

He was uncertain what to do. Options open. He approached the woman and children. He fingered the knife in his pocket. The inexperienced operative would strike the woman first. But she might fight, giving the twelve-year-old the chance to run. No: First kill the older child. The woman would instinctively turn to shield the younger child, leaving herself exposed. And then the younger child.

And then the lawyer.

Melissa looked up at him, cheeks streaked with tears. "Thank you for killing him. I know it wasn't an easy thing to do."

She was wrong about that, of course. But the anomaly—being thanked for his butchery—caught him by surprise. "You're welcome," he replied.

The girl smiled, and he was won over for the time being.

There had been enough killing for one night.

He turned to the woman. "You're lucky to have such a fine daughter. It's obvious this isn't a good time to have a business meeting. Tell Mr. Beck I'll call him."

He turned to leave, walked a few yards, then stopped and looked at the older girl. "Melissa, please tell your uncle he's lucky to have you for a niece. He doesn't know how lucky he is."

53

"This morning," said Father John Fitzpatrick, "our Gospel reading from Luke contained this passage. 'Forgive, and you will be forgiven.' "

We were at St. Bernard's Church on Friday morning. It was the regular weekday Mass. And it was the memorial Mass for Sandi O'Neill.

"Forgive and you will be forgiven. What a powerful notion that is."

Melissa, Veronica, and I were seated on the second row, alongside Roy Stamis. Steven sat in front, along with a half dozen of Sandi's friends and an elderly aunt who had made the trip from New York. Kay Wheaton had entered the chapel a few minutes after the service started; she sat in a rear pew.

"It's easy to love a friend. And it's simple to forgive that friend. But God asks us to love *all* of his children, even those who hate us and hurt us. And to forgive them.

"This isn't easy. But true happiness lies in following the example of Jesus. Returning kindness for unkindness, love for hatred, good for evil. God made you, and you, and me. And to love God, we must love one another. And forgive one another."

My friendship with John Fitzpatrick had brought me to Mass a few other times. There was nothing new to me in what he was saying. And as always, I didn't accept what he said. Surely some people were deserving of hatred. I was fond of something I read in college: *One should forgive one's enemies, but not before they are hanged.*

Now he looked directly at me. "Some of you are skeptical. Let me tell you about something that happened to me before I entered the priesthood."

He turned toward the rest of the people. "My brother and I had a falling out. For a year I refused to speak with him, and he refused to speak with me.

"On Mother's Day I went to my mother's house with gifts. But she wouldn't accept them. She said, 'I want only one gift from you. I want you to forgive your brother. I want the same gift from him. I love both of you. If you won't give me that gift, then your other gifts mean nothing to me.'

"That's how it is with God. We hurt Him when we hurt another of His children. And we show our love for Him by loving others. And by forgiving them.

"God loves Sandra O'Neill. He forgives her sins. But He also loves and forgives the tortured soul responsible for her death. He wants us to do the same. And to pray for both of them."

It was pretty standard stuff, delivered with no particular flair. But in the pew in front of me, Steven Farr was crying quietly.

54

Veronica had arranged a modest catered brunch for the small group of mourners. And so all of them—Steven, Roy, and Sandi's aunt and friends—came to the house directly from church.

Melissa asked to be excused from the affair, and I agreed. Then she asked if she could ride her bike to Bobby's house to pick up her bracelet; she had come home the previous night immediately after the incident with the cat, not waiting for Bobby to return from walking his dog.

"Uncle Bobby's not home," I said. "He drove up to Maine early this morning to join Aunt Cheryl and Kenny. They'll be back at the end of the weekend."

"Oh. Then maybe I'll ride over to a friend's house."

"No, sweetheart. That's not a good idea."

"Why not?"

"Because I'm not comfortable with you going anywhere on your own right now. It isn't safe."

I expected an argument, but she didn't offer one. She went upstairs to watch a video.

Kay dropped by to pay her respects. She had nothing new to report on the murder investigation. She greeted a few of Sandi's friends; she had met them when she went to New York a few days earlier.

Veronica was playing the role of hostess. Roy was in the kitchen, swapping cooking hints with the caterer.

Steven walked over to Sandi's friends but couldn't seem to work his way into their conversation. He grew tired of trying, and he retreated to the rear porch. I joined him there a few minutes later.

He looked out at the field, and at the woods beyond. "Pretty place," he said. "A lot different from the city. Sandi loved coming up here."

"Can I get you something to eat? Something to drink?"

"Not in the mood, thanks."

"It was nice of Sandi's friends to make the trip."

"Uh-huh. I tried to thank them, but they didn't seem interested in talking to me."

"Why is that?"

He shrugged. "I don't know. It's almost as if they blame me for what happened."

"I know what that's like. My wife died from cancer. But for a long time her father acted as if her illness were somehow connected with her decision to marry me."

"That doesn't make much sense. Hell, that doesn't make any sense at all."

"It's how he coped," I said. "He was angry that he lost her. He needed something to focus the anger on."

"So he focused it on you?"

"Yes."

"I guess I won't have that problem. Someone actually did this to Sandi. I'll have someone to focus on."

"You and a lot of others. Whoever he is, he's caused a lot of anxiety in this town."

"I don't understand what you mean."

"The killer. Three victims already. Who knows how many more?"

"Oh. I wasn't even thinking about that. I was just thinking about Sandi."

"That's understandable."

"Your friend Father John has been very helpful. He persuaded the funeral home to handle the cremation immediately so I can finish up my business here tomorrow. But I don't know about that forgiveness stuff. I don't think I'm ready for that."

"That's understandable, too."

"I figure it was probably Max Rothman, or someone working for him. He had the most to lose. And Sandi always said he wasn't to be trusted. She didn't get along well with him, and she didn't like him at all. Everytime she mentioned his name, she referred to him as a money-grubbing so-and-so."

In my mind I substituted "Jew" for "so-and-so," since that was the only word I had ever heard in connection with the term "money-grubbing." I wondered whether it was intended as an anti-Semitic remark. And if it was intended as such, was it a reflection of Steven's sentiments, or was he merely reporting what Sandi had said?

Veronica stepped onto the porch to ask if we needed anything. Then she returned inside.

Steven watched her leave, then turned to me and said, "I appreciate your letting me stay here this week."

"Not a problem."

"If Sandi had wanted to let an old boyfriend stay with us, I don't think I would have been so understanding."

"Offhand, I can't think of anything Veronica could ask me to do that I wouldn't do."

He smiled. "Is that because you love her, or is it because she carries a gun?"

I laughed. "Because I love her. But with a killer on the loose, I suppose I should look upon the gun as an extra added attraction."

"Let's hope she doesn't need it."

"As my grandmother used to say: 'From your mouth to God's ears.'"

He sighed. "Well, if God plans on doing anything about this, I'd say he's a little late."

55

Friday night passed in Concord without another visit from the True Believer.

On Saturday morning the five of us hiked single file along the north shore of Walden Pond. It was just past sunrise, and we had come to scatter Sandi O'Neill's ashes at the site of Thoreau's cabin. There was a taste of autumn in the air, and we all wore jackets against the unseasonable chill.

Melissa knew the way, and so she walked at the head of the line. I had been to the cabin site only once, several years earlier. The others had never been there. Veronica walked behind Melissa, followed by me and then Roy Stamis. Steven lagged several yards behind, understandably reluctant to arrive at the place where his fiancée was slain.

More than once Veronica had tried to dissuade Steven from his plan to scatter the ashes at that particular place. But each time he said, "This is what Sandi would have wanted." And so we walked on.

Steven carried the small box he had picked up the previous afternoon from the funeral home. It measured about eight inches on each side. It was cardboard, and it was wrapped in unmarked white paper. A small gold seal, embossed with the name of the crematorium, held the paper secure around the box.

It took us about fifteen minutes to walk from the lot on

Route 126 to our desination. We passed no one else, and nobody was at the cabin site when we got there. I assumed that
was due to the early hour. But maybe people were especially
reluctant that day to go for a walk in the woods—the woods at
Walden in particular.

A small, bare patch of ground marked the place where
Thoreau built his cabin in 1845. Nine granite posts, all the
same height of between two and three feet, marked the
perimeter. Nearby was a sign with a quotation from *Walden*, a
board with information about the excavation of the site, and a
large pile of rocks—some of them as big as a softball—that
had been left over the years as remembrances by visitors to the
site.

Steven's eyes darted back and forth, surveying the scene.
Perhaps he was wondering exactly where Sandi's body had
fallen. I knew from speaking with Kay where that spot was but
decided not to volunteer the information unless he asked me.

We stood directly in front of the cabin site. Steven placed the
box on the ground and said, "Just give me a minute. I'll be right
back." He walked down the short, gentle incline to the edge of
the pond.

From the direction of the nearby tracks, I heard the rumble
of an eastbound train as it headed past Walden on its way from
Fitchburg to Boston. Its whistle made a mournful sound.

Melissa said to me, "I changed my mind. I don't think I want
to be here to see him empty the ashes out of the box. Is it all
right if I walk up that path over there?"

"Yes," I replied. "Just stay within sight."

"I'm going to turn my back so I don't have to watch. Call me
when it's time to go." She walked to a spot about forty yards
away.

Steven rejoined us. He was crying. He said, "I guess I should
get this over with."

He unsealed the carton. Inside, atop the ashes, was a small
envelope with a metal tag. The tag had a serial number on it.
Steven put the tag in his pocket.

He circled the perimeter of the cabin site, scattering ashes as he walked. The box was empty by the time he rejoined us in front of the site.

Steven placed the empty box in the ground. "This will sound really stupid. I feel like I should say something, but the only thing I can think of is this old football cheer from high school. 'Ashes to ashes, dust to dust. You can beat anybody but you can't beat us.' "

Roy Stamis smiled. "The lady would have liked that. She was a good one, and now she's gone, but she would have laughed at that. The only one I remember is, 'Push 'em back, shove 'em back, w-a-a-a-y back.' "

Steven said, "We also had, 'Hit 'em high. Hit 'em low. Hit 'em where the Trojans go.' "

"Trojans?" said Roy.

"A brand name for condoms. But back then we called them rubbers."

I said, "I remember two cheers from high school. A few of the honor students went for, 'Repel them. Repel them. Compel them to relinquish the ball.' Most people preferred, 'Hit 'em with a pitchfork. Hit 'em with a broom. Fuck 'em up, fuck 'em up. Boom, boom, boom.' "

And so the three of us continued, laughing at our own juvenile humor.

Veronica smiled in spite of herself and said, "Men are very strange creatures, indeed."

And then, gradually, the laughing stopped.

And then the four of us stood there, each one lost in private thoughts.

And then I said a silent prayer for a woman I had never known.

And then . . . the first shot rang out.

56

The gun's retort echoed in the woods.

With his one good arm, Roy Stamis shoved Steven to the ground. Almost in the same movement, he knocked me over with a cross-body block, falling on top of me.

A few yards away, Veronica dropped to the ground at the same time.

"Dad!"

Roy's large form blocked me from seeing Melissa. His mass kept me pinned to the ground.

Veronica and I shouted to Melissa at the same time. "Get down!"

Another shot sounded and echoed. Veronica looked around, trying to locate its source.

"*Dad!*" Melissa sounded closer now, moving toward us instead of falling to the ground.

"Get down!" I tried to push Roy off of me.

Veronica said, "She isn't listening. I'll get her."

"*Daddy!*"

Veronica jumped to her feet. In that same instant, a third shot rang out.

The bullet's momentum knocked her body forward. Her head snapped back, her arms stretched out, and she fell to the ground with a whimper.

Melissa screamed. Still unable to see her, I feared she had

been struck. With a burst of adrenaline I pushed Roy Stamis away and rose to my feet.

Melissa was still on her feet, running toward Veronica. We both reached her at the same moment.

Roy yelled at us to stay down, but we were too focused on Veronica to pay attention to what he was saying.

Veronica writhed in obvious pain. Her left leg was soaked with blood. Her body quaked. Her pallor and unfocused gaze indicated she was already going into shock: either from pain, or from blood loss, or both.

I removed my jacket and placed it over Veronica to help keep her warm. I gave my cellular phone to Melissa and instructed her to call 911. That gave her something to do to keep her from becoming hysterical, and it left me free to work on Veronica.

I elevated her feet. She groaned when I moved her left leg. The wound was situated a few inches below her knee. I ripped my shirt off, wrapped it loosely around her calf, and applied pressure. She screamed again.

Steven and Roy rushed over. Now we were all open targets for the unseen shooter.

"Damn," Roy said.

Steven said, "This is all my fault."

I didn't know what he meant by that and didn't have the time to wonder.

Melissa told the police where we were and what had happened. In a quavering voice she said, "In the leg . . . Yes, that's what we're doing. My father is here, and he's a doctor . . . I don't know. I don't see anyone, and there haven't been any more shots . . . Okay. Please, please hurry."

When she was off the phone, I told her to lie on the ground behind one of the granite pillars.

Roy kneeled next to Veronica. He unslung his injured arm, wincing in pain. He grabbed both of her shoulders and kept her still, making it easier for me to keep the pressure constant on her leg.

Suddenly Steven shouted, "I think I see the bastard!" He pointed toward the railroad tracks, and he started to run in that direction.

Roy and I both yelled for him to stop, but he didn't listen. As he ran past the pile of rocks, he grabbed one without breaking stride.

Veronica's eyes were closed. Her breathing was rapid and shallow. I held the pressure on her leg as steady as I could. Each time I shifted my hands, Veronica groaned. She mumbled something; I couldn't tell for certain what she said, but it sounded as though she were asking me to stop hurting her. I thought it probable that the bullet had hit bone; that would account for her intense pain.

I was stuck with two unattractive options. If I applied pressure, the added pain could send her reeling into shock. If I loosened the pressure, the added blood loss could have the same effect. I knew my only choice was to keep the pressure on and hold the bleeding down.

I fumbled again with Veronica's leg, and she shook and made a sound of ungodly pain.

Roy said, "I have bigger hands. Let me do that." He took over the job of applying pressure.

I held Veronica's hand and pressed my lips to her forehead. She was ice cold.

Keeping low to the ground, I scurried to where my daughter lay.

"Will she be okay?"

"Yes, sweetheart," I replied, hoping I sounded more confident than I felt. "It's just a leg wound. The ambulance should be here soon, and the hospital is only a mile down Route 2."

"But . . . all that blood."

Yes, I thought. *All that blood.* I hoped the bullet hadn't severed her anterior tibial artery. If it had, it might be impossible to save her.

She sat up. "I'm scared, Daddy."

"I know, honey. I know." I pulled her toward me and held her in my arms.

Suddenly there came the sound of someone running, and Melissa said, "It's *him*! It's the man who killed the cat for me!"

I turned around. A familiar figure with a gray ponytail was rushing toward us. It was Davey Waterstone. No doubt he had heard the gunshots and was coming to help. The realization brought me instant relief.

But Davey ran past us, looking frightened and exhausted. And then I saw Steven, in close pursuit, still holding the rock he had taken from the pile.

When they were thirty yards beyond the cabin site, Steven closed the gap and leaped onto Davey's back. In the same motion he swung the rock forward onto Davey's skull.

Davey crumpled to the ground with Steven on top of him. The rock tumbled from Steven's hand and rolled away.

Steven sprang to his feet and began to kick Davey's prone form: here, there, and everywhere—repeatedly, and very, very hard.

"Oh, God," my daughter exclaimed.

I turned her around. "Don't watch this."

I ran toward Steven. Davey lay motionless, and still Steven continued to beat him. I shouted out for him to stop, but he didn't.

When I was almost upon them, Steven reached into Davey's jacket pocket and pulled out a handgun. He grasped it with both hands. I heard the click of the hammer as he cocked the gun.

I came to a halt ten feet away from Steven. Davey lay between us, moaning.

Steven aimed the gun barrel at Davey's back.

"Steven—no!"

He looked at me but kept the gun pointed toward Davey. "Self-defense, Harry."

"No, it's not."

"Justifiable homicide."

"You've practically killed him already."

"They'd never convict me."

"Yes, they would. I would see to that." I stepped over Davey Waterstone and stood between the two of them. "Put the gun on the ground, Steven."

I was bare-chested, shivering from the cold and from fear. We stared at each other for several seconds. And then he slowly lowered the barrel, and he placed the gun on the ground.

"Thank you," I said. "Go help Roy. Wait—leave your jacket here."

He dropped his jacket over the gun and walked off.

I moved the jacket aside. The gun was still cocked. I didn't know how to undo that, and I worried that someone would accidentally discharge it. I grasped the handle and fired a bullet into a nearby tree.

"Daddy!"

"It's all right, sweetheart! Stay where you are!"

I kneeled next to Davey. He whispered my name. I told him not to talk.

A light inspection of his body revealed probable rib and leg fractures. He bled profusely from the mouth, no doubt from internal injuries. His pulse and breathing were weak. There was little I could do. I doubted he could be saved. I placed Steven's jacket over him.

"Davey, can you hear me?"

He mumbled something.

"Stay as still as you can, but try to move your fingers and your feet."

There was no movement at all.

"Good," I lied. "Very good. An ambulance is on the way. Just hang in there."

He began to shake. Blood pooled by his mouth. His breathing was labored and he struggled to get words out. "Tell her . . . sorry . . ."

I glanced at his gun on the ground. "Why did you shoot at us?"

He shuddered. "I'm so cold . . . cold . . ."

I leaned closer to his ear and spoke loudly. "Why did you do it?"

"Didn't mean to hurt . . . just scare . . ."

"Why?"

"Walden," he rasped. "To save Walden."

"I don't understand. How is shooting at us going to save Walden?"

"Just scare . . . no more killing . . . done enough already."

"What are you talking about?"

"Alex Mason . . . Abigail . . . done enough."

It took a moment to sink in, so unexpected and unfathomable was the news. He was almost gone. I looked directly at him. And in that final moment our eyes met, and he knew that I knew. I said, "You killed them."

He nodded, almost imperceptibly.

"And you wrote the letters."

He nodded again.

"Why did you do it?"

"Sacrifices for the cause . . . old woman, nearly dead already . . . a man no one liked . . ."

"And Sandi O'Neill," I said. "Don't forget what you did to her."

"No," he said, with as much force as he could muster. "Not her. Someone else. But it started me thinking . . ."

And then he went still. There was no pulse and no breath, and I knew he was gone.

I rushed back to the cabin site, where my daughter was still facing away as I had told her to do. She was whimpering, trying to contain a scream.

"I'm all right," I said. "Let's help Veronica."

We hurried to Veronica's side. Roy had a firm grip on her leg, applying constant pressure.

Sweat poured down my bare chest, and I was shivering badly. Melissa draped her jacket over my shoulders.

I took Veronica's hand and checked her pulse. It was weak but steady.

Her eyes fluttered open. She looked at me and said, "I don't think I'll make it."

I held on to her hand. The words she had spoken Wednesday night found their way back to me. I said, "I refuse to let this be happening. You will *not* die on me. I refuse to lose you."

Roy kept hold of Veronica's bloodied leg. I kept hold of her hand. Melissa held the other hand and pressed her lips to Veronica's cheek.

Steven was nowhere in sight.

I heard sirens moving east on Route 2, along the northern border of the park.

57

I rode in the ambulance with Veronica. Roy Stamis and Melissa followed in a police cruiser. Steven was still nowhere to be found.

A police officer remained at the scene to guard Davey Waterstone's corpse until the medical examiner arrived.

Veronica was in and out of drowsy consciousness during the mercifully short ride to Emerson Hospital. I held her hand all the way there, and all the way until they wheeled her gurney into the surgery area.

While they were prepping Veronica for surgery, the doctor spoke with me. "We'll run a CBC, check her platelets. We'll zap the bleeders to keep her from losing more blood. I don't think the artery was severed. I hope I'm right. We'll do a scan, check for bone fragments, take them out if there are any. She's too shocky for general, so she'll have a spinal."

"Good luck."

"Yeah, good luck," he said, and then he was gone.

Melissa and I sat quietly for several minutes. Roy Stamis was having his gunshot wound redressed.

"I did this to her," Melissa said. "I got scared when the shots started. Too scared to know what do to. I ran toward you instead of falling down like you told me to do. That's why Veronica got shot, trying to protect me."

I touched her arm. "No, honey. You didn't do this. It was a frightening situation. If Roy hadn't knocked me over, I might have wound up doing the same thing you did. The important thing now is to say a prayer for Veronica." I paused. "What? What is it?"

"I don't remember you ever asking me to pray before. When Mom was sick, or even after she died."

I sighed. "There are things I would do differently if I had the chance."

She took hold of my hand and we sat waiting for some word on Veronica.

After another quarter hour Roy Stamis rejoined us. "How's it going?"

"They're still working on her."

"Well, I hope she's okay. She's a gutsy lady."

"You don't know the half of it."

He shifted in his seat, taking care not to bump his wounded arm. "You knew that guy?"

"Yes."

"Why did he do this?"

"He said he was just trying to scare us."

"Well, hell of a town you got here. And I thought Bed-Stuy was rough."

More time passed. There were no other people in the waiting area. There were no magazines. A television screen, sound muted, was set high on one wall. "That makes no sense," I said.

"What?" Roy replied.

"CNN without sound. It's like listening to radio with the sound off."

Suddenly the doors to the emergency room waiting area swung open. Kay Wheaton and a uniformed officer walked in. Kay approached us.

"How is she?" Kay asked.

"We're waiting to hear."

"I just came from Walden. Can I speak with you over there for a minute, Harry?"

She gestured toward an empty couch on the far side of the waiting area. We walked there together.

She said, "Let me see if I have this straight. Davey Waterstone shot Veronica, and Steven pummeled him to death."

"Those are the highlights."

"I saw the body. Steven really beat him badly."

"Yes."

"Too badly, I think."

"Yes."

"What the *fuck* was that all about? And where the hell is Steven?"

"As to your second question, I have no idea. As to the first—"

Someone called my name. I turned around and saw the emergency room physician standing in the middle of the room removing his mask and gloves.

The four of us—Melissa, Roy, Kay, and myself—walked over to him.

"Her platelet level is good. A clean chip off the tibia. Got the fragment, no other floaters. Must have hurt like holy hell. The bullet missed the artery or we wouldn't be having this conversation right now. Even so, she lost a lot of blood. But she's one lucky woman, except for the fact that she was shot, of course. Without the first aid she got on the scene, she might not have survived. Might not even have made it here alive."

Melissa spoke up. "You're talking too fast. How *is* she?"

The doctor turned to Melissa and smiled. "I'm sorry. What I'm saying is, your mother is going to be just fine. A few days in the hospital to make sure she doesn't develop an infection. But in a couple of weeks, she'll be good as new."

No one corrected him for referring to Veronica as Melissa's mother.

Kay identified herself and flashed her police badge. "I'd like to speak with her."

The doctor shook his head. "In a few hours, maybe. Father and daughter, you can see her now, just for a few minutes. She's sedated, may not make much sense. But I'll take you in."

Veronica lay on her back in an intensive-care cubicle: very, very still. Her eyes were closed. She was hooked up to two IV lines: fluids feeding into one arm, blood into the other.

Melissa and I stood on opposite sides of the bed. She pointed with alarm to a line leading into Veronica's neck with a monitor at the other end. "What's that?"

"A CVP line. Central venous pressure. It's standard procedure. I'll explain later."

Veronica heard us talking. She opened her eyes partially. "I was shot," she said.

"Yes," I replied. "You're all right now."

"But . . . why?"

"I'll tell you later. You need to rest. The important thing is you're all right, and they got the guy who did it."

"And the two of you?"

"We're fine, other than being scared senseless."

"Steven and his friend?"

"They're all right, too."

She looked at Melissa. "I'm sorry if I scared you, honey."

"Oh, God," Melissa said, sniffling. "I was afraid you were going to die."

"You heard what your father said, didn't you? He refuses to let me die."

Melissa laughed and cried at the same time. Her nose began to run. She started to wipe it with her sleeve, then thought better of it and reached for the tissue box on Veronica's nightstand. She kissed Veronica's cheek and said, "I love you so much."

"And I love you. I also love whatever drug it is he gave me, and I hope he gives me a prescription for it. With many refills."

I patted her hand. "You should rest. We'll see you later."

She looked around the room. "No mirrors," she said. "I guess that's because I must look like hell."

"No," my daughter replied. "No, you don't. I think you're beautiful, inside out and outside in."

We returned to the waiting room. Melissa sat next to Roy.

Kay was standing by the exit. I walked over to her and asked if she would drive me back to Walden so I could get my car. I planned to drop Roy and Melissa off at home, then come back to the hospital in case Veronica needed me.

I said, "I assume sooner or later Steven will make his way

back to my house. You probably want to question him about what happened."

She looked very grim. "I'd like that very much, but it's not in the cards."

"What do you mean?"

"I'll have one of my officers drive your daughter and your friend home. I need you to come with me. There's a note in a sealed envelope, and it's addressed to you. Steven Farr had it in his pocket about twenty minutes ago when he walked out of the woods and stepped in front of a train."

58

"Believe it or not," the medical examiner said, "there are some days when I actually like this job." He looked at Kay and me. "This is *not* one of those days."

We were standing beside the commuter train track, at a spot about a quarter mile from the site of Thoreau's cabin. Nearby was the underpass that takes the track beneath Route 2.

A few yards away was a corpse, covered by a canvas tarpaulin. Farther down the track two teenage girls, visibly agitated, were sitting beside the embankment under the watchful eye of a police officer.

Kay said, "Have you released Waterstone's body yet?"

"The one up by the pond? Yes. The cause of death there is internal bleeding from a variety of injuries, apparently suffered from a blunt object or objects. The manner of death, of course, is homicide. You said someone saw the attack occur."

"Yes." Kay nodded toward me. "This is the witness."

"I'm Harry Kline."

"Ah," he said, "then you would be the gentleman to whom the deceased—this deceased, over here—addressed this." He reached into his jacket and produced a small sealed envelope with my name written on its front. He handed it to me.

Kay said, "I need to be present when you open that, Harry."

"Should I open it now?"

"Hold onto it for a couple of minutes." She gestured toward

Steven Farr's lifeless form. "Doc, tell me what happened to him."

"He was struck by an inbound train. The train was due to leave Concord station at twenty minutes after eight. Assuming it left more or less on time, the decedent was struck more or less at eight twenty-two. The engineer apparently didn't realize he hit anyone. He kept going. Your officer radioed the MBTA and asked them to hold the train at North Station in Boston, just in case you want to inspect it. Those girls witnessed what happened. One of them climbed up the embankment to Route 2 and flagged down a motorist. The motorist had a cell phone, and here we are." He shook his head. "I've never had a week like the one I've had this week."

"Me, neither," Kay said.

The medical examiner turned to me. "Do you have any idea who killed Waterstone?"

"Yes. Steven Farr. They're—they *were*—both acquaintances of mine."

"So Farr killed Waterstone, you witnessed it, and then he killed himself, and he left a note for you. Interesting."

Kay said, "Are you certain it was suicide?"

"It was suicide, if your witnesses over there are to be believed."

Kay and I walked alongside the track to the spot where the two girls sat. They looked about fifteen, high school age. They were huddled closely together, shivering and tapping their feet nervously. Kay identified herself and asked them to tell her what they had seen.

The first one said, "My mother is gonna kill me when she finds out I'm here. I promised her I'd never go near the tracks."

The second one said, "We were sitting up there, near the top of the slope. And we see this guy standing right next to the track, near where the trains to Boston come out after they go under Route 2. And I yelled to him, 'Hey, mister, train's gonna come through there in a few minutes. I was you, I'd get back.' Didn't I, Carla? Didn't I tell him to get back?"

"Kill me," the first one said. "She's gonna *kill* me."

"Anyway, he waves and yells something like, 'Sure,' or

'Okay.' But he keeps standing there. We heard the train in the distance, and he looked down the track. Then he pulled back out of view, so, like, the train wouldn't see him. And he did that a couple of times, and then just as the train starts underneath Route 2, he jumps onto the track. Isn't that right, Carla?"

The first one stood up. "She is absolutely gonna fucking *kill* me." She rolled her hand into a fist, placed it against her mouth, bit down on a knuckle, and screamed.

"Jesus, Carla. Lighten up. It's not like we knew the guy."

Kay turned to the uniformed officer. "You took their names and phone numbers?"

"Yes."

"Have their parents been called?"

"Yes. I told them I would bring the girls to the station after you finished interviewing them."

"Good. You girls can go now. This officer will take you to meet your parents."

"Great," said Carla. "That's just fucking, fucking, fucking *great*!"

The police officer helped the girls up the embankment.

Kay said, "I think Carla is having a bad day."

"I can relate to that."

She pointed to the envelope that was taken from Steven's pocket. "Let's take a look at that."

I opened the envelope. Inside was a single sheet of paper, and on that paper was a single line. It read: *Forgive, and you will be forgiven.*

59

It was only ten-thirty. Already that morning I had witnessed the scattering of Sandi O'Neill's cremains, a homicide, the aftermath of a suicide, and the shooting of the woman I loved. The last place I felt like being in was Alfred Korvich's Naugahyde palace. And yet that's where I was.

He was seated at his desk when we arrived. With a nod he bade us sit down across from him. He said, "I just got here. This was supposed to be my day off. On a scale of one to five, this sucks six ways to Sunday. Fall foliage season is coming. Rampant murder tends to drive away the tourist dollars. Especially unsolved rampant murder. And now I hear you have two more corpses for me, detective. I'm hoping I hear wrong."

"No, unfortunately, you heard correctly."

"Aaagh." He threw his hands up in the air. "Tell me none of this is happening. Tell me it's like Bobby Ewing on *Dallas*, and everything that's been happening is just a bad dream."

Kay said, "I can't tell you that. But I can tell you that I don't think there will be any more killing."

"Oh?" He paused. "I like that. Tell me more."

At Kay's request, I told Korvich about the sunrise visit to Walden: Davey Waterstone shooting Veronica, and Steven Farr killing Davey.

"Wait a second," he replied. "Two corpses. Veronica isn't . . ."

"No. She's all right. She lost a lot of blood. They have to guard against infection. But there's no serious injury."

"Good. Continue your story."

"Just before he died, Davey Waterstone told me he was the killer. He wrote the letters, and he killed Abigail Claymore-Whitley and Alex Mason. He said he was shooting at us just to frighten us, that hitting Veronica was a mistake."

"But . . . why was he doing all this?"

I shook my head. "I'm not sure. Every word was a struggle for him. He said something about making sacrifices for the good of the cause. I know he wanted to stop Max Rothman's development project. The only thing I can figure is, he was trying to arouse sentiment against the project by making it look like someone was murdering its opponents."

"Christ, what a nutty thing to do."

Kay said, "I have his house and his trailer sealed off. I'm heading there soon with a state police forensics team. We'll go over the place inch by inch, looking for evidence to tie him in. The running shoes he was wearing when he died look like they might match the style of the footprint at Abigail Claymore-Whitley's house. I'll know more in a couple of hours."

Korvich smiled. "Well, now. You put Waterstone's name on those three murders and this turns into a pretty good day, after all."

"Only two," I said.

"Huh?"

"I asked him about Sandi O'Neill. He specifically denied killing her."

He furrowed his brow. "I don't get it."

"He said her murder gave him the idea for the others, but that he didn't kill her. He knew he was dying, and he was already admitting to two murders and to shooting Veronica. So I can't think of any reason for him to lie about *not* killing Sandi."

Kay said, "Sandra O'Neill was murdered a week ago Thursday evening. Her body was found the next morning. But we didn't identify her until Monday night. Waterstone didn't leave his letter in the library—didn't claim responsibility for killing her—until Tuesday, after word got out about the identification."

I said, "Her copy of *Walden* probably gave him the idea to steal the ones from the gift shop."

Kay said, "He called the shop Tuesday morning and asked how many they had in stock. Then he went there and stole ten copies. He wanted it to appear that one person was responsible for all the murders. For the good of the cause."

I said, "He probably figured that the more fear he could whip up, the greater his chances were of drawing negative attention to the development project."

No one said anything for several seconds. We were all piecing things together in our minds.

I said, "He got a little sloppy when we spoke with him on Thursday."

"What do you mean?" Kay asked.

"He knew he had planted clues in the letters that would get you to focus on Robert Butler as a suspect. But they were very subtle clues, and neither one of us saw them. He was probably waiting for you to show him the letters so he could point them out to you. But when you didn't show them to him, just as we were leaving he asked you if he could see them. He said, 'Maybe I'll see something you overlooked.' "

"I hesitated before I showed them to him."

"I know. I saw that."

"I thought it was an unusual thing for him to say, but I didn't stop to think it through."

Alfred Korvich leaned back in his chair. "Well, if Waterstone didn't kill Sandra O'Neill, who did?"

Kay shrugged. "Most likely it was Steven, I suppose. When I eliminated him from consideration, it was because I assumed there was only one killer, and I knew Steven couldn't have killed Alex Mason. I screwed up. I disqualified him too quickly."

"Well, where the hell is he?"

"He's the second corpse," Kay replied. "Threw himself in front of a commuter train."

"One thing is certain," I said. "We know now that Steven was capable of beating someone to death if he was angry enough."

Kay sighed. "It may be difficult to prove for sure."

"What about the developer?" Korvich asked. "Any luck trying to figure out who took Sandra O'Neill's car to that parking lot?"

"No," Kay replied. "Checking out alibis for everyone who has had business at that site is difficult. But I find it hard to believe that Max Rothman or anyone else who has anything to do with his construction company would leave the car in such an obvious place. Almost begging us to make the connection between Sandi and Rothman."

"Wait a second . . ."

Kay faced me. "What is it, Harry?"

"I don't know. I'm thinking . . . That first night . . . *Damn!*" I smacked my palm against my forehead. "I'm so stupid."

"Now what?" Korvich asked.

"When I spoke with Steven at my house on Monday night, he said he had never heard the name Max Rothman. He said the same thing to Kay on Wednesday night."

Kay said, "And Rothman's story was consistent with that. He said he had never met Sandi."

"Right. But yesterday after the memorial Mass, Steven said something quite different to me. He told me he assumed Rothman was behind Sandi's death. He made it sound like Sandi definitely knew Max Rothman, and that Sandi had mentioned Rothman to him by name on several occasions."

"I don't get it," Kay said.

Korvich furrowed his brow. "Me neither."

"It means he was lying—either with his first story, or his second. Those are two very different stories, about something very important. He had to know that one of them was a lie. Now, I ask you—if the man sincerely wanted you to discover the truth about his fiancée's murder, why would he try so hard to mislead you?"

60

Psychiatrists deal with language and context: what a person says, and when and why he says it. We are trained—and paid—to listen in a very special way: with our own concerns and needs divorced completely from the picture.

But in our personal relationships, we are just as likely as anyone else to let our own issues get in the way of understanding what another person is communicating to us. When Steven made his comment about the money-grubbing Max Rothman, my sensitivity to the possible anti-Semitic slur blinded me to the more paramount issue: He had lied about something very important, one way or another—something that no innocent person would lie about.

The most parsimonious explanation: He was trying to frame Rothman all along. But Kay Wheaton would never know that for certain, and neither would I.

I wondered what difference it might have made if I had picked up on his changed story the day before, when he made his comments about Rothman. Would I have confronted him, called him a liar? Would I have called Kay to tell her what had happened? If things had unfolded differently, perhaps we wouldn't have gone with him to Walden and Veronica wouldn't have been shot.

Well, I would never know that for certain, either.

That evening, when Veronica was more rested and alert, I brought her the news about Steven's suicide. I told her about his note: *Forgive, and you will be forgiven.* She asked me what I thought it meant.

"Two things. First of all, I think it means he killed Sandi."

"No. Kay Wheaton cleared him."

"Kay Wheaton was wrong." I told her about Davey Waterstone's confession to murders number two and number three, and the mistake Kay made in eliminating Steven as a suspect in the first murder. And I told her about the lie Steven told me. "He killed her, darling. It was probably an impulsive thing. For some reason he changed his original plans and came up to Massachusetts with her that day. They must have argued about something at Walden that evening. I've seen firsthand what he was capable of when he was angry. And then he improvised a plan to cover his tracks. It wasn't a very good plan, but when the letters appeared and other people began to turn up dead, it complicated things for Kay and worked to Steven's advantage. I don't know that Kay will be able to prove it now, but I believe Steven killed Sandi O'Neill."

She reached for my hand. "You said you think Steven's note had two meanings. What's the second?"

"I think seeing you get shot pushed him over the edge. At some level, he probably knew instinctively that it was related to what he had done to Sandi. As soon as it happened, he said, 'This is all my fault.' He probably thought you were going to die. When he jumped in front of that train, he thought he was responsible for your death as well as Sandi's, and that was too much for him to forgive himself."

She pondered that in silence for several minutes. Then she said, "Once upon a time I thought I loved him."

"Yes, I know."

"But that was a long time ago." She paused. "God, if I had stayed with him, now where would I be?"

"If you had stayed with him," I said, "now where would *I* be?"

61

Veronica was shot on the Saturday of Labor Day weekend. She came home from the hospital on Tuesday.

On Wednesday I resumed my work schedule and Melissa started the seventh grade. I wanted to hire nursing help, at least for a few days, but Veronica would have nothing of it. She was never one for pampering. She had a crutch for support but within a couple of days was able to get around the house without it. She was determined not to let her temporary incapacity interfere with the plans for Melissa's thirteenth birthday party on Saturday.

It was a week of funerals. Steven Farr's elderly parents lived on Long Island. I helped make arrangements to transport Steven's body to their town for burial, thus saving them the trauma of traveling to Concord to handle the matter.

Alex Mason was buried on Wednesday. I attended the service at Trinity Episcopal Church on Elm Street. I had never liked the man, and Veronica thought I was foolish for going, but it felt like the right thing to do.

Davey Waterstone was buried without a service on Thursday.

In the wake of all the publicity about the Logan tract that the murders generated, Max Rothman's investors got cold feet. Rothman abandoned his development plans and, paying a hefty penalty, reneged on his agreement to buy the land from the Logan heirs. Eventually the land was purchased by the project to save Walden Woods, its coffers having swelled in the wake of that same publicity. Ironically, then, Davey Waterstone's actions had their ultimate intended effect.

The final irony wouldn't come until the following year: Max Rothman purchased Davey's ten-acre estate and, with nary a word of opposition from the various town regulatory boards or citizens' groups, constructed several units of affordable housing.

Within a few days after Davey's death, Kay Wheaton uncovered enough forensic evidence—shoe prints, fiber analysis, blood samples—to tie him definitively to the murders of Abigail Claymore-Whitley and Alex Mason.

Sandi O'Neill's murder remains officially open to this day. But Kay Wheaton doesn't doubt that Steven Farr killed the young woman, and neither do I.

That Friday afternoon my office phone rang shortly after my final patient for the week left. "Hello, Harry. It's Jamie Ray. How are you?"

"I don't know. You tell me. How am I?"

"According to the biopsy results I received five minutes ago, you're very well, indeed."

After I finished the phone call I walked upstairs to Veronica's study. I said, "My urologist just called. The biopsy results are negative."

"Oh, Harry. I'm so glad."

I touched her cheek. "Neither one of us is going to die."

She placed her hand over mine. "Ever?"

I smiled. "Wouldn't that be nice?"

That night we lay in bed listening to the Canada geese as they flew through the darkness toward the wildlife refuge. I propped myself up on my elbow and looked down at her. I said, "Do you think your battered, fragile body has recovered enough to handle some gentle pounding?"

"As long as I remain in the traditional subservient supine position, and you don't try anything exotic."

And so we made tender and very satisfying love.

I lay on my back afterward. I took her hand and placed it on my chest, holding it there with my hand.

"I can feel your heart," she said. "It sounds happy."

"It is," I replied. "I am."

"And so am I."

She turned onto her side, facing the window. I moved next to her, my front to her back, and wrapped my arm around her.

She said, "It's a beautiful night."

"Yes, my love, it is."

And so we lay together, until sleep came at last, and the semicircle moon hung high above us in the Concord, Massachusetts, sky.

62

My late wife was buried in Sleepy Hollow Cemetery, a mile from our house. Her grave was on the side of a low hill, less than a hundred yards from Authors Ridge: the steep rise that holds the graves of the Alcotts, Emersons, and Hawthornes—and, of course, Henry David Thoreau.

It was Saturday, my daughter's thirteenth birthday, and she had come to pay her respects to her mother.

I watched as Melissa approached the grave. She stood quietly for a few minutes. Then she turned to me and said, "Do you think she's mad at me?"

"Mad at you? Why in the world would she be mad at you?"

"For not getting bat mitzvahed."

"Oh, honey—"

"It's just . . ." Her eyes teared up. "It's just that sometimes I get so confused, and I don't know what's the right thing to do."

She fell into my arms and held on tightly.

"Sweetheart, there's nothing you ever did, and nothing you

could ever do, that your mother wouldn't find a way to forgive. If there's one thing I know, it's that she's not angry with you."

"Do you still miss her?"

"Yes," I replied. "I still miss her."

"What do you do about that?"

I thought of Janet, her honey hair flowing in the breeze, reading to me as we sat on a hill when we were in college. I said, "Sometimes I think about a poem she once read to me."

"How does it go?"

"It starts like this," I said, still holding Melissa in my arms. " 'Let love go, if go she will. Seek not, O Fool, her wanton flight to stay. Of all she gives and takes away, the best remains behind her still.' "

"But how does that help?"

I stepped back and looked at her, this lovely child who would soon be a child no more. "It reminds me of what she gave me. I see her in you. 'The best remains behind her still.' "

Melissa and I arrived home about a half hour before the guests were due. A large tent was set up in the field, with tables and chairs underneath. Veronica's father and stepmother were coming, as were Janet's parents—Melissa's grandparents. Bobby and Cheryl would be there. And about three dozen boys and girls from the Sanborn and Peabody middle schools were invited.

At a few minutes before one o'clock, we went outside to wait for our guests. Melissa and Veronica stood near the house. I walked over to the tent for a last-minute check on the food and beverages.

A minivan came up the driveway. I walked back toward the house. Three girls got out of the car. I didn't know the driver. I heard her introduce herself as the mother of one of the girls. And then she said to Veronica, "You must be Melissa's mother."

Before Veronica could reply, my daughter touched her lightly on the shoulder and said, "She's sort of my stepmother." Then she and her three friends headed out into the field.

I reached the house and stood next to Veronica. She said, "Did you hear that? She said that I'm sort of her stepmother." She paused. "Wow."

"Well, you could be, you know."

"I could be what?"

"You could be her stepmother, so long as you're willing to take me as part of the package."

"Are you saying what I think you're saying?"

"You know I am." I clasped her hand in mine. "I'm saying that I want us to be married."

Neither one of us spoke for several seconds.

I said, "This is the part where you always say, 'What's wrong with leaving things the way they are?' Or something like that."

She smiled. "Yes, I know."

"But you didn't say that."

"No, I didn't."

She kissed my cheek, and then the two of us stood there silently, holding hands and smiling at one another.

Melissa walked over to us. She smiled and said, "You guys look happy."

"We are," I replied.

"Me, too," Melissa said.

And then my daughter laughed, and in that moment I saw all the ages of my child's life in her eyes: the little girl she once was, the adolescent she had become, the woman she would one day be.

Melissa said, "This may be the happiest day I've ever had."

Veronica smiled. "I feel the same way. Let's walk over to the tent. I want to meet all your friends."

The three of us walked hand-in-hand into the field. The far side of the field was lined with trees, each one flashing its September colors for us. I wished I could freeze that moment, keeping all of us safe and happy together, forever.

Melissa pulled her hands free and buttoned up her sweater. "I'm a little chilly."

Veronica said, "I am, too. I have a feeling we're going to have a cold winter."

"That's not a problem," I said. "I gave the snowblower a tune-up last week, and in a few days they'll deliver three cords of firewood. We have everything we need."

I looked at them: the loves of my life. *Yes,* I thought. *We have everything we need.*

A CONVERSATION WITH PHILIP LUBER

Q. Phil, we know that you're a forensic psychologist who works with mentally ill and violent patients. Could you tell us exactly what a forensic psychologist does?

A. A forensic psychologist practices at the interface of psychology and the law. I have twenty years of experience evaluating and treating criminal offenders—jailed and otherwise—and violent mentally ill people. I advise psychiatric hospitals regarding their planning for patients who have histories of mental illness and violent behavior. I consult with lawyers and judges regarding criminal cases. And I travel once a week to a state prison to interview and evaluate inmates.

Q. Do you make use of your professional training and experience when you write your novels—particularly the Harry Kline–Veronica Pace series?

A. Absolutely. My work has brought me face-to-face with perpetrators of very vile, very vicious acts. It has given me a first-hand acquaintance with evil. For every wretched fantasy, I know someone who has lived it. For every unsavory impulse, I know someone who has acted it out. And I've learned that each of us has a little of that inside ourselves.

Deadly Convictions, my first novel, was about a mass murderer who beats the system by feigning insanity. It was set at a maximum-security hospital for the criminally insane, not unlike the one where I spent several years learning about violent mental illness.

My doctoral dissertation research focused on women who had suffered the death of a young child. *Forgive Us Our Sins*, which was the first book featuring Harry Kline and Veronica

Pace, was largely inspired by that research. It revolves around a serial killer who has been driven into madness and revenge by grief over his dead child. The sequel, *Deliver Us From Evil*, was inspired in part by my professional interest in the controversial area of so-called forgotten memories. Some therapists believe that a patient can repress traumatic memories for years—including memories of abuse that happened repeatedly over the course of several years—and then regain those memories in their entirety and without distortion, often assisted by suggestive therapeutic techniques. Some people think this is a scientific breakthrough, but a growing number of mental health and legal professionals believe it to be a modern-day version of the hysteria about witches.

Q. You're a psychologist. You write in the first person in the voice of Harry Kline, who is a psychiatrist. Like Harry, you live in Concord, Massachusetts. Readers often wonder if an author's protagonist is based on himself. Is Harry, essentially, you?

A. No, I don't think so. Harry is smarter, richer, and better looking than I am. He also has more hair.

Q. Then perhaps he's the person you would like to be?

A. I wouldn't say that, either. Harry has suffered much more than I have. His wife died, his daughter was kidnapped, one girlfriend was attacked and almost murdered, and another girlfriend committed suicide. Harry has been attacked and almost murdered, and he has found it necessary to kill. None of that sounds like fun to me.

Q. You've written one stand-alone book, and (with the addition of Pray For Us Sinners *and* Have Mercy on Us*) you now have four Harry Kline–Veronica Pace thrillers under your belt. What are some of the attractions of writing a mystery series?*

A. Writing a series gives me the opportunity to create characters and relationships that mature over time. This in turn allows me to stretch my writing skills and develop my craft.

Although many good series revolve around protagonists who remain essentially the same from book to book, as a reader I have always been drawn to series in which protagonists age, change, and grow. I think there are three challenges that the author of a mystery series faces. First, you have to maintain continuity and consistency across books. It's hard enough remembering what you had for dinner two nights ago. Now try recalling who said what to whom—about this, that, or the other thing—one, two, or more books ago. When I write a series book, I not only have to keep the events and chronology of that book in my mind as I write, I have to keep the contents of the earlier books in mind as well. That's a lot to juggle. It makes me appreciate Fawcett's editorial staff even more. They help me watch out for inconsistencies. Second, when you write a series you have to appeal to two types of readers at the same time: new readers, and people who have read one or more earlier books in the series. You have to provide enough information to new readers to bring them up to speed on the story arc, yet refrain from boring your old readers when you recount things that have appeared in earlier books. Also, you don't want to reveal too much about the earlier books, because you want new readers to go back and catch up on what they've missed. Third, we all know at least one married person who, as years pass, begins to look more and more like his or her spouse. Well, the more time you spend writing a character, the harder it can be to remember where you end and he begins. This is especially risky when the writer uses his own town as the setting for his books. My protagonist, Harry Kline, lives in the same town I live in. There are places in town that have emotional import for my characters, but none for me in my own life. Yet sometimes I'll feel a little adrenaline rush when I drive past those sites, and it unnerves me to realize that it is my characters—not me—to whom that rush properly belongs.

Earlier today I drove past the spot where a murder occurred in *Deliver Us From Evil*. It was unnerving.

Q. You're a busy man. When do you find time to write?

A. I have an active practice as a forensic psychologist. I'm married and I have a school-age daughter. I write very early in the morning or very late at night, and whenever possible I'm more likely to sacrifice sleep than time with my family. When I'm writing intensely, and therefore losing a lot of sleep, I can be very difficult to be around. I develop short-term memory problems, I get very irritable—did I mention that I develop short-term memory problems?

(This interview originally appeared in somewhat different form on Murder on the Internet.*)*

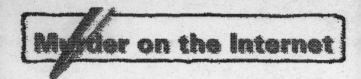